THE BLOOMSBURY GROUP MEMOIR CLUB

The Bloomsbury Group Memoir Club

S. P. Rosenbaum (1929–2012)
University of Toronto

Edited with an Introduction and Afterword by
James M. Haule
University of Texas–Pan American

First published 2014 by
PALGRAVE MACMILLAN

Palgrave Macmillan in the UK is an imprint of Macmillan Publishers Limited,
registered in England, company number 785998, of Houndmills, Basingstoke,
Hampshire RG21 6XS.

Palgrave Macmillan in the US is a division of St Martin's Press LLC,
175 Fifth Avenue, New York, NY 10010.

Palgrave Macmillan is the global academic imprint of the above companies
and has companies and representatives throughout the world.

Palgrave® and Macmillan® are registered trademarks in the United States,
the United Kingdom, Europe and other countries.

ISBN 978–1–137–36035–9

This book is printed on paper suitable for recycling and made from fully
managed and sustained forest sources. Logging, pulping and manufacturing
processes are expected to conform to the environmental regulations of the
country of origin.

A catalogue record for this book is available from the British Library.

A catalog record for this book is available from the Library of Congress.

Typeset by MPS Limited, Chennai, India.

This history is dedicated to
Naomi Black

Contents

Introduction

James M. Haule

When S. P. 'Pat' Rosenbaum died in the spring of 2012 after a short illness, he left uncompleted his book on the Memoir Club. Some months earlier, I spoke to him about his plans and what he hoped to achieve, offering the same easy encouragement I had numerous times before. I was sure he would succeed, I said, even though what he proposed seemed nearly impossible. I had reason for optimism. He had done this before when composing each of his books on Bloomsbury. Pat was not just an accomplished literary historian, but a fine philosopher and literary critic. The intellectual quality I admired most in him, aside from his searing honesty, was his ability to remember. He could speak with authority on even the most disparate details of twentieth-century literature and history, marshalling the elements of many disciplines to illuminate not just a manuscript but an age. His loss was deeply felt, most especially by his family. Once the shock of Pat's death began to ebb into grief, another loss seemed likely. The Memoir Club book, unfinished and in pieces, was surely gone as well. In this, happily, I was wrong.

Naomi Black, Pat's wife, sent me what he had completed and asked that I read it with an eye to its disposition. I was surprised by what I found. It was not merely a series of notes and outlines, but over five chapters, provisionally edited and proofread. It was Pat's voice not just telling the story of one of the most fascinating associations in the history of English letters but also explaining it, linking the papers they presented with the work of their lifetimes, work we rightly see as critical to our understanding of literature and politics and history in the early twentieth century. Although *The Bloomsbury Group Memoir Club* is unfinished, his account of the Club's early years is nearly complete. In it he provides a firm basis for our understanding of how the group was formed and how it operated, and marks a path through the remaining evidence to allow us, in time, to complete the work he began. It was clearly among his most valuable contributions, and I knew it must be shared. The current volume is the result.

S. P. Rosenbaum's plans for his book were described in his keynote address at the exhibit entitled 'A Room of Their Own: The Bloomsbury Artists in American Collections' held at Cornell University in October 2009.[1] He knew that he had a problem at the outset: what was the Bloomsbury Group and who were its members? This would be

> difficult to say for several reasons. First of all, essentialist definitions won't work because the members of the Group display [no] common and peculiar characteristics but rather an overlapping interconnected similarity of ideas and attitudes such as their values and beliefs concerning individual consciousness, external nature, isolation, time and space, love and death. Unlike most other kinds of intellectual or artistic groups, the Bloomsbury Group was not formed out of common beliefs or shared aspirations. Bloomsbury originated rather in families and old friendships which predated any of the Group's achievements or fame. From these relationships they developed into a collectivity whose work deeply influenced modern English literature, visual art, aesthetics, criticism, and international economics as well as modern attitudes towards feminism, pacifism, and sexuality. The development of Bloomsbury over two generations is another reason why notions of the Group can be elusive. Some members of the Group itself were convinced it ended with the First World War while others distinguished between Old Bloomsbury before the war and Later Bloomsbury that flourished in the 1920s and 30s.

Few outside Bloomsbury knew of the existence of the Club until publications by members eventually acknowledged its existence. In the spring of 1949 a posthumous book by John Maynard Keynes appeared entitled *Two Memoirs*. In his introduction, David Garnett noted that the memoirs were first 'read to a small audience of old and intimate friends . . . to whom the writer could speak entirely without reserve . . . '[2] Virginia Woolf had alluded to the Club years earlier in her 1940 biography of Roger Fry when she said Fry's childhood memoirs were 'written for friends who took a humorous rather than a reverential view of eminent Victorians' and 'no doubt owed a little to the temper of the audience'.[3] This context is important since, 'David Garnett's and Virginia Woolf's emphases on the context of Keynes' and Fry's memoirs are fundamental to understanding these memoirs and the Club for which they and others were written.' This is a topic to which Rosenbaum returns often in his book.

Membership in the Club changed with the years as members resigned or died and others were added. Their memories are our first source of information. Second are the memoirs they read to the Club in whatever condition they now exist, supplemented by published and unpublished diaries and member correspondence. In 1975 Rosenbaum edited a number of these memoirs in a collection that was revised twenty years later.[4] Aware of the memoirs, correspondence and diaries that had come to light in recent years, Rosenbaum knew it was possible to sketch a history of the Memoir Club and of the Bloomsbury Group that formed it. He begins at the beginning:

> Let's start, as all accounts of Bloomsbury seem to, with a cast of characters. The original members of the Memoir Club included the novelists and essayists Virginia Woolf, E. M. Forster, and Mary or Molly MacCarthy, the biographer and essayist Lytton Strachey, the economist John Maynard Keynes, the painters Duncan Grant, Vanessa Bell, and Roger Fry, and the critics Clive Bell, Leonard Woolf, Desmond MacCarthy, in addition to Fry, Strachey and Keynes.

Rosenbaum is careful to draw attention to a central fact: all of these people were either related to one another or were undergraduate friends at two Cambridge colleges. Many brothers, sisters, friends, partners, husbands and wives never belonged to it, not Lytton Strachey's companion Carrington, not assorted Strachey and Stephen siblings. Like the Cambridge Apostles before it, the Memoir Club was a very private group with highly selective admission. It all began with a letter of invitation:

> In the Spring of 1920 . . . Molly MacCarthy . . . sent out a letter to a group of people inviting them to the first meeting of what was to be a secret Memoir Club. They were all friends of the MacCarthys and included those who have come to be known as Old Bloomsbury as well as others such as Bertrand Russell . . . and the future diplomat Sydney Waterlow. . . . The original members of The Memoir Club consisted of the MacCarthys, Woolfs, Bells, Duncan Grant, Roger Fry, and Maynard Keynes. Shortly afterwards E. M. Forster expressed a desire to belong and joined the Club only to have characteristic misgivings over the years as to whether he really wanted to belong or not. And in addition to Waterlow, Mary Hutchinson – a cousin and confidante of Lytton Strachey's as well as Clive Bell's current lover – also belonged at the beginning of the Memoir Club . . .

Molly had an ulterior motive. She hoped it might encourage her dilatory husband Desmond to write his memoirs. She had tried something similar six years earlier when she started a Novel Club. Neither effort worked; Desmond wrote nothing. There was a second impulse behind the founding of the Memoir Club that was more successful; it brought together friends and relatives of Old Bloomsbury dispersed by World War I. As Rosenbaum notes in his address, 'the First World War remained the most disillusioning historical event in Bloomsbury's own history, and many of the Club's memoirs are about antebellum life'. This gathering of old friends and the companionship and entertainment it promised is a central point in Rosenbaum's book.

So is irony. Just before the founding of the Club three of its members published books that were deeply ironic: Lytton Strachey's *Eminent Victorians* in 1918, Maynard Keynes' *The Economic Consequences of the Peace* in 1919, and Leonard Woolf's *Empire and Commerce in Africa* early in 1920. Rosenbaum notes that it

> did not . . . escape the members of the Memoir Club that there was something rather ridiculous in a group of middle-aged friends . . . meeting regularly to read one another their memoirs. Irony is a pervasive characteristic

of Bloomsbury memoirs. They were meant to amuse their friends, but they were also serious.

There were other influences on the founding of the Memoir Club. Roger Fry had been reading Marcel Proust since 1914 and urging him on his friends. In 1929 Clive Bell wrote the first book in English on Proust.

> Forster felt Proust helped him finish *A Passage to India*, and Virginia Woolf's development in the Twenties might be described as from the Joycean *Mrs Dalloway* to the Proustian *To the Lighthouse*. . . . The Shakespearean title of the translation of Proust's novel that Scott-Moncrieff began in 1922 better describes the remembrances of things past in Bloomsbury's memoirs than the French *À la recherche du temps perdu*. Bloomsbury memoirs are not searching for the past. Proust's title better describes my quest for the Memoir Club's history.

Rosenbaum identifies another formative inspiration for the Memoir Club: the secret undergraduate discussion group known formally as the Cambridge Conversazione Society. All the Bloomsbury men of the Memoir Club except Clive Bell and Duncan Grant were Cambridge Apostles, as the group was known. The Apostles read papers to close male friends with the utmost sincerity and humour. This was the model of the meetings of the Memoir Club. Rosenbaum notes that

> the Apostles' papers were objective, dispassionate sometimes irreverent discussions of almost any subject. The Memoir Club, confined to auto-biography, made their memoirs reminiscences rather than apologetics or confessions. . . . The members were neither exercising self-justification or exorcising accumulated guilt. Their memoirs were remembrances.

The most significant Apostolic characteristic of the Memoir Club is audience.

> The Memoir Club . . . was composed of old friends and family who were thoroughly familiar with the lives, characters and personalities of each

memoirist. Thus much could be taken [for] granted and not spelled out in the memoirs. What could be assumed on such occasions is sometimes overlooked by interpreters of the memoirs. The presence and pressure of intimate but critical listeners should never be forgotten in considering the Club's memoirs. . . . Indeed one of the Memoir Club's few rules was that no one should be affronted by anything read or said in the Club. That was the theory.

It was no place to go for comfort or support, certainly not applause.

The difference between a private and a public Bloomsbury memoir is, Rosenbaum tells us, a 'matter of tone'. Rosenbaum reminds us that a memoir for the Club was to be not only candid and serious but also entertaining. This tone, developed by a lifetime of association and deep affection, must be kept in mind as we read and interpret what the members presented in private meetings and then edited, often substantially, before publishing to the world.

The private nature of the Memoir Club is illustrated by a 1943 painting by Vanessa Bell.[5] Seated in a circle are Desmond MacCarthy, Molly MacCarthy, Quentin Bell, Forster, David Garnett, Vanessa Bell in a hat, Duncan Grant, Leonard Woolf, Maynard Keynes, and Lydia Keynes. And on the wall are Bloomsbury portraits of the three deceased members, Virginia Woolf, Lytton Strachey, and Roger Fry. Desmond MacCarthy, appropriately, is reading a paper. The number of Club members, about twelve, seems to have remained steady over the forty years of its existence. During that time, there were a total of 25 members. After the first meeting on 4 March 1920, Molly's original memoir plan proved too ambitious. The Club settled into having two or three memoirs read of an evening, some of them continuations of earlier ones.

One of the main sources of Memoir Club history are Virginia Woolf's diaries. Rosenbaum tells us why. 'No records were kept of the Club – no register of meetings, no minutes of them, no archive of memoirs.' One of the difficulties was that the writers often took their memoirs home after they were read. There seems to have been some initial interest in keeping track of them, since 'Virginia Woolf once donated a handsome ledger to the Club in which to record the meetings. The members all inscribed their names, but when Quentin Bell, the last secretary of the Club, came to examine it, he found it was blank.' This makes the scattered accounts of meetings that survive in letters and diaries of special importance, as are the memoirs themselves, especially those that refer to previous ones.

Facing these limitations, Rosenbaum used three basic sources to construct his history: the members, their meetings, and finally the memoirs themselves. We know a good deal about many of the original members of the Club. All of them except Clive Bell have biographers. Some later members, most notably Frances Partridge and Julia Strachey, have as well. Membership in the Club was an issue that the members discussed in their letters and diaries over the years. With the deaths of Lytton Strachey in 1932, Roger Fry in 1934, Virginia Woolf in 1941 and Maynard Keynes in 1946, new members were invited to join. First sons, daughters or nieces of members were added; later a few friends, the men often Apostles, were elected. The Memoir Club met six times the first year, two or three times in the next two years. In 1922 Molly MacCarthy proposed quarterly meetings before meetings abruptly stopped. For five years there were none.

This did not mean that memoir was abandoned entirely. Rosenbaum tells us that the

hiatus of Memoir Cub meetings corresponded, oddly, with an activity at Charleston . . . that resulted in a mocking juvenile commentary on some Bloomsbury lives. From 1923 to 1927 Vanessa and Clive's children Julian and Quentin produced a newspaper called *The Charleston* or *New Bulletin* for which Virginia Woolf wrote some of the commentary. Special numbers included a life of Vanessa, dictated by Virginia. Another number had the Strachean title *Eminent Charlestonians*. Anecdotes about Duncan Grant were nicely called *The Dunciad*, and a life of Clive Bell was entitled *The Messiah*, while the life and adventures of Maynard and Lydia Keynes took the name *The Tiltoniad* from Tilton, their Sussex home next to Charleston.

In 1928 Molly MacCarthy announced a last meeting of the Club to hear Virginia Woolf read something on Bloomsbury's beginnings. What was supposed to signal the end of the Club, however, seems to have resuscitated it. It met at least three times in the late Twenties and then at least a dozen times in the Thirties. There were a few meetings during World War II and another twelve in the Forties. In the Fifties and early Sixties the Club met once or twice a year. The end came with the death of four original members: the MacCarthys in 1952 and 1953, Vanessa Bell in 1961 and Clive Bell in 1964. Only three original members survived it: Leonard Woolf, E. M. Forster, and Duncan Grant.

Rosenbaum tells us that 'approximately 60 meetings took place during the 45 years of the Club's existence and some 125 memoirs were read. A number of these are lost . . . and others cannot now be identified with any certainty. But it appears that around 80 memoirs have survived. The existence of these memoirs is the principal justification for an interest in the Memoir Club and its history.' About a quarter of these remain unpublished.

> Those that have been published are scattered in books of memoirs (there are two now by Virginia Woolf), in collected essays (such as Clive Bell's and Desmond MacCarthy's, all of which are out of print), in the appendices to collected works (such as E. M. Forster's), and in multiple-volume autobiographies (such as Leonard Woolf's and David Garnett's). That the dispersed memoirs need to be brought together, if only in a history, is indicated, I believe, by their interrelations. . . . When presented in their historical context, the memoirs can illuminate one another by their shared or even by their contrasting subjects.

Rosenbaum's discussion of this aspect of the Memoir Club is one of his most important contributions. He begins with an illuminating discussion of John Maynard Keynes' extended, two-part memoir 'Dr Melchior: Defeated Enemy' and moves to a memoir read at the same meeting, Clive Bell's unpublished account of his experience as a teenager with a powerfully sexual woman in her late thirties. E. M. Forster's 1922 memoir read on his return from India shows that the Memoir Club continued to provide an outlet for frank sexual discussion and may have encouraged Virginia Woolf to produce what has become the most significant example. In November of the Club's first year, Rosenbaum tells us,

> Virginia Woolf read a memoir that has survived. Her account of home life at Hyde Park Gate centred on her obtuse, erotic half-brother George Duckworth and his attentions to Vanessa and herself after their mother's death. The description of George – 'though he had the curls of a God and the ears of a faun he had unmistakably the eyes of a pig' – Keynes in turn thought the best thing Virginia had written, which of course depressed her.[6] Like Keynes' and Clive's memoirs, Virginia's breaks off on a note of suspense, in this case a hyperbolic one that calls the cuddling George his sisters' 'lover'. In so writing Virginia Woolf could count on the amused response of her audience that has escaped some later readers of her memoir.

This did not end the discussion of sexual matters. Years later Vanessa Bell returned to the scene in a memoir that

> presents George as a chaperone-cum-nursemaid rather than as an incestuous half-brother. An earlier sequel to Virginia's memoir of her Kensington home and its extended Victorian family was given in 1922 by Lytton Strachey on his Kensington home. In his only memoir written for the Club, Strachey's 'Lancaster Gate' also ends with sexual encounter in a relative's bedroom – in this case his cousin Duncan Grant's. Strachey's memoir focuses on that quintessential Bloomsbury symbol . . . [of] the room. In the drawing rooms and bedrooms of their houses the energetic chaos of Victorian family life is played out in the Memoir Club's memoirs.

While memoirs continued to be written about the proclivities of the living, the dead were topics too. Lytton Strachey, Roger Fry, Virginia Woolf, and Maynard Keynes all became subjects of memoirs after their deaths. Rosenbaum also notes the

> substantial memoirs . . . written about members' lives – Leonard Woolf's on his colleagues in the Ceylon Civil Service, E. M. Forster's on his difficulties with his Surrey landlords who drove him out of the house whose architect was his father, and Duncan Grant's on his comic involvement, through Strachey and Keynes, with the Apostles. . . .

This is how S. P. Rosenbaum saw the scope and purpose of the book he had in 2009 already begun to write. The five chapters of his *The Bloomsbury Group Memoir Club* presented here follow this plan. They explain the origins of the Club, document its initial members and their contributions, and explore the impact of these meetings on the work each of them pursued individually. It concludes with a chapter on the hiatus in Club meetings from 1922 to 1928, a prolific period of production that included fiction, criticism, and a large variety of published and unpublished autobiographical work. For example, the resumption of meetings in 1928 marked the completion of Virginia Woolf's *Orlando* and the beginning of her work on *A Room of One's Own*. That first meeting after the hiatus began with Woolf reading a memoir entitled 'Old Bloomsbury', a text that has become an essential source in the biography of Virginia Stephen.

Rosenbaum was able to complete only a few paragraphs of Chapter 6, stopping just before Virginia Woolf read 'Old Bloomsbury', the same year that saw the publication of Clive Bell's *Proust*, Strachey's *Elizabeth and Essex,* and Forster's *Eternal Moment and Other Stories.* Some of the most significant work of the Memoir Club members was yet to come: Fry's *Matisse* (1930), Woolf's *The Waves* (1931), Leonard Woolf's *After the Deluge* (1931 & 1939) and Keynes *Essays in Biography* (1931). We do not know what Rosenbaum might have told us about the Memoir Club's influence on these texts or what we might have learned about later members: Francis Partridge, whose diaries he admired, and Quentin Bell, Angelica Garnett, Julia and Oliver Strachey among others.

S. P. Rosenbaum was a careful and determined scholar, and while his work on the Memoir Club was cut short, the evidence he found and how he was able to organize and understand it is important to those of us who wish to continue this essential work. Among the last things he said was that he had to 'get out of [the hospital]' because he 'had a book to finish'. That task now falls on us. We miss Pat terribly but are deeply grateful for who he was and what he gave us. And we are fortunate to be able to depend on his remarkable work as we complete the story of this special group of friends who transformed the twentieth century.

Acknowledgements

I regret that I cannot name and thank the many colleagues, scholars, librarians, and archivists on whom S. P. Rosenbaum depended as he gathered his information and organized it. Since I do not know the many, I dare not name the few. One person, however, was essential to my work here and to Pat's work for a lifetime: Naomi Black. A distinguished teacher and scholar in her own right, Naomi's encouragement and material help Pat long acknowledged as essential. It was for me as well. Without her insight and energy, the typescript would have been lost. Without her wisdom and encouragement, this volume never would have been possible. I add my voice to Pat's as I repeat one last time the dedication that opened so many of S. P. Rosenbaum's Bloomsbury books: 'This history is dedicated to Naomi Black.'

James M. Haule
June 2013

Outlines

1

In the spring of 1949 a small posthumous book by an economist appeared in London under the title *Two Memoirs*. Economists' memoirs are not often of general interest but these turned out to be among the twentieth-century's most interesting works of what is now called life-writing. Part of that interest comes from the remarkable origin of the memoirs.

The economist was John Maynard Keynes. His memoirs were introduced by David Garnett who noted that they were not written for publication but rather 'read to a small audience of old and intimate friends' who had been meeting over the years to listen to one or two of their memoirs. The memoirs were written without reserve or veils, Garnett continued, noting that their personal allusions and jokes would have been understood by the listeners, who would not have been shocked by their truth and wit.

Garnett's brief introduction is virtually the first published description of the Memoir Club that had been meeting since the 1920s, though he does not give its name. Virginia Woolf had alluded to the Club earlier in her 1940 biography of Roger Fry when introducing a memoir of his that was written, she said, 'for friends who took a humorous rather than a reverential view of eminent Victorians' and thus owed something 'to the temper of the audience'.[1]

The Memoir Club was named for the first time in print by Leonard Woolf when he reviewed for the *Listener* Keynes' *Two Memoirs* in 1949. Leonard doubted if the memoirs could really be understood by outsiders, for they

are private papers read to a small circle of people who had been intimate friends for thirty years and more, and who met from time to time in what they called their 'Memoir Club'. At each meeting of the 'Club', members, in rotation, after a dinner, read a 'memoir' which was intended to be quite frank and truthful and was, therefore, almost always indiscreet.

Leonard goes on to discuss the subjects of Keynes' two memoirs, defending the first, which is entitled 'Dr Melchior: A Defeated Enemy' and mostly agreeing with the brilliant second memoir, 'My Early Beliefs', but about which he has one serious reservation (he will have others later). He thought Keynes confused the efficacy of reason with the rationality of human beings. Woolf, Keynes, and their college friends believed in the former, but not the latter. And in making this distinction, Leonard invokes the book Virginia had alluded to by another Cambridge friend and Memoir Club member: Lytton Strachey's *Eminent Victorians*, which appeared two years before the Club was founded.[2]

Since the publication of Keynes' *Two Memoirs*, the Memoir Club has become widely known as biographers have used its papers in their lives of Keynes, Strachey, the Woolfs, Vanessa Bell, Duncan Grant, Desmond and Molly MacCarthy, E. M. Forster, and Roger Fry – to stop with these founding members. But sometimes the Memoir Club context of these memoirs has been inaccurately represented. Even David Garnett, himself – a later member of the Club, as he says – rather exaggerates in claiming that Keynes' memoirs wore no veils. 'My Early Beliefs' is concerned, among other things, with D. H. Lawrence's hostility to Keynes and his friends, but the memoir omits any mention of their crucial 'early belief' having to do with homosexuality that so upset Lawrence. Keynes' audience (which included at least one of his former lovers) would not need to have his sexual history spelled out.

The circumstances of the Memoir Club are essential to understanding its memoirs, and not only because of the shared experiences of its members. A number of the memoirs are interactive, as it were, stimulated by other Club memoirs and contingent on the occasions of their readings. Then there is the pervasive use of humour in the recollections of old friends. Leonard Woolf refers to the sharp edge of Strachey's irony, which is present in many of the memoirs.[3] More than one of Virginia Woolf's interpreters, for instance, have cut themselves handling the irony in her memoirs.

*   *   *

Ours has been called the age of the memoir. (This is not new. E. M. Forster in the 1930s thought his an age of recollectionism.) Memoirs are now seen to rival novels in popularity. It is rather surprising, then, that so little attention has been given to one of the most notable manifestations of memoirs in modern times. Despite the frequent citations of its memoirs in various accounts of and commentaries on the members and their works, there has still been no detailed account of the Memoir Club.

The main reason for this is simply the absence of accurate information about the Club. Scattered comments in biographies are based on allusions in letters, diaries (Virginia Woolf's are an important source), autobiographies, and most especially in the memoirs themselves. The Club appears to have kept no records, no minutes of meetings, no inclusive record of memoirs read. When Vanessa and then Quentin Bell became secretaries of the Club in the 1940s, Molly MacCarthy – the founding 'secretary and drudge', as she called herself – passed on a handsome log-book that Virginia Woolf had originally presented to her. Quentin found it blank. Molly also thought there was a suitcase of Club memoirs somewhere but it has never been found.

Over the forty-some years of its existence, the Memoir Club underwent frequent changes in membership, the frequency of its gatherings, and the focus of its memoirs. Members, meetings, memoirs – these are the components of the Club's history. They can be reconstructed in varying degrees as the following pages will show. The founding members of the Memoir Club were the following: Mary (Molly) MacCarthy, Desmond MacCarthy, Roger Fry, John Maynard Keynes, Vanessa Bell, Clive Bell, Duncan Grant, Virginia Woolf, Leonard Woolf, Lytton Strachey, and E. M. Forster as well as Mary Hutchinson and Sidney Waterlow, who did not continue as members.[4]

Meetings

Molly MacCarthy called the Memoir Club into being early in 1920. Her intention has been variously described. One account has her trying once more to get her charming, dilatory husband to write a book – this time his memoirs. Another purpose was to bring together old friends, scattered by the war, to share their memories. It was not lost on these friends or their convener that there was something absurd in an early-middle-aged group of people reading one another their memoirs.

The original plan was to have the invited members read a section of their memoirs at a monthly meeting. For reasons that will become clear later, the existence of the Club was to be a secret; there were no stated rules at the beginning, just an understanding that the memoirs should be completely frank. But as Leonard Woolf observed, 'in our reminiscences what we said was absolutely true, but absolute truth was sometimes filtered through some discretion and reticence'.[5] Such was the case certainly with Keynes' 'My Early Beliefs'.

The meetings of the Memoir Club, however, are the most difficult aspect of the Club's history to recapture. The dates of many meetings are uncertain, and the number of meetings held each year changed. Indeed the Memoir Club underwent various vicissitudes over the years, stopping for a while, starting up again, changing with the death of members and the addition of new ones. Even after the Club finally ceased with the death of Clive Bell in 1964, surviving members sometimes misremembered who had belonged.

How many meetings there were over the years it is not possible to say definitely. Molly MacCarthy wanted to have a so-called centenary dinner of the Club in 1931, and this led some commentators, misled by her hyperbole and her original intention of meeting eight times a year, to conclude that there had been nearly a hundred meetings over the previous decade. From letters, diaries, and the memoirs themselves it now seems clear that the Club had only around sixty meetings during the forty-four years of its existence.

More critical for a history of the Memoir Club than the uncertainty about the number of meetings at which memoirs were read is the absence of records about what was talked about at them after the memoirs were read. The general procedure of the Club that developed was to meet at a restaurant and then adjourn to a member's house or flat for the reading of memoirs. The domestic setting was appropriate for the intimacy of the memoirs and the conversation they brought about. Comments, anecdotes, questions, and laughter usually followed, but not much more than that is now known about the post-memoir talk.

The fact of this talk brings out, however, perhaps the most striking feature of the Memoir Club memoirs, and that is their performative aspect. The memoirs were read to an audience of old friends – people, Forster said later, they had grown up with – who would know how to take the memoirs. Thus questions of authenticity that bedevil modern memoirs did not arise. Which is not to say that the Club's memoirs were not spiced with irony and spaced with things that did not need to be said. The uses of silence in Bloomsbury, often remarked upon by themselves and others, carried over into the Memoir Club.

It was a formidable audience, these friends and relatives. Reading a memoir to them was taken seriously though never solemnly. In assessing the Club's memoirs their performative context should never be ignored. The memoirs were shaped in part by the audience they were intended for. And the interactive character of a Memoir-Club reading appears not just in the reactions of the listeners, which are unrecoverable, but in other memoirs as well that were written in response to previous ones. The departure point of Keynes' early-belief memoir was David Garnett's recollection of D. H. Lawrence at the previous meeting of the Club. And the subject of Old Bloomsbury that Molly MacCarthy proposed to Virginia Woolf in the late Twenties resulted in a series of memoirs that are among the primary sources for our knowledge of the Group.

Memoirs

The lives of the memoirists, especially the original ones, being well known, and the particulars of their meetings being largely unknown, the emphasis of a reconstructed account of the Memoir Club falls on the memoirs themselves. Their history is therefore essentially a literary history.

Before beginning it, the many meanings of the term *memoir* so widely used today may need some clarification. Molly MacCarthy's original intention, it seems, was to use its plural sense of collected recollections: the members were to read chapters from their memoirs at subsequent meetings. A few memoirs continued their narratives from one meeting to another but most were self-contained essays, episodic rather than diachronic, to use a current terminology.[6]

Autobiographies have been traditionally classified by genre according to whether they were primarily confessions, apologies, or memoirs. That is whether they are essentially concerned to admit things about the memoirists' lives, to explain and defend them, or to reminisce about them. The categories are not absolute, and most autobiographies contain elements of the confessional and the apologetic as well as the reminiscent.[7]

Until fairly recently the term *memoir* in the singular seems to have meant a selective recollection as distinguished from a birth-to-writing autobiography. (All true autobiographies are necessarily incomplete.) Now however *memoir* has become the common term for autobiographies of self-justification, testimony, redemption, nostalgia, therapy, or just plain misery. There is not much confession or apology in Memoir Club memoirs; they did not bear witness to the past or try to exorcise it. And they were not nostalgic. Sharing recollections for the amusement of intimate friends was their abiding purpose, which distinguishes them from many memoirs today.

A memoir for the Memoir Club could be about almost anything, from childhood memories and pre-war reminiscences to the recounting of quite recent experiences. The platform of time, in Virginia Woolf's metaphor, from which the memoirist looked back, could be quite low at times, as in Keynes' peace-treaty memoir. Subjects might range from childhood recollections through sexual encounters to imperial experiences or current servant problems. Later some members took to reading letters, ancestral and otherwise, though this was considered not quite fair by other memoirists.

The Memoir Club habit also appears to have influenced other short memoirs by members that may not have been written particularly for the Club. Occasionally it is difficult to determine whether or not a memoir was originally written for the Club. Some non-Club memoirs were done under intensely personal circumstances, such as grief – E. M. Forster's for his Egyptian lover, or Virginia Woolf's for her nephew Julian Bell. Others were written for various commemorative occasions, and still others for their own sakes. The relevance of these diverse memoirs to those written specifically for the Memoir Club is frequently worth noting.

From correspondence, diaries, and the memoirs themselves, it looks as if about 125 memoirs were read during the some sixty meetings of the Memoir Club. A number of the memoirs can no longer be identified. About a dozen others have been lost. Still others can no longer be distinctly separated from longer autobiographies or essay collections in which they are embedded. Despite these obstacles, it remains possible to identify ninety memoirs from the Club's history. Many of these have been published, but in scattered places, ranging from diverse collections of memoirs to the appendices of collected works. At least twenty-five Club memoirs remain unpublished. Others may emerge as more collections of papers become available. Part of the problem was that various memoirists – especially the writers among them – took their memoirs home after reading them. The memoirs, currently known and unknown, published and unpublished, are listed in Appendix 2.

It is a considerable corpus of twentieth-century life-writing that needs to be considered together as a complex whole and not just as body parts of biographies. Contributing to that unity were some of the most remarkable figures of twentieth-century English culture. The memoir papers of E. M. Forster, J. M. Keynes, and Virginia Woolf, to stop with the most well-known of them, cannot be fully understood or appreciated apart from the settings for which they were written and performed.

Twenty-five members over the forty-some years, around sixty meetings at which some 125 memoirs were read: such are the outlines of the Memoir Club. The aim of a history of the Memoir Club is to fill them in as much as possible with discussions of the memoirs and their contexts.

* * *

Before beginning that history, the pre-history of the Memoir Club needs to be considered. In the next chapter the tradition of family autobiography and the influence of Cambridge that shaped the Club and its memoirs will be discussed. Here, the more immediate backgrounds of the First World War and, in the decade preceding it, the formation of Bloomsbury, should be outlined.

Bloomsbury

The history of Old Bloomsbury is best told in the various Memoir Club memoirs that recall it. It need only be sketched here. The family of Leslie Stephen – Thoby, Vanessa, Virginia, Adrian – minus their Duckworth half-brothers George and Gerald, moved from Kensington to Gordon Square in Bloomsbury after Sir Leslie's death in 1904. The Bloomsbury Group began to coalesce when Thoby invited his Cambridge friends to meet his sisters at home in that part of London later classified, to the amusement of Virginia Woolf and others, as W.C. 1. Among the old friends and relations who would later form the Memoir Club were three close Trinity College friends of Thoby's: Clive Bell, Lytton Strachey, and briefly Leonard Woolf, who soon departed for seven years in the jungles of the Ceylon Civil Service.

Lytton's cousin Duncan Grant soon became associated with his friends (Mary Hutchinson was another cousin with whom Lytton was close), as did John Maynard Keynes and other somewhat older Cambridge acquaintances Desmond MacCarthy and Edward Morgan Forster. Virginia Stephen found Forster's Edwardian novels, culminating with *Howards End* in 1910, to be about people like themselves. In 1906 Desmond married Molly MacCarthy, whose aunt Anne Thackeray Ritchie had been Leslie Stephen's sister-in-law. The year after Thoby Stephen died of typhoid fever in 1907, Vanessa Stephen married Clive Bell. They settled in Gordon Square while Virginia and her brother Adrian moved out to Fitzroy Square where they continued to see their Cambridge friends. 1910 – a century ago at this writing – saw Virginia, Adrian, and Duncan involved in the *Dreadnought* Hoax of the Royal Navy early in the year, and Vanessa, Clive, Duncan and Desmond MacCarthy occupied at the end of the year with Roger Fry's first post-impressionist exhibition.

The older Fry changed Bloomsbury, making visual art and criticism as important for them as literature and the Cambridge philosophy of G. E. Moore. The division between painters and writers would be continued in the Memoir Club. A second post-impressionist exhibition was held in 1912 with Leonard Woolf, returned from Ceylon, as secretary, succeeded by Sydney Waterlow. Clive Bell's *Art* (1914) with its doctrines of significant form and aesthetic emotion, introduced post-impressionism along with Fry's lectures and articles to a wide English audience.

The Woolfs married in 1912. Leonard wrote novels out of his Ceylon experience (*The Village in the Jungle*, 1913) and then from his disillusioned re-encountering Bloomsbury (*The Wise Virgins*, 1914), while Virginia struggled to complete her first one. 1913 also saw the founding of Fry's Omega Workshops for the purposes of extending post-impressionism to applied arts and of helping struggling artists; the war eventually brought it to a close. The waning of the Bells' marriage, Lytton Strachey's settling in Berkshire in 1912, and the move of the Woolfs, following another of Virginia's breakdowns, to Richmond in 1914 began Old Bloomsbury's dispersal which the coming of the war continued.

Even the briefest outlines of Old Bloomsbury's history is incomplete without a mention of the complex emotional relationships of its members. Duncan Grant was in love at various times with Lytton Strachey, Maynard Keynes, Adrian Stephen, David Garnett, and finally Vanessa Bell, with whom he spent most of his life amidst other affairs. Roger Fry's love for Vanessa was only briefly reciprocated; Clive Bell's flirtation with his sister-in-law and brief affair with Molly MacCarthy adversely affected both the Bell and MacCarthy marriages. Lytton Strachey and Sydney Waterlow proposed to Virginia Stephen at various times; Lytton was briefly accepted then declined, to the relief of both. Despite these diverse affairs, there were no divorces in Bloomsbury. Old friends remained friends, which made the Memoir Club possible.

The First World War

Unlike Old Bloomsbury, the First World War was significantly not a subject of any Memoir Club memoirs, though it profoundly affected their lives and books. The chasm of the war, as Virginia called it, was the foreground of the Memoir Club. No one in the Club fought in the war but brothers of Leonard Woolf and Molly MacCarthy were both killed in action. Strachey, Grant, and Clive Bell among the original members became conscientious objectors. Clive appeared to do some agricultural work at Garsington, Ottoline and Philip Morrell's Oxfordshire manor house, while Duncan Grant and David Garnett worked at Wissett Lodge, the farm of a Grant relative in Suffolk, while living together with Vanessa Bell and her children in 1916, before moving to Charleston in Sussex. (Life at Wissett was described by the visiting Lytton Strachey in a diary account that reads a little like a Club memoir; Strachey also made some characteristic memoir notes in 1918 on his encounters with Asquith.[8]) Desmond MacCarthy served with the Red Cross and then naval intelligence, and Sydney Waterlow was in the foreign service. Roger Fry did some Quaker relief work, as did David Garnett. Leonard Woolf was disqualified for service by an inherited tremor. E. M. Forster, after completing his unpublishable homosexual novel *Maurice*, went to Egypt with the Red Cross to interview wounded soldiers. Keynes, who also had conscientious objections to the war, remained in the Treasury, despite the criticism of his Bloomsbury friends whom he helped when he could with testimonials at their conscription tribunals.

The two main memoirs he wrote for the Club on his involvement with the peace treaty in Paris and his encounter during the war with D. H. Lawrence in Cambridge are virtually the only Club memoirs connected with the First World War.

During the war and just after, however, a number of works – some very influential – were written by members directly or indirectly about the war that are relevant to their later memoirs. Clive Bell, Bloomsbury's most unyielding pacifist, wrote *Peace at Once* – a pamphlet arguing for peace negotiations which was confiscated and destroyed by the police in 1915. Desmond McCarthy wrote of the boredom and horror of war for the *New Statesman*, describing his experiences with the Red Cross ambulances in France in 1914–15.

Forster too made notes in greater detail on the terrible experiences described by wounded soldiers recuperating in Alexandria from the Gallipoli campaign. From these he could extract characteristic wisdom, such as 'The obverse of Love is not hatred but fear. Hatred is only one of the forms fear takes, cowardice being another and efficiency a third.'[9] Forster's four war years in Alexandria were productive for his writing. About Egypt, or what he liked to call The Nearer East, he wrote journalism for Egyptian newspapers, notes on the government of Egypt for the Labour Research Bureau (1920), a guide to Alexandria (1922), and then a collection of essays for the Hogarth Press entitled *Pharos and Pharillon* (1923). If there is a theme connecting these writings, it is Forster's implied and sometimes outspoken criticism of imperialism – a theme that links his work to that of other Memoir Club members Lytton Strachey, Maynard Keynes, and Leonard Woolf. Yet Forster was happy in Egypt, as he wrote, finding Egyptians easier to live with than Indians. Two Alexandrians in particular affected his outlook. One was the great modern Greek poet Constantine Cavafy, whose historically deflationary poetry Forster helped introduce to England. The other was an Egyptian tram conductor, with whom he was in love. But of his memoir with letters of his affair with Mohammed el Adl, the Memoir Club would hear nothing.

The most widely influential works written by Memoir Club members during the war and just after were by Lytton Strachey and Maynard Keynes. Writing in the midst of the ruins of nineteenth-century civilization that ended with the first of the world wars, Strachey used modernist methods of irony and selectiveness to treat his Victorian subjects. As he says in his preface to *Eminent Victorians*, he used 'fragments of truth' to expose 'the lives of an ecclesiastic, an educational authority, a woman of action, and a man of adventure' – and not just their lives, but also their times. Both are subjected to Strachey's pervasively ironic, often humorous tone but his interest, like the Memoir Club's, is ultimately more biographical than historical. 'Human beings', he writes in his manifesto of a preface,

> are too important to be treated as mere symptoms of the past. They have a value which is independent of any temporal processes – which is eternal, and must be felt for its own sake.

Here and elsewhere the values of ends and means emphasized in Moore's philosophy are to be distinguished, with consequences that changed the art of biography – and influenced autobiography too, as the Memoir Club will illustrate.

Implicit throughout Strachey's critique of the Victorian Age is a comparison of English civilization with French, and it emerges again in a crucial question at the end of a wartime review of a Victorian statesman's memoirs that typified for Strachey the age's incapacity for criticism, its complacency, egoism, and religiosity. If eighteenth-century French cynicism and scepticism produced the French Revolution, Strachey shrieked rhetorically, 'The Age of Victoria produced – what?'[10]

Answers were offered in two books by Memoir Club members in 1919 and 1920. Maynard Keynes' best-selling *The Economic Consequences of the Peace* was written at Charleston after Keynes left in despair and disgust the Versailles Peace Treaty negotiations where he was the Treasury's representative. Parts of the book were read aloud at Charleston, as Strachey's had been – a practice that would be continued in the Memoir Club. In his brief third-person preface, Keynes states the objections of 'the writer' to the policy of the peace conference and its economic consequences for Europe are entirely public in character. The personal dimension will be given to the Club in 1920–1. The purpose of Keynes' polemic, he says, 'is to show that the Carthaginian peace is not *practically* right or possible', and he dedicates his book, in the last sentence, to the formation of future opinion.[11] The emphasis is on consequences, as the title proclaims, rather than the insincere morality of the treaty (which Keynes says he will not treat) because his moral theory – and Bloomsbury's – were derived through G. E. Moore from a consequentialist ethics that concerned itself with means and ends rather than intuited duties or obligations. Keynes' book has been criticized for its preoccupation with personalities and its lack of social and political theory, but it did have an ethical one that emphasized, as with Strachey's *Eminent Victorians*, the fundamental value of personal relations.

The most enduring parts of *The Economic Consequences of the Peace* have not been its controversial economic analyses; Keynes, it appears, underestimated Germany's ability to pay reparations. What remains memorable are his account of the fragile international structure of nineteenth-century empires, the puritan psychology of society's accumulative habits and its non-consumption of cake, and especially his depiction of the eminent statesmen responsible for the treaty. Clemenceau was always gloved, which for Keynes with his fascination with the appearance of hands was significant: 'he had one illusion – France; and one disillusion – mankind . . . ' President Wilson was like a nonconformist minister: 'his thought and temperament were essentially theological not intellectual . . . '[12] As for Lloyd George, Keynes' cut the florid description of him, reprinting it more than a decade later and explaining he was unsatisfied with it at the time and also felt some compunction as he had been close to the Prime Minister at the conference. Besides, Lloyd George was so many things: a *femme fatale*, a Welsh witch on a broomstick, a prism, a vampire, a medium.[13] The mocking exaggerations seem Stracheyan in origin.

Maynard Keynes ended *The Economic Consequences of the Peace* quoting lines from Shelley's *Prometheus Unbound* about the good wanting power and the powerful goodness – lines also read by William Butler Yeats whose version in *The Second Coming*, also written in 1919, was 'The Best lack all conviction, while the worst / Are full of passionate intensity' (ll 7–8).

The other book answering Strachey's question of what the Age of Victoria had produced was Leonard Woolf's *Empire and Commerce in Africa*, published in 1920 and completing a trilogy of Memoir Club war works along with *Eminent Victorians* and *The Economic Consequences of the Peace*. Analysing the economic imperialism of African colonization, Leonard started to develop a theory of political history based on the beliefs, desires, and ideals of individuals' states of mind that constituted what he termed 'communal psychology' and which he would describe later in three books of what he would call *Principia Politica*. More influential, however, were his two reports on international laws and organizations (1916) that contributed to the formation of the League of Nations and then the United Nations. Much later after the demise of the Memoir Club, Leonard devoted the autobiographical volume entitled *Downhill All the Way* (1964) to the war years. (David Garnett had also treated the war rather obliquely in *The Flowers of the Forest* [1955], the second volume of his autobiography.) Leonard's volume describes the founding of the Hogarth Press and also the 1917 Club – named for the year of the Russian revolution – at which left-wing friends such as the Woolfs, various Stracheys, and E. M. Forster gathered for a few years. It was one of a number of clubs involving Bloomsbury that preceded the Memoir Club. Another was Roger Fry's Omega discussion club whose meetings W. B. Yeats, T. S. Eliot and Arnold Bennett sometimes attended; it ended with the close of the Workshops in 1919.

Finally, when she was not ill Virginia Woolf spent the war years finishing and publishing her first novel, *The Voyage Out*, and writing her second, *Night and Day*. Both are autobiographical and pre-war, with characters modelled after Vanessa and Clive Bell, Leslie Stephen, Lytton Strachey, Leonard and of course the author herself. The more experimental and contemporary fiction she was now beginning to write was different. In Virginia's 1917 story, included in 'Publication No. 1' of the Hogarth Press, the conclusion to the narrator's far-flung speculations as to a mark on the wall that she cannot be bothered to get up and examine is as follows:

> 'I'm going out to buy a newspaper.'
> 'Yes?'
> 'Though it's no good buying newspapers . . . Nothing ever happens.
> Curse this war; God damn this war! . . . All the same, I don't see why we should have a snail on our wall.'
> Ah, the mark on the wall! It was a snail.[14]

Ancestral Voices, Cambridge Conversations

2

Two traditions, one literary and one discursive, fundamentally influenced the formation of the Memoir Club after the First World War had dispersed the old friends of Bloomsbury. The literary tradition is to be found in the members' family histories of life-writing; the other very different discursive tradition came from a notable Cambridge University Society.

❊   ❊   ❊

The founding members of the Memoir Club were great readers and some frequent reviewers of autobiographical writings. The French tradition was the favourite model; among its many examples they enjoyed Saint-Simon's memoirs and valued Rousseau's confessions over Augustine's, not always for literary reasons. But it was Montaigne who in several ways was one of the most significant precursors of the Memoir Club. His domestic and private intention of writing for his relatives and friends resembled those of their ancestors' autobiographical works; his self-described humorous and familiar style well describes many of the Club's memoirs. Montaigne's mixture of frankness with reticence was also practiced in the Club; and perhaps most important, the short, tentative, reflective and reflexive prose genre that he originated found a twentieth-century expression in their writings.

Among other autobiographical traditions, the Italian and Russian were most familiar to the Memoir Club, though Forster reviewed and praised some Indian memoirs, including Babur's. Of the Italians Cardano seems to have been preferred to Cellini or Casanova. Russian autobiographies such as Avvakum's, Aksakov's, Herzen's, and Gorky's were enjoyed, several of which the Woolfs' Hogarth Press published in translation. Gorky's reminiscences of Tolstoy, published in the first year of the Memoir Club, became the Press's most successful publication so far.

Life-writing in English they knew best. Browne, Gibbon, Pepys, Sterne, Boswell, Wordsworth, Coleridge, De Quincey, Lamb, Hazlitt, Emerson, Thoreau, Mill, Carlyle, Borrow, Ruskin, among many others, and in their own century Adams, James, Conrad, Gosse, Blunt, B. Webb, and T. E. Lawrence were read and reviewed. Lytton Strachey undertook with help the editing of Greville's memoirs at the end of his life. And Virginia Woolf sought for, encouraged, admired and enjoyed the autobiographies of women such as – to give them their usual gendered titles – Mrs Leticia Pilkington or her friends Dame Ethel Smyth and Lady Ottoline Morrell but not others such as Ladies Dorothy Neville and Georgiana Peel or Mrs Humphry Ward.

Behind this heritage, however, was the more immediate influence of an extensive and varied tradition of family life-writing – the letters, diaries, biographies, and autobiographies of the ancestors of the Memoir Club's members. Ancestral voices, public and private, echo around the founding of the Club. The various forms of family life-writing are reflected in the intimate domestic character of the Club's memoirs. The history of English autobiography has yet to record this complex continuity. Ancestral life-writing expressed evangelical, utilitarian, liberal, and aesthetic values which the memoirists inherited and transmuted.[1]

The nineteenth and even eighteenth-century life-writing of their predecessors both impressed and bored their twentieth-century descendants. Memoir Club memoirs shunned the hopeful idealism, the reserve, the sentimentality, and the piety or agnosticism of many of these records, but they continued the practice of sharing domestic memories, experiences and especially affection with their families and close friends. To these they added a secular integrity and candour that valued truth, affection, and aesthetic experience above all else.

The tradition of domestic memoirs in which the writing of women appears prominently was tempered nevertheless by a very different kind of atmosphere that the men of the Memoir Club encountered when they left their families for Cambridge. But first the ancestral voices should be heard.

* * *

In 1919, the year before the Memoir Club began, Virginia Woolf published her second novel. *Night and Day* is a melancholy comedy of manners that represented, among its dualities, the generation gap between the Victorians and pre-war moderns. The heroine's mother in the novel is modelled on Anne Thackeray Ritchie, elder daughter of William Makepeace Thackeray, sister of Leslie Stephen's first wife, and also the sister-in-law of Molly MacCarthy's mother. Funny, scatty and shrewd, Mrs Hilbery is attempting by fits and starts to write the biography of her great poet-father with the assistance of a daughter who escapes from ancestor worship into sorting out her own love life.

'Aunt Anny' to both Virginia and Molly had died eight months before *Night and Day* appeared. As the author of more than twenty works of fiction, essays, and memoirs, she was accorded a tribute in the *Times Literary Supplement*, written anonymously by Virginia Woolf. Lady Ritchie's memoirs, said Virginia Woolf, 'would be the unacknowledged source of much that remains in men's minds about the Victorian age' rather than the official lives that Lytton Strachey had debunked the year before in *Eminent Victorians*. Tennyson, Ruskin, Carlyle, Dickens, and above all Thackeray himself, whose works she wrote introductions to in lieu of the biography he had forbidden, were among her English memoirs. Not sustained recollections but rather *Chapters from Some Memoirs*, as she called one of her volumes, describes her range. Her skill in suggesting without analysis or criticism 'the mood, the spirit the look of places and people defies any attempt to explain it', Virginia wrote.[2] In addition to her reminiscences of Charlotte Brontë, Trelawny, and George Sand, there were others of Chopin, Elizabeth Barrett Browning, and of course Thackeray. Anne Thackeray Ritchie's impressionistic recollections were the most familiar public memoirs of the Memoir Club's ancestors, and essential to their success is what Woolf called 'her flitting mockery'.[3] Aunt Anny herself attempted a description of humour in an essay on the memoir by Thomas Bewick, the wood-engraver of *British Birds*. Subtitling her essay 'Written from a Poultry Farm', she wrote,

> Bewick, besides his love for Nature and his power to depict it, possessed that delightful play of mind which some call humour and which is assuredly the characteristic of true sympathy. I write advisedly, for humour seems to me interest combined with affection and truthful criticism, as opposed to that interest without light or shade which is apt to grow monotonous in its unvarying note of reverence and blind reiteration, or painful in its modern attitude of shrug and sarcastic laughter.[4]

The description illuminates her own art as well as various Victorian memoirs, and, some might add later, those of the Memoir Club.

Several critics, including Desmond MacCarthy, have found resemblances between Anne Thackeray Ritchie's lyric prose and Virginia Woolf's. A more direct influence, however, appears in the Memoir Club memoirs of Desmond's wife Molly and her depiction of Aunt Anny. The story in *A Nineteenth-Century Childhood* of how Molly was taken by her aunt to Westminster Abbey for the trimming of Thackeray's marble whiskers is an example in a modern memoir of the humorous combination of sympathetic affection and criticism.

Mary MacCarthy's droll view of things may well have been an inheritance from her eccentric mother. Blanche Ritchie Warre-Cornish was a niece of Thackeray's (she published some family letters of his together with her recollections) and wife of the Vice-Provost of Eton. Remarks of hers to family, friends, and Eton schoolboys were collected anonymously by Logan Pearsall Smith in a privately published pamphlet entitled *Cornishiana*. Her mind is described there as moving like the knight in chess: two squares forward and one around the corner. Among her best known remarks were what she always said to herself in disagreeable circumstances: 'I am an Englishwoman, I have been born in wedlock, I am on dry land.' And to a daughter – perhaps

Molly? – who expressed shock at 'a scandal of the usual sort at Eton', Mrs Cornish responded 'Don't be a prig! . . . It's the ancient, aristocratic vice of Eton. What do they know of it in those modern, sanitary, linoleum schools?'[5] Her husband Frank Warre-Cornish was the author of a number of works including a history of the English Church (which did not, however, keep his wife from converting to Catholicism). Molly described her imaginative mother at greater length than her mild father in *A Nineteenth-Century Childhood*, summing her up as someone who allowed no one to be commonplace.[6] At her family's request, however, she concealed their names.

When Anne Thackeray Ritchie died, Virginia Woolf noted in her diary that it was almost the end of the nineteenth-century Hyde Park Gate world in which she had grown up. Virginia admired Aunt Anny sincerely 'but still the generations look very different ways' (5 March 1919). Nowhere are those generational views more distinct than in the public and private writings of her father who, portraying her with exasperated affection, admitted his sister-in-law's influence.

How Leslie Stephen figures as father in the memories of his daughters appears in their memoirs. His significance for the biographies of Lytton Strachey (who found *The Dictionary of National Biography* the most amusing of books) and the criticism of Desmond MacCarthy (who devoted the Leslie Stephen lecture at Cambridge to him) has been variously discussed. What needs to be noted here is his importance for the Memoir Club. Stephen's voice resonated for the Club in his extensive life-writings: hundreds of articles for the *DNB*, two full-length authorized biographies (of his brother and Henry Fawcett), five men-of-letters volumes, four volumes of *Studies of a Biographer*, some of which are indistinguishable in subject-matter from his three-volume *Hours in a Library*, several collections of essays, and innumerable uncollected ones – not to mention his histories of English thought in the eighteenth and nineteenth centuries.

Stephen's is an understated yet incisive voice, dryly sardonic, reticently self-conscious, commonsensical, unaesthetic, freethinking and plain speaking (as he titled a collection of essays) without ceasing to sound firmly moralistic. As he said of human nature in an essay on autobiography, it is 'in some sense a contradictory compound', adding that until you 'can take delight in the queer results which grow out of them, you are hardly qualified to be a student of autobiography'.[7] It was a qualification the members of the Memoir Club met without difficulty. Stephen maintained he had written no autobiography. Yet he published *Sketches from Cambridge by a Don* at the beginning of his literary career and *Some Early Impressions* at the end of it (republished by the Woolfs in 1924). The life of his good friend Henry Fawcett (1885) includes passages on their time together at Cambridge. The biography of his brother James Fitzjames (1895) is a kind of reticent family biography. And for the *Dictionary of National Biography*, Leslie Stephen wrote the lives of Fawcett and Fitzjames again as well as Fitzjames' son J. K. Stephen, Leslie's father Sir James Stephen, his grandfather James Stephen, an uncle and two grand uncles. And finally after the death of his second wife he composed the private grief-stricken letter-memoir for his children – dubbed by them *The Mausoleum Book* – a copy of which, typed out by Virginia, circulated among their family and close friends, and was used by some of them in their writings and by F. W. Maitland in his authorized life of Stephen.

By Stephen's own definition, however, none of these works was a real autobiography. Leslie Stephen disliked and avoided formalistic literary analyses, making few generic distinctions in his discussions of life-writing (a term he would have detested). He does not use the word 'memoir'. Autobiography was the fundamental term, as he indicated in his essay on the subject. It could include confessions – such as Rousseau's, which he found remarkable and repulsive – but not reminiscences. Reminiscing was a kind of attitudinizing, he wrote in an essay on biography; it was replacing authentic autobiography and adding a new terror to life, just as unsympathetic biographies had added a new one to death. Stephen does not discuss *apologias*, though he used the term (with its veiled allusion to Newman's *Apologia Pro*

Vita Sua) in the titles of his collected essays on agnosticism and plain-speaking.

The genuine autobiographer, Stephen said in his essay was one 'who had deliberately written down a history of his own feelings and thoughts for the benefit of posterity'.[8] In the early *Sketches from Cambridge* his feelings are only implicit in what his editor described as its *nil admirari* attitude. And in the impressions he published the year before he died, Stephen pronounced his memory unreliable and his inner life – which he would keep to himself – uninteresting, yet he admitted to some reminiscing. With the life of his brother Fitzjames, Leslie argued he had the advantage of the sympathetic appreciation necessary for good biography, but even there he was inhibited from expressing his thoughts and feelings about such things as his brother's attitudes and work.

As for the private *The Mausoleum Book*, that was to be about his beloved Julia. He had no intention, he told his children, of writing an autobiography, except in an incidental way. One reason, he repeated, was a poor memory for facts and incidents:

> Another reason is that I could give you none of those narratives of inward events, conversions or spiritual crises which give interest to some autobiographers. . . . I could give a history of some struggles through which I had to pass – successfully or otherwise; but I have a certain sense of satisfaction in reflecting that I shall take the knowledge with me to the grave.[9]

The Mausoleum Book is a complex, carefully rewritten work by a fluent professional writer of lives. It begins as a letter to his and Julia's children hoping to fix memories of their idealized mother for them, and it ends as a diary with obituaries – hence the title given it by his children. Though based on his letters to Julia, *The Mausoleum Book* is, of course, an autobiographical work even on Stephen's own terms, for the history of his feelings and thoughts cannot be kept out of the account that becomes at times confessional and at others apologetic. 'The terrible havoc wrought by death' is the theme, and the only agnostic consolation is the transmutation of grief's affliction into affection for survivors.

Stephen's grieving lamentations, literal and literary, left his children cold, but the emphasis on affections remained a fundamental value of theirs and their friends in the Memoir Club. Maitland in his 1906 biography of Stephen quoted a passage from *The Mausoleum Book* about how regretting love because it brought sorrow was what Stephen called a sin against the Holy Ghost of one's best affections. Lytton Strachey quoted the passage to Maynard Keynes as a 'rather magnificent thing'.[10]

About the source of one's best affections, however, the children of Leslie Stephen and their Memoir Club friends differed radically from him, and this distances their memoirs from his. They all express the very great value of personal affection, and the expression, as with Anne Thackeray Ritchie, is quite consistent again with acidulous humour. For Anny and Leslie as well, despite his protestations, the affection expressed could be quite sentimental. Their memoirs are wet as well as dry. Stephen abhorred gush, as he says in his Cambridge writings, but there is lugubrious gush and sentimentality in his *Mausoleum Book* grief. Yet more than the expression of feeling it is the sources of affection that separate Stephen from his descendants and their friends.

For Leslie Stephen personal affection was heterosexually centred in the patriarchal family. The family as a cohesive, evolving primitive relation formed the basis of his *The Science of Ethics*. The terms 'manly' and 'effeminate' recur in his writings. (A scandal-causing homosexual relative is dismissed as a 'blackguard' in *The Mausoleum Book*.) For the Memoir Club and Bloomsbury, what mattered was the quality of love, not the gender of the lovers. The monogamous, often very large hierarchal family was what they escaped from as they matured. Domesticity was the carefully preserved basis of their lives, as the arrangements for the Memoir Club show, but it was not the traditional family domesticity. 'I loved my parents', Quentin Bell wrote in a retrospective essay, '(and I had more than the usual number to love).'[11]

Quentin Bell also commented on *The Mausoleum Book* before it was finally published in 1977. Coming from a later member of the Memoir Club, his account is part of its history. Quentin calls the book 'a sentimental autobiography', and summarizes the story his grandfather tells of his two marriages, describing for example the amusing contrasts Stephen depicts between himself, his sister Caroline Emelia, and his sister-in-law Aunt Anny. Quentin's commentary also notes the aesthetic side of his inheritance that is mostly absent from *The Mausoleum Book* and concludes stressing the remarkable personality of Julia Stephen that through *The Mausoleum Book* 'lived on in the consciousness of the next generation'. For her daughter, however, there was in the 'noble lamentations' of the *Mausoleum Book* 'no semblance of a woman you could love'.[12]

Yet the beautiful Julia Stephen lived on in the memories of her contemporaries. Once at a party where 'the beautiful, sibylline Mrs Leslie Stephen' was established apart in a small room into which guests were led in one by one, Mrs Cornish was heard to exclaim 'Such a killjoy!'[13] Julia wrote no memoirs apart from the brief *DNB* notice of a celebrated aunt, but something of her voice might be heard in stories and essays she wrote, especially in her brief *Notes from a Sickroom* on the arts of nursing and of being ill, to which a daughter would return in a well-known essay.

Julia Stephen's aunt was the great photographer Julia Margaret Cameron. The famous photographs of her niece and others were hung in the hall of the Bells' Gordon Square home, and later selected and prefaced by Virginia Woolf and Roger Fry in 1926. The famous men, hairy and pouched, the fair women, beautifully vacuous, were the blurred visual symbols of the Memoir Club's Victorian past. In Cameron's unfinished posthumous autobiography *Annals of My Glass House*, she recorded her eccentric enthusiasms even more indistinctly than in her photographs, but they come out in Anne Thackeray Ritchie's memoir of life with the Tennysons and others at Freshwater on the Isle of Wight, about which Virginia Woolf would write a play for family and friends.

'Is no one normal?' Anny quotes her despairing friend Caroline Emelia Stephen when visiting Freshwater. Leslie Stephen's sister, if not exactly normal, was less assertive a personality, as became an inspirational Quaker. Her niece's brief, anonymous obituary does not express the ambivalence of Virginia Woolf's fondness for the old Quaker, her disdain for her mystical writings, and her appreciation of a bequest that would be mythologized in *A Room of One's Own*.[14]

Yet it was the valetudinarian Caroline Emelia Stephen rather than her literary brothers who edited the letters of their father Sir James with biographical notes in 1906. James Stephen's great influence as undersecretary for the colonies was reflected in epithets such as 'Mr Oversecretary Stephen'. He was also a historian and the author of *Essays in Ecclesiastical Biography*. Both his sons abandoned the evangelical puritanism of their parents, but Fitzjames maintained his father's faith in imperialism, and Leslie seems to have inherited something of his skinless shyness and his interest in biography as well.

Leslie Stephen also continued the Stephen family tradition of autobiography that various Stephens had carried on in unpublished or privately printed memoirs. It began with Leslie's abolitionist grandfather. *The Memoirs of James Stephen Written by Himself for the Use of His Children* were read by the four generations of Stephens, including members of the Memoir Club, before the Woolfs' Hogarth Press brought out an edition of them in 1954. Covering only the years 1758–1783 (Stephen died in 1832), the memoirs, like *The Mausoleum Book*, were private and domestic, written for posterity, but not simply to record memories. James Stephen's intention is to justify God's ways to his children, to instruct and improve rather than to interest or entertain them. Yet the passionate, penitent world of his late eighteenth-century youth, which included his simultaneous love of two women, the birth of an illegitimate son (concealed by Leslie in his *DNB* life of James), and an involvement in a homosexual scandal make for more lively reading than the elderly mournful, agnostic memories of his grandson. Both memoirs are connected, however, with those of the Memoir Club through the practice of domestic life-writing and the great value they all placed on human affections.

Later in his life James Stephen moved to Clapham Common and became very effective in the anti-slavery movement, acting with men such as William Wilberforce and Henry Thornton, the great-grandfather of E. M. Forster. Stephen's remarks on what Sidney Smith dubbed the Clapham Sect anticipate some of the criticism levelled at their descendants:

> It is not permitted to any Coterie altogether to escape the spirit of Coterie. Clapham Common, of course, thought itself the best of all commons. . . . A critical race, they drew many of their canons of criticism from books and talk of their own parentage; and for those on the outside of the pale, there might be, now and then, some failure of charity.[15]

Banker and economist as well as an evangelical abolitionist, Forster's great-grandfather wrote two influential books exemplifying his worlds of religion and the rise of capitalism. Henry Thornton's book on paper credit is said to have anticipated elements of John Maynard Keynes' *General Theory*; his posthumously published *Family Prayers* was enormously successful. Forster, in an essay on Thornton, found the prayers characteristically evangelical, consisting 'of vague contrition, vague thankfulness, and somewhat precise instructions to God on the subject of His own attributes'.[16] Their remaining aroma for Forster is of a vanished, pious, prosperous society that helped to abolish African but remained uninterested in industrial slavery.

Ancestral Thornton voices are preserved by Forster in the biography he finished in 1956 of Henry's daughter, his great aunt Marianne Thornton. (Aunts more than clergymen seem to proliferate in Bloomsbury's ancestral writing, rather like Forster's fiction which Katherine Mansfield once described as 'alive with aunts and black with chaplains'.[17]) Marianne Thornton was even more generous than Virginia Woolf's aunt, bequeathing Forster the means to go to Cambridge and become a writer. Among the family papers that Forster uses in her biography are Henry Thornton's diary, his recollections written for his children, Marianne's more extensive recollections, and those of another aunt, as well as numerous family letters. *Marianne Thornton*, Forster announces on the title page, is a domestic biography, not a public one, which Forster turns into autobiography at the end. The Thornton voices, patriarchal and matriarchal, are all private, unpublished, as most of the Stephen ones were, in the convention of domestic autobiography that the Memoir Club in its own way continued. Marianne Thornton's voice conveys humour and warmth in Forster's excerpts; he likes her eighteenth-century faith in reason, except for the indulgence in deathbed grief that leaves her great nephew as unresponsive as Leslie Stephen's children. For all the Thornton piety and belief in personal immortality, Forster finds their attitude to life surprisingly dry. The great defect of the Clapham Sect, as compared he thought with the Quakers, was their 'indifference to the unseen. . . . Poetry, mystery, passion, ecstasy, music, don't count.'[18] Leslie Stephen's agnostic family affection was not as indifferent.

E. M. Forster's ancestral memories, like those of others in the Memoir Club, are more topographical than temporal. From his earliest memoir to the last extended one that he read to the Club, his recollections are about houses he had loved and lost. It is a theme of *Marianne Thornton* too; she had to leave Battersea Rise (the name of the Thornton family home on Clapham Common that still thrills Forster) because her brother married his deceased wife's sister. For Marianne the marriage was a shame not a sin. For Forster this is another illustration of stupid English sex laws.

Again, it is puritan morality rather than the mystical unseen that can be heard in the autobiography of Roger Fry's father, Quaker though he was. Forster knew Caroline Emelia Stephen as a friend of his aunt's and visited her at Cambridge, but he seems never to have met Edward Fry. A year after the founding of the Memoir Club, Roger's sister Agnes edited *A Memoir of the Right Honourable Sir Edward Fry, G.C.B. . . . . Compiled Largely from an Autobiography Written for His Family*. 'The pages were certainly not written for publication, but for the perusal by his children after his death' she explains in a preface to justify her alterations and omission of domestic, personal details in the interest of producing 'a record not discordant with a life at once austere and tender'. Included were some brief recollections of

Roger's grandmother about a Quaker childhood in which denial prevailed over desire. (Virginia Woolf in her biography of Roger also made use of some autobiographical remarks by his mother.)

Austerity more than tenderness is the atmosphere of Edward Fry's autobiography. Another formidable, shy, sensitive, sentiment-disliking, family-centred patriarch, Fry nevertheless has little to say about his family in his edited memoirs. He was distinguished as a jurist, diplomat, and naturalist. He speaks of his idealistic faith in transcendental morality, his conflicting feelings about body and spirit, and his experience of wonder and mystery. Yet his religious life was solitary after he came to disagree with Quaker habits of dress and address. As a scientist (he was a Fellow of the Royal Society) Fry wrote on Darwin, whom he accepted. He was amused, he admits, by Darwin's discussions of the immorality of lower animals. To art, however, he was quite indifferent. As for love, his editor-daughter says few words need be said about his marriage, but she does record that he admitted to a probing lady he had been in love only once and that was 'with his wife'; he remembered her comment: 'How dull of ye!'.[19]

Reading some of his father's memoir to Vanessa Bell and Duncan Grant, Roger Fry was torn between the desire to see what fun Virginia Woolf would find in it and terror at what his family might feel if she had reviewed it: 'I think it's very well done', he wrote to her, 'and it is a kind of concentrated essence of Victorianism which will be a cordial to you.'[20] He also thought Lytton Strachey might profit by it, as Dr Thomas Arnold was a major influence on his father. (Edward Fry died a few months after *Eminent Victorians* with its belittling portrait of Arnold was published.)

The Victorian essence of the Frys' family life may be conveyed by the fact that none of his six sisters married. Roger became anti-family in theory, if not in practice. He remained close to his sister Margery, and another, Joan, helped with his children when his wife became insane. And again, as with Morgan Forster and Virginia Woolf, he profited from the grand Victorian puritan vice of saving, about which Keynes would have much to say.

A bequest from his chocolate-manufacturing uncle Joseph in 1913 allowed Roger to start the Omega Workshops.

Puritanism again coloured the family history of John Maynard Keynes, his grandfather being a Congregational minister, a successor to and biographer of John Bunyan. The only family memoirs of the Keyneses, apart from the largely record-keeping diaries of the father John Neville, are those by his mother, written in her eighties and published in 1950 (four years after her famous older son's death), and by his younger brother Geoffrey, published in his nineties. Florence Ada Keynes' *Gathering up the Threads* was written for publication rather than privately for her children. More a modern 'Study in Family Biography', as it is subtitled, than an ancestral memoir, the book describes her parents' religious backgrounds, her own education at Newnham, married life in academic Cambridge in the 1880s and 90s, her own career as an activist especially in women's issues, and the early lives of her three children. Maynard's mother was an accomplished administrator, like her husband, eventually becoming mayor of Cambridge. Both her study and Geoffrey Keynes' *The Gates of Memory* suggest, as Geoffrey noted, in an essay on his brother's early years, how unusual his family was in its absence of generational antagonisms, though the brothers were not close.

The mother of Lytton Strachey and aunt of Duncan Grant also began dictating her memoirs in her eighties, during the early years of the Memoir Club. Excerpts from 'Some Recollections from a Long Life', written once again for the amusement of her children, were published by Leonard Woolf in 1924 while he was literary editor of the *Nation*. Vanessa Bell cautioned Virginia later that if she did not start her memoirs soon, she would be too old and forgetful, like Lady Strachey.

Jane Maria Strachey née Grant remembered her Indian years as the great epoch of her life. Through her father, Sir John Peter Grant, then her husband, General Sir Richard Strachey, she was familiar with the administrators and administration of India, even assisting her much older husband in drafting documents (he was not literary, she said). Lord Lytton became a particular friend and the godfather and namesake of her fourth son. It is striking how many of the Memoir Club families were involved with imperialism, especially in the East: Ritchies, Stephens, Stracheys, and Grants all served there in various capacities. Among the exceptions were the families of the two Memoir Club members who actually lived for a time in the East, E. M. Forster and Leonard Woolf.

In England Lady Strachey's anecdotal memoirs included her friendship with Huxley, George Eliot, Carlyle, Tennyson, Browning, Anne Thackeray Ritchie, and others. Her memoirs, only a quarter of which were published, also describe her unwavering faith in Indian imperialism, her Scottish family home, her children (she bore 13 in 28 years), her travels with her husband in America, her public works and ardent crusade for women's suffrage, and her love of English especially Elizabethan literature. Leonard and Virginia Woolf remembered her voice not in the stories she told but in her unforgettable readings of her beloved, albeit expurgated Elizabethan plays.

A large, dominant, sometimes formidable and vital, if at times vague and distracted Victorian matriarch living well into the twentieth century, Lady Strachey was an unpredictable mixture of the conventional and the unconventional. She was an agnostic rationalist, like her distinguished scientist husband, proud of Lytton's literary achievement, but prudishly oblivious of his and James's homosexuality. Unfortunately her late memoirs are an expression of her conventional side – disjointed, sometimes sentimental, though unself-centred, reminiscences of the type Leslie Stephen deplored. Like Leslie, however, she admitted she could not express her emotions. Her ancestral voice remains rather indistinct.

More memorable than Lady Strachey's own recollections, however, were the extensive journals of her aunt that she edited in abridged and, of course, expurgated form in 1898 under the title *Memoirs of a Highland Lady . . . Elizabeth Grant of Rothiemurchus Afterwards Mrs Smith of Baltiboys, 1797–1830*. Lady Strachey's edition, originally printed privately by subscription, was an immediate success, being reprinted four times in one year. Various editions succeeded it, including finally an unbowdlerized edition by Duncan Grant's friend Angus Davidson in 1950. A complete edition was published in 1988, followed by editions of *A Highland Lady in Ireland*, with its insightful and compassionate account of the Irish famine, and *A Highland Lady in France*.

The memoirs of Elizabeth Grant's early life were begun in 1845 and written, she says, to please her children and niece. Her vivid recall of scenes from her early life is narrated with 'lively simplicity', Lady Strachey understatedly notes in her preface.[21] Elizabeth Grant was something of a professional author, who began writing to help her financially troubled family. Her uninhibited, pre-Victorian voice fluently retells her Grant family history as the eldest daughter of a laird in the Highlands, which she returns to again and again in her memoirs. She also tells of her youthful life in Edinburgh, London, Oxford, Holland, and finally India where her bankrupt father had been appointed an Indian judge (the result of a gift of some special scotch, grudged by Elizabeth, to George IV), and where she met her Irish husband. Elizabeth Grant Smith can and does write of her feelings: a broken engagement is remembered with pain and regret into old age; other hurtful events she finds it useless to remember. She is opinionated, willful, amusing, passionate, self-conscious, waspish (on Sir Walter Scott, his novels, wife, castle, for example), gossipy, and forthright on such subjects as her disagreeable mother (partly expurgated by Lady Strachey). These are reminiscences but not of the familiar commemorative kind. Her stay at Oxford with an uncle, the Master of University College, happened, for instance, during the expulsion of a trouble-making undergraduate named Shelley, whom she describes as half-crazy.

The *Memoirs of a Highland Lady* is regarded as an invaluable social document of late eighteenth and early nineteenth highland life recalled by a woman. As literature her memoirs are a notable addition to the journal genre. About them she had some doubts, however. Sometimes Elizabeth thought of giving them up or burning them because she feared 'they are all like the wretched, flippant, egotistical diary of the celebrated Miss Burney. I never read such odious stuff.' The tone is authentic, and remained so into widowed old age, when she wrote ' . . . I am all alone, and I really think the less I have to say to myself of myself the better'. [22]

A last example of ancestral life-writing, appearing four years after the Memoir Club began, is the endearing eighteenth-century diary of the Highland Lady's grandmother, kept when she was a young woman. It was selected and edited with commentary by her great-grandson Bartle Grant, then published posthumously with a portrait and decorations by his son Duncan in 1924 (the same year as Lady Strachey's memoirs appeared in the *Nation*). *The Receipt Book of Elizabeth Raper and a Portion of her Cypher Journal* was one of the first publications of *The Nonesuch Press*, which, unlike the Hogarth Press, was dedicated to printing fine editions of classic works. Duncan Grant's close friend David Garnett was an early partner and probably responsible for getting the book printed in a handsome limited edition.

The journal portion of Elizabeth Raper's receipt book was written between 1756 and 1770. As published it consists of two parts, journal and cookbook, and two voices. There is Elizabeth's young, whimsical, funny, flighty, yet shrewd, linguistically inventive self-communings chiefly about her would-be kissing and squeezing prospective lovers. Then there is her elderly great-grandson's historical family commentary along with his dry observations and appreciations. Elizabeth was attracted to Captain Richard (later Admiral Lord) Howe, and when he married someone else, ' . . . thought I should have died, cried heartily, damned him as heartily, and walked about loose with neither life nor soul'. Later she 'fizzled about all morning' or was 'vastly sociable'. She meets a doctor and his wife, 'the Dr. very much my humble servant and all that egad'. Difficult to detach is an unwonted admirer, dubbed 'the statue'. Another admirer, a rector (later Bishop) turns out to want her parents' money more than her. She finally married the physician William Grant, which eventually brought her to Rothiemurchus, where she became the subject of anecdotes by her granddaughter Elizabeth. One from the Highland lady describes Elizabeth Raper riding pillion to Rothiemurchus with high-heeled pointed shoes, a yellow silk petticoat, hoops, and a black hat with a feather stuck on one side of her powdered hair – an irresistible description illustrated by Duncan Grant for his father's book.

'How very odd, how individualised were the people of those old days!' Bartle Grant concludes, using some of Elizabeth Raper's favourite words to describe his great-grandmother as 'immensely notable' and 'vastly agreeable'.[23] As for her eighteenth-century recipes, her descendant, who was something of a cook, notes that they are closer to French cuisine than English cookery. How characteristic of the family memoirs of the Memoir Club that the earliest one should be combined with that quintessential domestic text, the cookbook.

It seems a long way from the *Receipt Book* to the *Mausoleum Book*: more than a century of diaries, recollections, confessions, apologies, prayers, laments by Stephens, Ritchies, Thorntons, Frys, Stracheys, Grants. Pious, agnostic, mournful, irreverent, reticent, uninhibited, these life writings, most of which were done affectionately for the domestic family circle, constitute an autobiographical heritage, in which the voices of women are at least as memorable as those of men.

*   *   *

Reading the memoir of Edward Fry until she was 'filled with blank despair', Vanessa Bell wrote Roger wondering 'How did you emerge?'[24] The answer is to be found in Cambridge. In Cambridge the future members of the Memoir Club emerged from Victorian patriarchy and matriarchy – even those who never went to college. If the legacy of ancestral autobiography can be seen to have influenced the content of the Memoir Club's memoirs, more than a little of its form as a Club came from Cambridge. Yet the Cambridge experience of the Memoir Club seldom appears in autobiographical writings that were read to the Club, for reasons that will become clear.

Virginia Woolf turns in the fourth chapter of *Night and Day* from the claustrophobic families of her heroine and hero to a meeting with their young friends. It was, she writes, a 'fortnightly meeting of a society for the free discussion of everything . . . '[25] Most of the members were artists or writers and the paper for the evening discussion was literary. The fictive origin of the society may have been Vanessa Bell's Friday Club that she started in 1905 for the exhibition and discussion of art, and at which over the years various papers were read by Desmond MacCarthy, E. M. Forster, Leonard Woolf, and others unassociated with Bloomsbury. There were also other Clubs in and around Old Bloomsbury – a play-reading one started and revived at various times by Clive Bell and friends, and a novel-writing one that Molly started to get her husband to finish his novel; in 1917 two new clubs started, a social one by Leonard Woolf and Oliver Strachey to celebrate the Russian revolution, and the same year an Omega Club started by Roger Fry to help his declining Workshop. But by far the most important discussion group preceding the founding of the Memoir Club, and the only one that engaged in the free and frank discussion of everything, was the celebrated Cambridge Conversazione Society, known informally as the Apostles, the Society, or the Brethren.

Much has been written on the Cambridge Apostles – on their nineteenth and early twentieth-century history, on their connection with G. E. Moore and their significance for Bloomsbury and the Group's writings. Relevant here, however, is the Society's pervasive influence on the Memoir Club.

Six of the Memoir Club's founding nine men had been elected as undergraduates to the Apostles; two were husbands of the women in the Club who also had Apostle uncles or fathers. Fry was elected in the eighties, MacCarthy in the nineties, Forster in 1901, Strachey and Woolf in 1902, and Keynes the next year. Two later members of the Memoir Club, Sebastian Sprott and Dennis Proctor, were elected in the twenties. Clive Bell, Duncan Grant (who never went to college) and Sydney Waterlow did not belong. Bell experienced something of the Apostolic spirit through the influence of G. E. Moore's *Principia Ethica*. Grant learned about the Apostles in his affairs with Strachey and Keynes, as he revealed in a late comic paper – the only Club memoir that actually names the Society. Secrecy among the Brethren was taken very seriously. When Grant read his paper, versions of which were entitled 'Where Angels Fear to Tread' and 'Intimations of Immortality', Forster and MacCarthy were much amused, but not Leonard Woolf, who waited into his eighties before writing about the Apostles in his autobiography.

When Leonard attempted to describe the spirit of the Society, he quoted from the memoir of the Victorian philosopher-Apostle Henry Sidgwick. (It was Sidgwick to whom Leslie Stephen turned for information about the Apostles for his brother's biography; Leslie, an academic success at Cambridge, was not elected to the Apostles, whereas Fitzjames, a failure, was.) In his memoir Sidgwick wrote,

> I can only describe it as the spirit of the pursuit of truth with absolute devotion and unreserve by a group of intimate friends who were perfectly frank with each other, and indulged in any amount of humorous sarcasm and playful banter ... Absolute candour was the only duty that the tradition of the society enforced ... It was rather a point of the apostolic mind to understand how much suggestion and instruction may be derived from what is in form a jest – even in dealing with the gravest matters. ... The tie of attachment to the society is much the strongest corporate bond which I have known in life.

Leonard adds that the Apostles of his generation were still in complete agreement with Sidgwick.[26] Intimate friendship, candour, and humour were certainly characteristic of the Memoir Club. But in memoirs truth is not so much pursued as recalled or recovered, sometimes filtered through discretion and reserve, as Leonard Woolf had observed later in his autobiography.

When Molly MacCarthy, wife and daughter of Apostles, wrote inviting Maynard Keynes to the Memoir Club, she alluded to the secrecy of the Apostles and, years later, when announcing her resignation as secretary, she used Apostolic jargon saying that she wanted to 'take wings'. Long after the Apostle members of the Club themselves had taken wings and become 'Angels', as the inactive members were called, they kept up their association, sometimes by attending meetings in Cambridge or going to the annual dinners over which they occasionally presided. One of the remarkable features of the Society was the continued association of up to a dozen undergraduate members with older Apostles visiting or resident in Cambridge. Thus an undergraduate like Leonard Woolf or Lytton Strachey might find himself at the weekly meeting in discussion with Roger Fry, Desmond MacCarthy, even Bertrand Russell, or the most influential philosopher-Apostle, G. E. Moore.

Nearly all commentators agree Moore had a great influence on Bloomsbury and thus on the Memoir Club but few agree on what exactly that influence was. Some think that it was mainly personal, others that it was *Principia Ethica*'s ideal of love and art, and still others that it was Moore's a rigorous analysis of commonsense meanings. Contention began in the Memoir Club itself in 1938, with Keynes' renowned memoir on his Cambridge experience, 'My Early Beliefs' – which never mentions the Apostles, however. Nothing mattered but states of mind, Keynes argued; Moore offered a religion but no morals – an attitude, that is, to the ultimate that ignored the intermediate.[27] In 1960 Leonard Woolf challenged Keynes' interpretation in the first volume of his autobiography, insisting that Moore's disciples were

fascinated by questions of what was right and wrong, what one *ought* to do . . . and argued interminably about the consequences of one's actions, both in actual and imaginary situations.

Woolf cited an early Apostle paper in which he had urged Moore to draft an education bill.[28] More broadly, Woolf thought Moore's influence came philosophically through an astringent dialectic that questioned one's meaning, and artistically in painting and writing through a purification that eliminated Victorian 'irrelevant extraneous matter', as Keynes had noted.[29]

At the root of Keynes' and Woolf's interpretations and funda-mental to an understanding of Moore's ethical thought and its sig-nificance for the Memoir Club is the distinction Moore draws in the preface to *Principia Ethica* between 'what things ought to exist for their own sakes' and 'what kinds of actions ought we to per-form'.[30] This distinction between ends and means or intrinsic and instrumental value is the moral warp and weft of Bloomsbury's writing, including their memoirs. Distinguishing ends and means was a familiar practice in moral philosophy, but what made the distinction so illuminating for Moore's followers in Cambridge and later in London was his conception of intrinsic value: the greatest intrinsic goods, he maintained, were personal relations, aesthetic experience and the pursuit of truth. In Moore's philo-sophy these goods were based on an indefinable, intuited notion of good and a conception of organic or complex unities, whose values as wholes are not proportionate to the additive value of their parts. The Memoir Club is itself an example of such a unity.

There were of course other discussion societies at Cambridge, such as the Trinity College Sunday Essay Society which heard papers on religious matters by Strachey and others, as well as the midnight reading society that met after the Saturday Apostle meetings and included Woolf and Strachey as well as the non-Apostles Clive Bell and Thoby Stephen. But it was the secret, exclusive, intimate, self-conscious, candid, humorous, and rig-orous discussion society of Apostles that more than any other provided the inspiration for the Memoir Club.

But with differences of course: the principal ones being that the Memoir Club was not a collegiate discussion society of brethren but a group of men and women, old friends, now middle-aged, who gathered to read and discuss their memoirs. And while they kept no records, the original Club members also became preoc-cupied, like the Society, with choosing new members. And some-thing of the Apostolic jargon that distinguished the real existence of the Society and its values from the phenomenal world outside survived in occasional memoir allusions to reality and unreality.

*   *   *

The Cambridge Conversazione Society underwent many changes, from its founding in the 1820s by twelve evangelicals through its domination by Marxists in the 1930s. (Even women were eventually elected.) Among the surviving papers by the Apostles of the Memoir Club are several that reflect changes during the Club's history from Roger Fry's election in 1887 to Maynard Keynes' in 1903 and beyond. These papers convey some idea of what the Apostles meant for various memoirists who, as was noted, never discussed or even so much as mentioned the Society in their Club memoirs. To have done so would, in the performative context of the Memoir Club's sessions, have invited the kinds of inquiries that Apostles customarily met with silence.

In a late Apostle paper written after 1914, Roger Fry reminisced about his incapacity for metaphysics in the Society's discussions; he went on to explain how he came to answer the posed question 'Do We Exist?' with a philosophy fashioned from Epicureanism and Taoism, in which our egos are linked to others through love in Proustian patterns of sensation and memory. This moral world is more real for him, Fry says, than an ethical one of rights and duties. Such conclusions are not all that inconsistent with Moore's, though Fry never considered himself one of his followers. Nor are they incompatible with his family origins. Curiously, however, Fry never mentions them in his Apostle papers, which refer to his 'phenomenal' studies in science and art, and allude to Hegelians, Epicureans, Stoics, Platonists, Buddhists, Taoists, but never Quakers. His emergence at Cambridge may have needed this disconnection.

There are no known writings by forbearers of Desmond MacCarthy but he was strongly influenced by his friendship with an older writer whose work he refers to in an Apostle paper delivered like Fry's when he had become an angelic brother. 'Is this an Awkward Age?' takes its title from Henry James's most recent novel. When MacCarthy looks at the Society in 1900 he still sees it as a collection of affinities; but in the self-conscious analytic spirit of the new century, he found the brethren had become more concerned with intimacy than with beliefs, and he wondered if truth should be pursued at all costs in personal relations. For MacCarthy and the younger Apostles of the Memoir Club,

James's influence combined with G. E. Moore's. The early correspondence of Lytton Strachey with Leonard Woolf in Ceylon illustrates this, as do the later writings of MacCarthy. In 1931, for example, MacCarthy – who was Moore's best friend – described how he and his fellow Apostles along with their successors found expressed in James's work,

> those parts of experience which could be regarded as ends in themselves. Morality was either a means to attaining these goods of the soul, or it was nothing.... These ends naturally fined themselves down to personal relations, aesthetic emotions and the pursuit of truth.... The tendency was for the stress to fall on feeling rightly rather than on action.

We suspected, MacCarthy continued, that James overvalued subtlety and was too social in his standards,

> but whether or not we always agreed with his estimate of values, he was pre-eminently interested in what interested us; that is to say disentangling emotions, in describing their appropriate objects and in showing in what subtle ways friendships might be exquisite, base, exciting, dull or droll.... Nor were we particularly interested in the instincts or the will compared with the play of the intelligence.[31]

On the whole it still seemed to MacCarthy a sound philosophy as it did to Maynard Keynes a few years later in 'My Early Beliefs'. The degree to which the rest of the Memoir Club remained committed to these values will be seen in its history.

E. M. Forster like Roger Fry also felt his incapacity for metaphysics among the Brethren, as he noted in the preface to a late Apostle paper where he welcomed the shift from philosophical topics of his youth, which he could hear but not understand, to literary subjects he now understood even if he could no longer hear them. Forster and Fry had been close friends of Lowes Dickinson, whose biography Forster managed to write without naming the Apostles or mentioning Dickinson's homosexuality. Both Forster's *Goldsworthy Lowes Dickinson* (1934) and Virginia Woolf's *Roger Fry* (1940) are in their sexual reticence closer to

Victorian lives, such as Leslie' Stephen's of his brother, than to biographies today. Forster did, however, suggest discreetly what the Society meant to Dickinson – and himself. After describing the procedure of 'one of those discussion societies which still flourish at Cambridge', Forster continues

> The young men seek truth rather than victory, they are willing to abjure opinion when it is proved untenable, they do not try to score off one another, they do not feel diffidence too high a price to pay for integrity. . . . Their influence, when it goes wrong, leads to self-consciousness and superciliousness; when it goes right, the mind is sharpened, the judgement is strengthened, and the heart becomes less selfish.[32]

The influence of the Apostles on the Memoir Club, for good or ill, is implicit in these remarks.

The impact of Moore on Forster was mediated through Apostle friends who enabled Forster to describe in a novel 'the Cambridge of G. E. Moore which I knew at the beginning of the century: the fearless uninfluential Cambridge that sought for reality and cared for truth.'[33] This was written more than half a century later as an introduction to *The Longest Journey*, which opens at Cambridge with an Apostolic discussion of reality. Forster summarizes how the metaphysical idea of reality, the ethical idea of facing reality, the ideal of the public school, and Shelley's belief (from which the title comes) in not loving only one person had all whirled around with the notion of an illegitimate brother to inspire the novel. And earlier, in a remarkable Memoir Club paper on his novels, Forster amplified, relating how a brief encounter with a shepherd in Wiltshire became the experience,

> which turns a key and bequeaths us something which philosophically may be also a glamour but which actually's tough. From this a book may spring. From the book, with the violence and persistency that only art possesses, a stream of emotion may beat back against and into the world.[34]

To test the significance of such an experience, Forster continues in his introduction, he stayed again in Wiltshire with Lytton

Strachey – 'not one to countenance fanciful transferences' – but even Strachey could not diminish the inspiration. It was an inspiration also influenced by an unpleasant uncle, described in yet another Memoir Club paper which also alludes to his great aunt Marianne Thornton.

Lytton Strachey, however, was not amused by *The Longest Journey*, and he agreed with Leonard Woolf, who was enduring the phenomenal realities of imperialism in Ceylon, that Forster in his novel did not seem to know what reality or experience really were. Other Apostles such as Maynard Keynes thought Forster had unintentionally caricatured the Society rather cruelly, while Desmond MacCarthy felt that Forster had 'hit off those miserable muffs the Cambridge Apostles pretty well'.[35]

Lytton Strachey's effect on the Apostles was greater than that of any of his contemporaries, moving their discussions in the awkward directions that MacCarthy had suggested. His impact on the Memoir Club was less so, partly because of his early death, but in his Apostle papers he conveys the sensitivity, integrity, ribald personality, and unerring detection of cant that the Woolfs, Bells, Grant, Keynes and Forster all enjoyed and valued. Apart from almost flaunting his homosexuality, Strachey's many Apostle papers are unautobiographical. Mainly they are attempts to apply Moore's ethics to questions of careers or aesthetics. In one, directed to Arthur Hobhouse whom he had competed with Keynes to sponsor, he defined the Apostolic state as one that was both analytic and passionate. Many years later, Duncan Grant's Memoir Club paper on the Apostles still wondered ironically just what the beautiful Hobhouse's Apostolic qualifications were.

Keynes' Apostle papers were largely focused on *Principia Ethica* but in a late lighter one he discussed the influence of furniture on love, which allowed him autobiographical digressions on how he had passed most of his life in the pompous rooms of Eton, King's College, and Whitehall where it was difficult to be at ease or in love because a room's shape influences our ideas and feelings. 'Who could commit sodomy', he asks 'in a boudoir or sapphism in [Trinity College's] Neville's Court?'[36]

Rooms are importantly symbolic in the writings of Forster and Virginia Woolf and in the paintings of Vanessa Bell, Grant, and Fry. They are significant as settings for the Memoir Club as well, but always they are domestic rooms, offering a relaxed, personal, and affectionate atmosphere for the meeting of friends and the reading of memoirs.

*   *   *

Virginia Woolf, writing of her mother in 'Sketch of the Past' as one of the definite 'invisible presences' which if not analysed make life-writing futile, mentioned some other presences that were less easy to describe. First among the given examples was 'the influence on me of the Cambridge Apostles' (others were the Galsworthy-Bennett-Wells school of fiction, women's suffrage, and the war).[37] How visible the Apostles were to other members, and how audible were their ancestral voices, the following history of members, meetings, and memoirs of the Memoir Club should indicate.

Beginnings

3

Two invitations to the Memoir Club written a generation apart illustrate the continuity and diversity of its history.

The first is an undated card to Maynard Keynes early in February 1920:

> The Memoir Club will have its opening meeting on Friday, the 27th inst., at <u>9 o'clock</u> precisely at 5 Wellington Square. It is expected that a few opening papers will be shown up [*sic*] by everyone – showing that people have thought out their probable manner of managing their memoirs, after that a chapter once a month is hoped for!
>
> Probable members of the Memoir Club: Roger Fry – Desmond – Maynard – Duncan – Molly – Virginia – Sidney Waterlow – Clive Bell – Vanessa Bell –
>
> It is advisable to be silent (as a Cambridge Apostle) to the tomb over it, or we shall get too many members. In the end we hope to have 12 members, but might as well wait a little.
>
> The first meeting will open with a short discussion.
>
> Mary MacCarthy. Secretary and drudge of the club.[1]

Other invitation cards from the secretary and drudge vary as to probable members – one to Mary Hutchinson does not mention Virginia or Leonard Woolf but includes Bertrand Russell (he never came). In the event the first meeting, which included the Woolfs, took place a week later – dates of meetings would continue to cause problems – but more surprising is Molly's initial plan of having monthly meetings at which members would read their memoirs rather than a memoir – chapters, that is, rather than the shorter papers they actually came to write from time to time.

Next a typed form letter of invitation from Quentin Bell some thirty years later.

15 February 1951
This is to invite you to become a member of the Memoir Club.

The club consists of eleven members viz: Desmond and Dermod Mac-Carthy, Oliver, Janie, Leonard, Frances, Duncan, Vanessa, Clive, Angelica, Bunny and myself. Our habit is to meet once or twice a year, to dine at a restaurant and then go to some place (not easily found) where we can listen to and gossip over the memoirs read by members.

Though the frequency of meetings and the membership had quite changed (Molly's deafness made her an inactive member) the wish for concealment at least remained. The letter continues:

In the thirteen years of membership, during six of which I have acted as secretary, I have managed to discover the following four rules, or perhaps I should say 'usages'.
1. Every member must read a memoir when his or her turn comes round; this should mean once in every three years; but in point of fact those members who are lazy read less often than that, because there are some who are willing to read more frequently, also we have taken to reading old memoirs which the young have not heard and the old have forgotten.
2. The memoirist may say what he or she likes and no one has the right to be shocked or affronted or aggrieved at what is read.
3. One black ball is sufficient to exclude a proposed member.
4. These rules may not be changed without the unanimous consent of the members.

Questions of membership began as the older members died, but problems of who would read and who might take offence at what was read were there almost from the beginning. Quentin's letter, written from Newcastle where he was a lecturer, concludes with an emphasis again on the enduring basis of friendship that underlay the Memoir Club throughout its history:

I do hope you will join us. We all feel that it would be a great gain to have you as a member and I personally should welcome some well defined opportunity of meeting you such as does not occur in the miserably rustic mode of life which is imposed on me by my work. Also I, like the others, look forward to the contributions that you would make.[2]

*   *   *

Virginia Woolf's diary is the source for the Memoir Club's beginning.[3] Throughout the first year of the Club her entries on meetings and members form a commentary on the Club and her relations with other members. She remarks critically on every member including Vanessa and Duncan, though not Leonard. In sympathy with Vanessa, she disdainfully called Clive Bell and his mistress Mary Hutchinson 'The Parrokeets'. Virginia's attitude to her Memoir Club friends is accurately described in her diary (8 September 1920):

L. at tea put me right: M. H. is one of the few people I dislike, I said. No: he replied: one of the many you dislike & like alternately. (D II 63)

And it is in her diary again on 6 March 1920 that Virginia records the first meeting of the Club:

Then on Thursday, dine with the MacCarthys, & the first Memoir Club meeting. A highly interesting occasion. Seven people read – & Lord knows what I didn't read into their reading. (D II 23)

The qualification is significant, not just for Virginia Woolf's descriptions of the Club over the years in her diary and letters, but for the reactions of other members as well. What was read into the readings is an essential part of the Memoir Club's history, however difficult it may now be to reconstruct. At the end of her entry on the Club Virginia added 'I doubt that anyone will *say* the interesting things but they can't prevent them from coming out'. That too is a significant aspect of the Club's memoirs for its members and their future readers.

But who exactly attended the first meeting is unclear, and of the seven memoirs read, only two can now actually be identified from Virginia's account. A self-conscious dream-memoir by Sydney Waterlow, which interested Virginia, is lost, and unidentified are the performances by Clive ('purely objective'), Vanessa ('starting matter of fact: then overcome by the emotional depths to be traversed & unable to read what she had written'), and Duncan ('fantastic & tongue – not tied – tongue enchanted'). The seventh memoirist is unnamed.

About Molly MacCarthy's and Roger Fry's memoirs, however, Virginia's diary is more forthcoming:

> Molly literary about tendencies & William Morris, carefully composed at first, & even formal: suddenly saying 'Oh this is absurd – I can't go on' shuffling all her sheets; beginning on the wrong page; firmly but waveringly, & carrying through to the end. 'These meagre Welsh, these hardheaded Scots – I detest them – I wanted to be the daughter of a French marquise by a misalliance with – ' That was the tone of it – & then 'these mild weak Cornishes'. Roger well composed; story of a coachman who stole geraniums & went to prison. Good: but too objective. (D II 23)

The presence or lack of self-consciousness that Virginia Woolf remarks upon in Vanessa's and Molly's readings brings out the importance of performing memoirs in the Club. For Virginia, as she will show when reading her first memoir at the next meeting, self-consciousness or the lack of it was part of the subjectivity or objectivity with which she classified the memoirs she heard. How consciously or unconsciously self-revealing they were of the memoirist is what seemed to interest her most at the start.

Although Molly MacCarthy's memoir can be identified, it can no longer be read in the form that the Memoir Club heard it. In rewriting her memoir as the first chapter of *A Nineteenth-Century Childhood*, Molly concealed the family names – at their request she said in the preface to the second edition – and softened the description of her family that Virginia quotes to 'very quiet, mild people' whose meatless skeletons she will not rattle.[4] From a short account of her upper-middle-class family background and its Tennysonian milieu and William Morris décor (without his socialism), Molly shifts to the present tense of her childhood point of view for the rest of her chapter about siblings, the nursery, and visitors to Eton where her father would be Vice-Provost. Class consciousness and a Victorian defensiveness remain characteristics of her autobiography, as does the understated humour which the viewpoint allows. *A Nineteenth-Century Childhood* is not another dishing up of eminent Victorians, Virginia Woolf commented again, this time when reviewing her book in 1924. Nor is it a sentimental revisiting of the age either. Traces of the self-consciousness Molly displayed in reading her memoir occur in the book, such as her noting how a memoir can be a trap for self-importance, and most prominently in the epigraph (dropped from the second edition) by Madame du Deffand for *A Nineteenth-Century Childhood* which Molly heads 'An Apology':

> Le Je et le Moi sont à tout instant. Mais enfin, quelles sont les connaissances qu'on peut avoir si n'est que le Je et le Moi?[5]

It is a basic question to be asked of the Memoir Club itself.

According to some accounts, including one by E. M. Forster, Molly MacCarthy started the Memoir Club in an attempt to get her wonderfully conversational, endlessly procrastinating husband to write his memoirs. It was to be a resurrection of the Novel Club that, as was mentioned, she had futilely started before the war to get Desmond to finish the novel he had begun. The Novel Club, which included neither Forster nor the Woolfs, seems to have failed because other members could not finish theirs either, or in some cases even start them. Memoirs might be easier, it seems; Desmond of course never wrote his either, though he did manage to read some pieces to the Club. One of them, according to Forster, he improvised as if reading it from a dispatch case on his lap, which was shown to be empty when he accidentally knocked it over.[6] In Vanessa Bell's 1943 oil sketch of the Memoir Club it is suitably Desmond who is reading.

The various descriptions of the Memoir Club's beginning often overlook, first, the crucial post-war context of the Club, and secondly, that among those whose memoirs were to be encouraged were those of the 'secretary and drudge' herself. Leonard Woolf, as literary editor of the *Nation*, serialized them as *A Nineteenth-Century Childhood* in 1923–4, interspersing them with the contrasting memoirs of a long life by Lady Strachey. Molly MacCarthy's were the first Memoir Club memoirs to be published; they appeared as a book in 1924. In 1918 Molly had brought out 'a novel of the nineties', as *A Pier and a Band* was subtitled – the only member of the Novel Club to write one. Her Memoir Club plan for members to read sequential memoirs was also carried out only by herself. Molly MacCarthy's bringing the Memoir Club into existence was something of a heroic endeavour for her too, for she was beginning to be affected with deafness as early as 1915. Meetings of the Club would eventually become a torment for her.

As for Roger Fry's 'too objective' performance, in its original form of 1500 words, it is the first complete memoir that we now have from the Memoir Club. It remains unpublished.[7] Fry begins subjectively enough with his first conscious impressions of patches of light on lime trees outside followed by gas lit indoor overtones of early twilight feelings of melancholy, intimacy, and security as the sound of the muffin man's bell '(though we never had muffins)' mixed with anticipations of tea. The memoir is well composed with such oblique suggestions of puritanism, and carefully written, with manuscript revisions, such as substituting 'I' for 'one' throughout. Fry soon shifts from early impressions to describing amusing childhood reactions to his hated Calvinistic nurse – convinced with an imperfect grasp of doctrine that her disobedient charge was going to hell – and the depredations his books and toys suffered from his twin younger sisters whom he called 'the twinges'. Then more objectively other characters appear, including a gardener interested in philosophy, and finally a coachman, indicative of their family's increasing prosperity, who was so desirous of flowers that he stole them.

Aspects of this earliest surviving Club memoir such as the lightly ironic humour and the frank class-awareness will reappear in many of the memoirs to follow.

* * *

Before the second gathering of the Memoir Club nearly two weeks later, Virginia Woolf published two reviews of life-writings that reflect on her reactions to the memoirs she heard and on the one she was about to read. 'A Talk About Memoirs' was written for the *New Statesman*, whose literary editor was Desmond MacCarthy. The talkers are two well-read girls, whom Virginia named after her brother's young children; the subjects of their conversation are five Victorian dropsical volumes of aristocratic and sporting memoirs. Though Judith and Ann disapprove of Mr Lytton Strachey for 'behaving disrespectfully to the great English art of biography', they adopt his point of view in their comments on the aristocrats under review ('Was death their only amusement, and rank their sole romance?'). The sportsmen, they found, at least enjoyed their lives.[8] Then for the *Athenaeum* Woolf reviewed a biography of the banker Thomas Coutts (1735–1822). Retelling the banker's life in her own way, which is how Woolf often reviewed such books, she contends that the diligent reader of memoirs seeks on every page 'the connecting word'; it may be 'something deep sunk beneath the surface, scattered in fragments, disguised behind frippery' but once found, it gives the work its form and the subject its force. (Money and love were the words in Coutts's life.)[9]

What is hidden, suppressed, or subjective is what interests Virginia Woolf most in her friends' memoirs too. 'Objective' memoirs could be triumphant, as she said in her diary about Leonard's memoir at the second meeting of the Club on 15 March which took place at Clive and Vanessa Bell's home in Gordon Square. Nothing can now be known of Leonard's performance, and very little of Virginia's own subjective 'chapter' other than her feeling 'most unpleasantly discomfited' with the result:

> 'Oh but why did I read this egotistic sentimental trash!' That was my cry, & the result of my sharp sense of the silence succeeding my chapter. It started with loud laughter; this was soon quenched; & then I couldn't help figuring a kind of uncomfortable boredom on the part of the males; to whose genial cheerful sense my revelations were at once mawkish & distasteful. What possessed me to lay bare my soul! (18 March)

One of Virginia Woolf's perceptive biographers cites this reaction as revealing everything about Virginia's problems of 'self presentation' and goes on to ask what Virginia had been telling the Club, why its men were discomfited, 'and why, in a group renowned for its openness, was there so much difficulty in speaking frankly?'[10]

The only evidence remaining of what Virginia Woolf had been telling the Memoir Club is the opening of her next memoir in November, which begins 'As I have said, the drawing room at Hyde Park Gate was divided by black folding doors . . . ' That memoir focuses on her family, especially her step-brother George Duckworth, rather than on herself. Of her memoirs' first chapter, that is all that can now be known. Nothing can be known of Leonard's triumphant memoir either, although Virginia records his dismissing her agony of self-consciousness as late-night miasma. Next month Morgan Forster told her he thought her memoir 'splendid'.

The questions raised about the Club's reactions to Virginia's self-revelations brings out again the importance of the context in which the Club's memoirs were written. Frankness, as Leonard Woolf remarked later, was filtered through discretion and reticence even in Bloomsbury. And the performance of reading a memoir seems to have been a daunting affair for Vanessa, then Molly, and now Virginia. For most of the men with their Apostolic experience, it may have been less so. Virginia's reaction also makes clear what would now would be called the gender imbalance of the Memoir Club, which the addition of Forster increased to nine men compared to four women (including Mary Hutchinson). Among the men besides her husband who may have laughed at Virginia's memoir were Desmond MacCarthy, Sydney Waterlow, Clive Bell, Maynard Keynes, Lytton Strachey, and Forster.

＊　＊　＊

Through her diaries Virginia Woolf appears to be the most prominent member in the early years of the Memoir Club, but it was

Morgan Forster who appears to have read the most memoirs over the years, though few of them can be dated precisely. They remain scattered in appendices to his works, collections of his essays, or archives of unpublished papers. Forster's relationship to the Club was unstable, however. The reasons for Forster's periodic misgivings about the Club arose from its history and his. Forster was the only one of the original continuing members (six of whom were married couples) who had not had a sexual relationship with another member. It is not even certain when he actually joined the Club. In March he attended the second meeting of the Club, heard Virginia's memoir, and read one of his own. But then in early September he wrote Leonard Woolf that he would like to join the Memoir Club, accepting the invitation to read a memoir at the next meeting and adding that he thought he could understand what had been happening to the Club.[11] Beyond the changing frequency of the meetings, it is unclear what may have been happening to the Club. In joining the Memoir Club, Forster may have been seeking a creative outlet; for ten years he had been unable to complete a printable novel, having lost interest in writing about heterosexual love in fiction.

Just which memoir Forster read at the second meeting is uncertain. Clive Bell reported to the absent Mary Hutchinson that the memoirs of both Virginia and Forster were excellent, his being perhaps the best. No mention was made of Leonard's memoir.[12] Three of E. M. Forster's early memoirs for the Memoir Club have survived: one on his uncle, one on his introductions to Bloomsbury, and one on his books. In the last one he begins by reminding the Club that they had already 'listened to my childhood, adolescence and undergraduation'. Among Forster's papers only the memoir about meeting Bloomsbury has been given a date: 17 November, 1920. What Forster read at the Club's second meeting, then, may have been the one about his nearest masculine Forster relative in a family of aunts, William Forster (1855–1910), his deceased father's only surviving brother.[13] The short early memoir is very different in tone as well as form from the fond, extended reminiscence of great aunt Marianne

Thornton that was Forster's last book. 'Aunt Monie' was Willie's aunt, Morgan's great aunt (to distinguish nephew from uncle, the names *Morgan* and *Willie* will be used here). Her bequest to Morgan made his writing career possible, as was mentioned; Willie, who quarrelled with her and practically everyone else, left his nephew absolutely nothing, which a decade later was still rankling him.

The memoir reads like the sketch for a Forsterian novel, with an amusing, judgmental narrator, a few characters in a social setting, some domestic and natural scenery, a little dialogue, and an unexpected ending. That the memoir should resemble Morgan's Edwardian fiction is not particularly surprising since he admitted in a late introduction that he had used his 'sedulously masculine' uncle and his Northumberland house for some of the traits of Mrs Failing and her house in *The Longest Journey*. Then in his memoir, Morgan says he attempted to give Willie's downtrodden, shifty wife Aunt Emily some immortality as Charlotte Bartlett in *A Room with a View*. Two features of the memoir, however, are uncharacteristic of Forster's fiction: the enigmatic sexuality of the principal character and the diffidence of the involved memoirist.

The memoir opens without preliminaries. (Later there will be a direct appeal to his audience as well as allusions to Virginia and Roger.) Forty years ago the lonely, unattractive, quietly rich Emily Nash sitting in the rain was proposed to by the younger, handsome, amusing, athletic William Forster. They married, then bolted around the world, bringing home Japanese rubbish from what Morgan, with his Indian and Egyptian experience behind him, calls 'the further east'. Willie had wanted to be a soldier but Morgan's scholarly clerical grandfather had forbidden it, so his son did nothing, grew corrosive, quarrelsome, unforgiving, revengeful, making fantastic judgements about people and scandal-mongering. Willie was acutely resentful of criticism and interference – a trait Morgan admits he shares, except that Willie 'let it be known he wouldn't be spoken to, which I don't do'.

Joining Willie and Emily in Northumberland was an adopted 'daughter' (the quotes are Morgan's and they could have been the disapproving Aunt Monie's) named Leontine Chipman and nicknamed *Leo* and also *Canada* because that is where she came from. Willie's relations with Canada remain obscure; he would become furious when his wife was away, leaving them alone, Morgan says, 'during the hours when copulation is possible in Northumberland'. (It never struck Willie, as it did his nephew, Morgan notes parenthetically, that the groom was also alone during those hours.) Courteous for a time to everyone, he was abominably rude to his wife, which Morgan illustrates with a quarrel over fish at mealtime, the only occasions when husband and wife seem to have met. Fishing, otter-killing, church-going, were Northumberland occupations described by Morgan. Visits by young girls whom Willy was fond of are also mentioned; sometimes he would set them roughly on his nephew. Also there were young male guests to whom Willie was briefly courteous before dismissing them because they were insolent, apathetic, or incompetent. Morgan was not insolent, but he makes no secret of his own apathy and incompetence, lagging and mooning around during his visits. To Canada he was 'quaint, pleasant and cynical' as he thought he was in *The Longest Journey*, but then she hardly considered him a man.

It is a very reflexive memoir, much concerned with Morgan's relationship to Willie as well as Aunt Emily and Canada. The uncle was not ridiculous, not an ass, the nephew insists: 'he satisfied one's aesthetic requirements and thus lulled one's critical faculty'. With the result that Morgan confesses in a direct appeal to the Memoir Club that he has trouble understanding his uncle's sexuality:

> For it will not have escaped such an audience as this that Sex played a large part in my uncle's life. The morbid marriage, the flight around the world, the coming of Canada, the increasing tendency to seclusion in irritability in a life that promised so fair – you work it out, can't you? I can't so well.

The aftertaste of the memoir, for all its critical humour, is regretful, almost bitter, as Morgan ends expressing his dismay

at inheriting nothing from Willie or Aunt Emily to whom, surprisingly, Willie left everything. And he is staggered when Aunt
Emily and Canada, who saw Willie through his fatal illness,
take a house together near Cambridge. Released from Willie's
'harness', they flourish a little during the war. Forster never
visits them. And he is dismayed when his aunt dies leaving everything to Canada, as Uncle Willie appears to have wanted,
except for some legacies to cousins, and nothing to the nephew.
No one, he concludes confessionally again to the Memoir Club,
appears to have quarrelled as completely with Uncle Willie as
he had. The result was 'Silence absolute. But this evening I have
broken it.'

There are relatively few references to Willie in Morgan's diary:
a quotation from him on suiting one's religion to one's host's that
is used in the memoir, and a last rude invitation easily refused.
But Forster briefly broke his silence again in alluding to Uncle
Willie in his Memoir Club memoir on his books, and then late
in life in the introduction to *The Longest Journey* where he is
referred to as a source for Mrs Failing and her house, and as 'a
meddlesome tease of a man' who bought up remaindered copies
of *The Longest Journey* for sixpence apiece and sent them to relatives they were likely to upset.

※　※　※

Records of Memoir Club meetings over the next few months,
when there was at least one meeting, are fragmentary and unin-
formative. '"How seldom we meet!" said Vanessa & yet we all
want to meet; & can't do it', (D II 27) recorded Virginia in her
diary toward the end of March. Then in early July the beginning of one of the most illustrious memoirs in the Club's history
was read. On 7 July memoirs by Molly MacCarthy, Maynard
Keynes, Clive Bell, and Duncan Grant were to be read. Two of
these still exist in their original form, and one of them is still
unpublished. Also surviving are some comments on the memoirs
and the Club's procedures.

Molly's memoir was read, perhaps one should say enacted in her unexplained absence by Desmond, who reported congratulations to his absent wife the next day on the great success of her memoir, with members laughing at all the funny bits:

> I enjoyed reading it *enormously* I began, as you would have done, by breaking down after the first sentence & saying it impossible to read a word more – as it was too stupid. I tried to do this in your voice & with one of your desperate gestures.[14]

Molly was encouraged to go on by Desmond's and other letters such as the Woolfs', who wrote together congratulating her on 'your brilliant & beautiful paper' and urged her to continue with it.[15] Sydney Waterlow also sent congratulations, though he would seem to change his mind when her memoirs were published.

But the exact nature of her memoir is again unclear; probably it was a further installment of her nineteenth-century childhood describing life at Eton from her young girl's point of view. The least feminist, most traditional of Memoir Club women, Molly does not comment on the ironies of hers and her sisters' education there, though her childhood recollections are interspersed with adult asides on the vanished Victorian past – on the contrast, for example, between Victorian poets, such as Tennyson (surrounded on the Isle of Wight by Mrs Cameron's photographs) who could not be silent about nature and the modern poets who seek inspiration in mathematics and dare not leave London. As for modern painters, including presumably those in her audience, they too are in a temper with the past, more interested in sands and rubble than landscapes with flowers, she feels. Even with her own medium, young writers think the great merit of modern prose is to mean absolutely nothing. For a long time, Molly concludes in her second chapter, the rose-coloured glass of nineteenth-century conservatories has been breaking up, while 'the detached biographess' can only murmur 'stones for bread!' And in a later lament she feels insulted as a member of 'the old "Curry and Rice" school' to hear that volume of the marvellous history of English rule in

India banged shut.[16] There was more diversity of opinion in the Memoir Club than is sometimes supposed.

The memoir Desmond performed, judging from the reported reactions, does not sound as if it was written by a very detached biographess. The funny bits he mentions may have had to do with the characterization of her absent-minded mother or quiet Warden-father. The comedy of their financial anxieties over the household account-book – dubbed 'Le Grand Livre' – which both kept and neither could understand, is quite different from the melodrama of Leslie Stephen's rages that Virginia Woolf would write of in her late memoirs. At Eton it was fast or feast, with Molly's father suggesting they cease their Camembert cheese purchases or wine expenses and her mother replying this was impossible, given their guests, and proposing how money could be saved by instantly putting down all the household pets, including the parrot of which the Warden was particularly fond.

How long Molly MacCarthy continued reading her childhood memoirs before publishing them in 1924 cannot now be determined. The queer, fascinating, muddle of Duncan Grant's continued ancestral stories, as reported by Desmond, appears no longer to exist. The two other surviving memoirs read at the same session were each presented in two installments, which suggests the plan for continued memoirs was still one of the Club's aims. Both memoirs entered very different territory from what had been read before. Clive Bell on his first amour and Maynard Keynes on his involvement with the Versailles treaty negotiations extended the range of Memoir Club subjects. Both memoirs stopped at thrilling points, Desmond wrote Molly, not to be continued until the next year. As the bulk of Keynes' long famous memoir was not read until then, the description of its considerable impact on the Club as well as its contrast with Bell's memoir, can be postponed until an account of the first meeting in 1921. At the 1920 meeting, however, Clive Bell proposed, according to Desmond, that only 'practicing novelists' read their memoirs aloud because they enjoyed doing so. An oblique comment on some of the performances, perhaps, the proposal exposes again the distinction between the literary and visual arts sides of the Club, both of which apparently combined to reject Clive's proposal.

* * *

There were two more meetings in 1920. Before the meeting on 17 November the Woolfs dined with the MacCarthys; Virginia's letters to the *New Statesman* the month before criticizing Desmond's (and Arnold Bennett's) demeaning views of the intellectual status of women apparently did not much affect their personal relations. The readers on the 17th were Roger Fry, Morgan Forster, and both Woolfs. Virginia this time was 'fearfully brilliant' (D II 77–8) in a memoir that has survived, as have Fry's and also Forster's, which Virginia described as 'very professional'. Of Leonard's, more impressive than her own she thought and with less pain, again no record remains.

E. M. Forster's 'very professional' second performance, if the archival date given the memoir is accurate, introduces a subject that will later preoccupy the Club's memoirs – namely Bloomsbury.[17] The short untitled memoir, less self-conscious than his first family memoir, is about Forster's first encounters with members of the Group. The manuscript is disordered, and at least one page is missing. Still, it remains a record of Forster's initial response to Bloomsbury's art and aesthetics as well as to the Memoir Club. While not quite equating Bloomsbury with the Club, Forster does directly address the members as representing Bloomsbury when he asks, for instance, 'when first did I stumble against your creative, as opposed to your critical rill?'

The memoir begins once more in late nineteenth-century Cambridge where as an undergraduate Forster was reluctantly persuaded to pay for some lectures by Roger Fry, the principal example in his memoir of Bloomsbury's critical rill. Yet seldom did he get more from such enjoyable lectures in which there were

hints of the coming reign of Mass and Line, and of Treatment, that undying worm. 'It's not the Subject that matters, it's the Treatment.' Roger didn't say this at the time, nor may he ever have said it, nor may anyone in Bloomsbury exactly have said it, yet it may fairly be called the Bloomsbury undertone . . .

Meeting Fry to look at photographs, Forster recalled, was something of a disappointment because of Fry's indifference to his remarks on painting, or maybe it was just the slight feeling

one has always, when recalling the past, to emphasize slightness because the mere effort of remembrance lends undue weight to what has been remembered.

Whether or not Fry's 'Bloomsbury undertone' is remembered with undue weight, it is the most interesting thing Forster has to say about Bloomsbury. While having his portrait done by Fry in 1911 after the post-impressionist exhibitions (Forster's mother hoped the face at least but would be 'clean' but Fry said this was impossible), Forster felt exalted to understand, again perhaps, what Fry 'was up to – to clear Art of reminiscences. Romanticism the enemy. To paint the position of things in space.' This insight lies behind his later memoir.[18] Indeed it is the subject of Forster's encounters with Bloomsbury's visual artists and critics rather than its casually organized treatment that seems to matter most as Forster recalls how the creative rill he first stumbled into became a river after the post-impressionist exhibitions and the Omega Workshop.

Among other recollected occasions on which Forster encountered Bloomsbury are a meagre lunch offered by the successful but uninfluential G. M. Trevelyan, a dinner party of the Sangers, and a visit with an obsessively punctual Arthur Cole to the young Stephens in Fitzroy Square. (Only Adrian is named, and there is no reference to Horace Cole's involvement of the Stephens and Duncan Grant in the 1910 *Dreadnought* hoax). As for meeting the members themselves, there was Fry and there was Duncan Grant, encountered comically in Greenwood's rooms borrowing a chair from under Forster's mother, and in whose art Forster saw some slight pornographic promise. There was also Lytton Strachey whose extraordinary voice coming, as it were, from the carpet in Trevelyan's rooms, startled Forster and dissuaded him from following up an introduction. And there was Clive Bell at Covent Garden, with whom Forster argued about the second French empire and the poor.

Forster apologizes for his erratic Bloomsbury recollections, explaining it would have been different if he kept a diary or letters – which in fact he did, as Virginia noted in her diary on 10 April (D II 27). There is something else, however, missing from Forster's recollected Bloomsbury encounters that may help explain the randomness of his memoir. Fry, Trevelyan, and Charles Sanger were older Apostles when Forster was elected in 1901. Leonard Greenwood, Lytton Strachey and Leonard Woolf would be elected the next year. Their role in Forster's Bloomsbury encounters, especially his Apostolic friendships with Strachey and Woolf – could not be easily discussed in the Memoir Club, at least in 1920, whereas the meetings with non-Apostle members Grant and Bell could be.

*   *   *

Roger Fry's own memoir read in November is unmentioned in Virginia Woolf's diary entry. It now exists only as a two-page fragment. In Virginia's later biography of Fry she quotes the entire fragment, and takes from it an organizing motif of the book as well as an illustration of the 'moments of vision' that are so significant in her fiction and non-fiction.[19] Fry's fragment also involves Virginia in another way, for it is accompanied by a rough sketch of two seated figures that have been plausibly identified as Mary Hutchinson and Virginia at a Memoir Club meeting. Whatever its origin, the sketch is clearly labelled 'Autobiography II', and it begins with the cancelled words 'As I said'.[20]

Fry's second memoir was read on the eve of the publication of his first collection of articles entitled *Vision and Design*. The attention there to vision, the 'Bloomsbury undertone' of formal design, and aesthetic emotion are reflected in what remains of Fry's memoir. The fragment also brings out again the familial puritanism of his upbringing. The Edenic garden of his first home was the setting of his first great passion and disillusionment as well as the imagined scene of subsequent seductions. The passion was for poppies. 'I had a general passion for red' wrote the foremost art-critic of his time looking back, and he worshipped the flowers more sincerely than Jesus and with greater affection than for anyone but his father. The poppy passion was laughed at by his family, 'for all passions even for red poppies leave one open to ridicule'. This becomes one of Virginia themes as she narrates Fry's life. The disillusion in which he discovered 'that justice is not supreme, that innocence is no protection' arose from his being reproved, 'apparently', (the last word of the fragment) for picking one of them in strict obedience to his mother's misunderstood request.

The shock of disillusionment, says his biographer, 'was still tingling fifty years later'. She explains its sharpness and permanence in connection with Fry's mother, but this is an added interpretation to the memoir fragment which itself breaks off with the sacrilegious plucking. The sequel was known, she says, without telling how, but she must have heard it at the Memoir Club, if not elsewhere.

Virginia will use another of Fry's memoirs a little later, again quoting it in its entirety, but it is Fry's second memoir fragment that she returns to when describing the success of his post-impressionist exhibitions. There she extends the significance of his early passion and disillusionment in a passage that is relevant to her own memoirs:

Such moments of vision, when a new force breaks in, and the gropings of the past suddenly seem to have meaning, are probably familiar to most artists. But most artists leave them unexplained. It would need a critic endowed with his own interpretative genius to single out and sum up all the elements in that long process which at last seemed to bear fruit. Unfortunately, though he traced many such spiritual journeys, he never traced his own. And even such a critic would have to admit that the origin of these moments of vision lies too deep for analysis. A red poppy, a mother's reproof, a Quaker upbringing, sorrows, loves, humiliations – they too have their part in moments of vision.[21]

The almost incantatory repetition of the luminous phrase 'moments of vision' was very much in Virginia Woolf's mind as she traced her own 'gropings of the past' in the memoirs she was beginning in 1939 as she finished her biography of Fry. Virginia had first explained the phrase in print in 1918 when reviewing *Trivia* by Logan Pearsall Smith (anonymous later editor of *Cornishiana*) where she describes them as moments 'of inexplicable significance, . . . almost menacing with meaning', which can neither be forgotten, explained, or written down.[22] Such moments will occur in her novels, as well as Forster's, where they can be menacing or ecstatic. That Virginia later credits the phrase to Thomas Hardy, whose *Moments of Vision and Miscellaneous Verses* was published in 1917, is also suggestive of the moments' varying nature.

*   *   *

Virginia Woolf's interpretive use of Roger Fry's second memoir illustrates what could be made of even fragments of the Memoir Club's memoirs. Nowhere is this more in evidence than with her own 'fearfully brilliant' first surviving Club memoir, which has become the most controversial of her autobiographical writings. All the biographies of Virginia Woolf – almost a dozen now and counting – need to interpret it. What has to be noted here is the extent to which her memoir was written in response to her audience. 'To know whom to write for is to know how to write', Virginia Woolf remarked in a 1924 essay (E IV 214). That might well serve as a motto for all the Club's memoirs. Yet a countervailing question is suggested in an earlier remark of Virginia's about Henry James's career when reviewing his letters during the first year of the Memoir Club: 'how far can one write for a select group?' (E III 202).[23] Both bear on the interpretations of Memoir Club memoirs.

To approach the memoir that Virginia read to the Memoir Club, one should try to put aside all the commentary and controversy that has accumulated over the memoir – beginning with Virginia's own changes to the text. What also should be noted is the distance in form and subject of her memoir from *Jacob's Room*, the fictive, modernist commemoration of her brother Thoby – unmentioned in her memoir – that she was also writing at this time.

The memoir published under the title '22 Hyde Park Gate' was apparently written quickly. (A week before the meeting Virginia records in her diary that she must prepare a chapter for the Club.) It exists in three states: there is the original surviving typescript, there are the handwritten changes to that typescript, and there is a revised typescript of a slightly more than half of the original script.[24] It is not known when Virginia made changes to the typescript or retyped it. The only evidence is a letter of 2 February 1932 to Ethyl Smyth that refers to

> 'an old memoir . . . that I wrote ten years ago about our doings with George Duckworth when we were so to speak virgins. It might amuse you but it needs copying such a mess it's in.'[25]

The more significant changes among many insignificant ones are the addition of a title to the memoir (the original typescript is untitled), the deletion of a sentence on George's natural lust and his inability to understand it, the removal of an appeal to her auditors to focus their eyes on the remarkable figure of George, and another added comment that George's lavish embraces of Vanessa were not entirely concealed from strangers. Then in the culminating bedroom scene with which the memoir closes, Virginia deleted everything but the first word from George's 'Beloved I have come to say good night' before continuing:

> and he flung himself on my bed, and took me in his arms.
> Yes, the old ladies of Kensington and Belgravia never knew that George Duckworth was not only father and mother, brother and sister to those poor Stephen girls, he was their lover also.

The scene ends the memoir on a thrilling point, just as Maynard Keynes' and Clive Bell's had the previous meeting in July, but whereas Keynes and Bell continued their accounts the next year, Virginia, contrary to what has sometimes been stated, did not return in a memoir to the bedroom scene for half a dozen years, when she briefly repeated the last scenes of the memoir and amplified a little her hyperbolic description of George as his sisters' lover.

Virginia began her 'chapter', as she called it in her diary, with 'As I have said', as Fry did his; she referred to the function of drawing room doors at Hyde Park Gate and the relic of a barrister's wig belonging to George's late father, but that apparently was the only allusion with her previous discomfiting memoir. There was to be little embarrassing soul-baring in her second memoir, but the laughter must have continued throughout for Virginia's was a wonderfully comic performance. The humour is less gentle than Molly MacCarthy's recollections, but then the Stephen family was more complicated than the Warre-Cornishes. Rather than exposing her soul this time Virginia exposed her family, though her own innocence and naivety were also on display.

To understand the memoir in its context, it is necessary to reclaim the comedy that has virtually disappeared under the mounds of speculation over George Duckworth's incestuous fondlings and cuddlings of his half-sisters. The comedy begins with descriptions of Hyde Park visitors – the women who seek consolation from Julia Stephen for having accidently poisoned their husbands or had their noses chalked with billiard cues, and the men visiting and boring Leslie with their talk which, if interrupted, could result in streams of tea and raisins erupting through their noses. Quickly, however, the time and place shift with the entrance of George Duckworth, as Virginia passes silently over her mother's and her half-sister's deaths and the gloom of her father's bereaved household to focus on her elder half-brother, now in effect the head of the family. What she described in her earlier biography of Vanessa as the 'shapeless catastrophe' of their lives is now turned into a comedy of manners.[26] Life with George, says Virginia, was like being a minnow in a tank with a whale. (The whale had his problems with the minnows too, as when Virginia sent a wire signed with her nickname 'Goat' that became garbled into greeting his fiancée as an aged goat.)

Virginia first tried characterizing George Duckworth in the early fragment of a novel that described his faun-like good looks and excitable stupidity.[27] In her memoir she continues the simile: one of his female admirers likened him to Hermes:

> but if you looked at him closely you noticed that one of his ears was pointed; and the other round; you also noticed that though he had the curls of a God and the ears of a faun he had unmistakably the eyes of a pig.

With an independent income he was generous with gifts and could be as self-sacrificing as a saint, but two other characteristics intervened, namely an emotionality and a stupidity that kept him from understanding his own feelings or judging their impact on others. Added to these were his snobbery and his obstinacy. George Duckworth was determined to rise to at least the lower aristocracy from the professional upper middle-classes, for which his density had ill-equipped him.

Describing his attempts to take first one suffering sister, then the other to dinner parties and dances where his social ambitions might be advanced, Virginia's memoir becomes a class comedy. The old ladies of Kensington and Belgravia invoked in Virginia's conclusion were shocked by George's young half-sister's talk of Plato's Symposium (which Virginia had been studying with Janet Case and which first enlightened her, she says elsewhere, about homosexuality). Yet these ladies proceeded to take her and George to a French farce, complete with copulating actors, from which they all had to flee. From there the memoir describes George's taking her to the more familiar world of artists and professional men, which he disdained, and then comes the final comic shock of the bedroom scene.

Relevant to that scenic conclusion is the observation Virginia made about her writing twenty years later toward the end of 'Sketch of the Past':

> But whatever the reason may be, I find that scene making is my natural way of marking the past. A scene always comes to the top; arranged; representative.[28]

Whatever the basis in reality of the scene, it makes a good comic climax – which is not exactly the right word. (George was completely chaste until his wedding, Virginia notes earlier in the memoir on the authority of his sister Stella's husband Jack Hills.)

Recalling the parties with George again in 'Sketch of the Past', Virginia ends again in the bedroom, but alone now with memories of party talk that remained as she read her Greek with Janet Case next morning. The only descriptions of sexual abuse there concern not George but his brother Gerald, whose molestation of her as a child she records uncomically.

It is in a letter to Vanessa (25? July 1911) about Janet Case that Virginia provides the most reliable historical testimony relevant to her memoir:

> She has a calm interest in copulation ... and this led to the revelation of all Georges malefactions. To my surprise, she has always had an intense dislike of him; and used to say 'Whew – you nasty creature', when he came in and began fondling me over my Greek. When I got to the bedroom scenes, she dropped her lace, and gasped like a benevolent gudgeon.

That there were 'malefactions' seems clear but they were public as well as private, and directed at both his half-sisters, which fits with the affectionate obtuseness of George that Virginia described. But this reality should not obscure the humour of the Virginia's Memoir Club memoir.

Vanessa's role in Virginia's family comedy brings out another important Memoir Club aspect of the piece Virginia eventually entitled '22 Hyde Park Gate'. Virginia's is the first Club memoir to involve another member of the Club in a prominent way. Eventually many of the memoirs will concern themselves with other members, but not at the beginning. Virginia's, of course given her subject, could hardly avoid being about Vanessa, as some of hers will be about Virginia and their involvement with George Duckworth. Virginia's memoir ends depicting George as dutiful father, mother, brother, sister to and lover of both 'those poor Stephen girls'. Earlier in her comedy, she will blame Vanessa, who could not help herself, for George's attentions, for if

> she had been born with one shoulder higher than another, with a limp, with a squint, with a large mole on her left cheek, both our lives would have been changed for the better.

She was, however, the touching spectacle of a beautiful, mother-less, eighteen-year-old that George could use for his own social advancement – except that her passion was 'for paint and turpentine, for turpentine and paint'. Yet curiously, there are places in Virginia's memoir when her mildly mocked sister seems not to be among her Memoir Club listeners, as when, for example, Virginia writes that what happened in the cab taking tearful George and the resisting Vanessa to another party 'will never be known'. Presumably Vanessa knew and even remembered.

As for Vanessa, her accounts for the Memoir Club written after Virginia's, including some before her death, present a slightly different view of George Duckworth, as shall appear later. Rather than a lover, Vanessa regarded him more, she would say, as a nursemaid cum chaperon, lavishing gifts upon her but ultimately failing to make her into his kind of social success. Desmond MacCarthy in another Club memoir recalled seeing Vanessa at a party looking like a slave in George's company, and this becomes the departure point for another of Vanessa's recollections. Her memoirs about Virginia's childhood, about life at Hyde Park Gate, about the awful weekend parties George made her attend, and about George's wife are part of the Memoir Club milieu in which Virginia's memoirs should be considered. And not only hers, for there would also be Lytton Strachey's later memoir of his ancestral home, which reads in part like a continuation of Virginia's. As the history of the Memoir Club unfolded, its accumulating memoirs influenced the writing of others. Always the context of the Club remains relevant to the interpretation and appreciation of them.

*   *   *

At the last meeting of the first year of the Memoir Club on 8 December, Molly MacCarthy continued her memoirs, perhaps on to the account of her being sent away unhappily to a High Church school for girls, but no details remain of her memoir. Nor is there any record of Mary Hutchinson's first memoir, other than the mention in Virginia Woolf's diary that she was going to read one, and Virginia's determination to laugh at her jokes although Mary never laughed at hers.

So ended what can now be recovered from the first year of the Memoir Club. 1920 was also the year that the Woolfs' press had its first big success with the publication of memoirs. In July, the month that Forster's *The Story of the Siren* was printed, the Hogarth Press also published Maxim Gorky's *Reminiscences of Leo Nicolayevitch Tolstoi*, translated rather strangely by the Woolfs' friend S. S. Koteliansky and then Englished by Leonard Woolf. Gorky had sent Koteliansky a copy along with the English translation rights. It was reprinted immediately and forty years later was still selling, Leonard Woolf wrote in his autobiography.[29] The memoir is a small masterpiece of twentieth century life-writing not only for the unvarnished picture of Tolstoy in old age but also for the response to him – the mixed admiration and the misgivings – of the much younger Gorky. Like the best reminiscences, Gorky's are a blend of biography and autobiography. It is only the picture of Tolstoy, however, that Virginia Woolf writes of in a brief *New Statesman* review. (Writing reviews of her own Press's publications did not continue for long.) Gorky shocks his readers, she thought, by showing Tolstoy like other men in his conceit, intolerance, and vindictiveness, and she quotes examples of his misogyny. Yet the vividness of Gorky's depiction of Tolstoy's power sends her back to Tolstoy's works to see if the conception of them has changed. Her review concludes that Gorky's incomplete memoir approached completeness because it did not attempt to explain or include everything: 'Here there is a very bright light, here darkness and emptiness. And perhaps this is the way in which we see people in reality.'[30] The memoirists of the Memoir Club wrote no great-man (or woman) reminiscences, but if they wanted a model for the brief lives they would be writing for one another, here was one that they could all read, and probably did.

Private and Public Affairs: 1921–1922

The memoirs that Clive Bell and Maynard Keynes began reading to the Memoir Club on 7 July 1920 were completed on 2 February 1921, the Club's first meeting in the new year. These memoirs indicate how in the course of a year the range of Memoir Club subjects expanded from the more remote past to the recent present, and from relatively impersonal childhood memories to intimately private or controversially public affairs.

As Memoir Club friends, Clive Bell and Maynard Keynes were not close. Keynes' closest Bloomsbury friends at the time the Club began and until the advent of Lydia Lopokova two years later were Clive's wife Vanessa and her partner Duncan Grant, which may have had something to do with Clive's feelings. The posthumous memoir of Maynard published in *Old Friends* brought protests from economists when it appeared in 1956. Clive and Maynard liked but did not love each other, according to the memoir; though he was the cleverest man Clive knew, Keynes' cocksureness irritated him, especially as Keynes lacked innate feeling for visual art. Bell's memoir opens with its own protest against the description of himself as 'a gay and amiable dog' in Keynes' early Cambridge beliefs memoir because they only met later.[1] Nevertheless the memoirs they read together at the Memoir Club are not inconsistent with images of their authors as cocksure economist and gay dog.

Clive Bell's lost first memoir – the 'purely objective' one of Virginia's description – was, he says at the start of his second, about the loves of his nonage having mainly to do with horses until one carried him to 'the first considerable affair of my life'. As a man of many affairs – the Don Juan of Bloomsbury as he has been stigmatized – Clive has often been underrated, sometimes by himself, but not in his second memoir where he presents himself as an accomplished lover while describing the charms of his first mistress. Here and elsewhere in his writing, the prose is always vigorous.[2]

Clive's memoir is about his affair with Mrs Raven Hill, wife of the well-known *Punch* illustrator and cartoonist, 'whom you, Vanessa knew' but eight years later; she was by then not so lovely, soft and sweet like a pear, partridge, or gardenia but had not yet turned old and whorish. What begins as his sexual initiation at eighteen in 1899 turns into the story of an affair that lasted through his marriage to the First World War, making the time covered by the memoir longer than others read to the Club so far. Clive keeps to his own point of view, explaining later that it would have been impertinent for him to describe the feelings of a mature, much sought after woman, but that view includes a frank account of the character Mrs Raven Hill (her first name Annie is never given). She was not stupid nor deficient in appearance, temperament, or technique. She was skillful with lips and fingers, but she lacked culture and intellect, hence could not be *une grande amoureuse*, which is Clive's supreme compliment for a woman. Besides, her bottom was too large for his taste. They were never in love 'but we had lust and some liking'. The relationship was without camaraderie, 'yet from her', Clive says, 'I learned the best of what I know'. She had lived in the Latin Quarter, and Clive Bell's son Quentin thought Clive first learned of French painters from her and thus had a Degas reproduction in his rooms at Trinity.[3] In his memoir Clive says her taste in art was genuine, if vulgar – but that conclusion may have come later in their relationship.

The first part of the memoir concerns Clive's seduction, how it started with Mrs Raven Hill's admiring Arthur's curls (his name when he had hair). The initial adulterous encounter Clive describes as a fiasco – like a duck-and-drake affair on Charleston Pond. He will not try to compete with Stendhal's Julien Sorel in telling of his humiliation, though he will lard his tale with French tags and references, including quoting a description in old French of Diane de Poitiers by a seventeenth-century memoirist that no one in the Memoir Club could have been expected to understand. The affectation, remarked on by Desmond in his report to Mollie, had its self-conscious ironies, as Clive turns to Meredith, Thackeray, Byron in describing his self-adulation for having had Mrs Raven Hill.

The rest of the memoir – and the first one in the Club about events directly affecting the personal relations of members – describes the off and on liaison and Mrs Raven Hill's management of it. She was 'a little cross when I married, because I did not come back to her – for a couple of years I think'. The casual uncertainty as to the exact time – what did it say to the Memoir Club about Clive and Vanessa's marriage and about his flirtation with his sister-in-law? The affair then went charmingly on again, and there were golden moments and multiple orgasms in his bachelor rooms in London (with Thoby and Saxon Sydney-Turner banging on the door for tea), in a house on, of all places, Clapham Common, at Brighton or at Bournemouth, in his family home at Seend, and finally even in his study at 46 Gordon Square for the last violent, indecent, abandoned time as the war was beginning to turn the world topsy-turvy.

Clive Bell in various writings claimed that only states of mind were real, which he thought he derived from Moore's philosophy, but in this memoir states of body are most real:

She had given me 'la grande volupté' and with that odd self-consciousness of mine, which gives me often a sense of Life flowing through me and of myself converting it into experience, I felt to myself as I drove home, 'I have had it. I have <u>almost</u> got it now, the thing we all desire.'

Clive's assertive, heterosexual amorousness is on display here for his Memoir Club friends. His amusingly explicit account seems almost to provoke the inhibitions of his fellow memoirists. Among his listeners was Mary Hutchinson. Vanessa invited Mary to the Club meeting in 1921, though she knew Clive and

Mary had agreed not to see each other for a while. Their affair had begun the year after he stopped seeing Mrs Raven Hill, and it survived the current interruption until 1927. (Mary Hutchinson's relations with the Memoir Club were not only through Clive; Lytton Strachey was also a cousin and confidante.) What Vanessa thought of Clive's memoir is unrecorded. She had met Mrs Raven Hill, as Clive says, and was impressed with the way she managed an old lover (not Clive). This was in 1908, before the affair with Clive had resumed; in a letter to Virginia that year, Vanessa mentioned Mrs Raven Hill's improper talk, adding that she hoped to learn something about birth control from her.

Virginia's reaction to Clive's memoir is known, however. Recording the Memoir club meeting in her diary on 5 February, she described Clive and Maynard's memoirs as 'elaborate & polished' with Clive's being 'mellow & reminiscent'. But she was surprised to learn from it that his affair with Mrs Raven Hill 'coincided with his attachment to me then. But she was a voluptuary. He was not "in love".' Clearly the Memoir Club was a place to learn more about one's relationships with old friends. (Virginia also remarked on the tactless Sydney Waterlow – whom she had told about Clive's and Mary's separation – congratulating Clive in front of everyone.)

Though Clive Bell never published his reminiscences of Mrs Raven Hill, he did explain at the end of his memoir that he had written of her freely because she was now an imbecile. In a note added in 1930, perhaps for another Club reading of the memoir (it was read again in 1950), he says she had now been dead for some years.

*   *   *

John Maynard Keynes did not publish his memoir 'Dr Melchior: A Defeated Enemy' either but left careful instructions for its posthumous publication along with the Cambridge beliefs memoir that he read later. With the appearance of *Two Memoirs* in 1949, as was noted, the public awareness of the Memoir Club began – an awareness, however, that even now does not yet extend to all the remaining memoirs and their subjects.

Keynes may have been moved to arrange for the printing of his 1920–1 memoir of Melchior when he was sent in 1942 some German minutes of his 1919 peace treaty negotiations that had turned up. They reminded him, he wrote, of 'an episode on which I wrote some elaborate memoirs, which have never yet been published'.[4] Elaborate memoirs they are, and may have done more than any others to draw attention to the Memoir Club. Saul Bellow, for instance, cited them in his novel *Ravelstein* as model memoirs. Despite the fame, however, the context in which Keynes read his memoir still needs to be described. The dates of the reading have yet to be given correctly: David Garnett in his editorial note for *Two Memoirs* thought it dated from the 30s; the collected edition of Keynes' writings added a correction dating the memoir 2 February 1921, but omitting the date of 7 July 1920 when the first part of the memoir was read. The earlier date is significant, for by then Keynes' polemic *The Economic Consequences of the Peace* (see Chapter 1), published at the end of 1919, had sold over 100,000 copies, which helps to explain why his memoir opens without any Memoir Club introduction or explanation. Parts of the book were indeed read at Charleston as Keynes was writing it there. (Leonard Woolf, who must have heard part of it, wrote Keynes that his psychological analysis of Wilson was absolutely right and hoped he was doing Lloyd George too.[5]) And before the book there were the despairing letters about the peace conference that Keynes had written to Vanessa Bell and Duncan Grant from Paris. The letters to Vanessa became, in turn, part of another Memoir Club memoir years after his death when some members were resorting to the reading of old letters as part of their turn to perform. It was to an audience that included much younger people in 1957 that Vanessa read excerpts copied out from Keynes' letters of how he was at the very first civilian negotiations in Germany, how later he was engaged in secret meetings with the enemy (which she must not mention), how he was living without any private life whatever in a state of nervous excitement for weeks, and finally, just before he resigned, how bad the treaty was despite Lloyd George's desperate wish now to change it.[6]

In addition to his unpublished letters to Charleston, Keynes' involvement as the Treasury's representative at the peace conference is documented by various official letters and memoranda that have been included in the Royal Economic Society edition of his collected writings. The mostly dry, official tone contrasts, of course, with the informal, personal remarks of the memoir. Keynes reveals his sensitivity to tone in the official documents where he notes at one point that he had to use the coldest tones possible to the Germans about a trick in their negotiations. The official records also show how Keynes simplified his narrative by omitting the financial complexities of his work on loans and such matters, including the useful negotiations he had with the Americans, in contrast with the French. The Melchior memoir also shows Keynes as less pessimistic than he was later, especially just before his resignation when he felt like an accomplice in what he saw as the tragic farce of the final treaty.

Leonard Woolf in his review of *Two Memoirs* described 'Dr Melchior: A Defeated Enemy' as 'a kind of secret appendix' to *The Economic Consequences of the Peace*. Virginia, reading the polemic in April 1920, found it 'a book that influences the world without being in the least a work of art: a work of morality, I suppose'.[7] Keynes' elaborate memoir is a work of literary art, however, as well as morality. His brilliantly written narrative, while not a work of fiction, can be described in the traditional terms of plot, setting, and character.

The plot of Keynes' memoir – and he actually uses the term – begins with an account of the uncertainty, encouraged by the Prime Minister Lloyd George, that surrounded the Conference at its beginning and throughout the whole process. Conflicts soon developed between the military, who had arranged the various armistices, and the civilian authorities concerned with the economic consequences of the blockade of Germany. Keynes is admirably clear in the ensuing welter of detail, centring it on the basic problems of how the food Germany needed was to be paid for by their gold, the transfer of their mercantile ships, or a loan from the Allies. He travelled with negotiators to Trèves ('as you know, is in Germany'), unwelcomed on Marshall Foch's train, to discuss directly with the Germans for the first time, and there he met Dr Melchior with whom, Keynes writes 'I was to have one of the most curious intimacies in the world, and some very strange passages of experience.'

That is the thrilling point, described by Desmond to Molly, on which Keynes ends the first part of his memoir that Keynes calls a 'section'. The second part is four times as long as the first part; it is the longest memoir read at a single meeting in the Club's history (the total length is over 15,000 words) and certainly deserves the 'elaborate memoirs' label Keynes gave it. 'Dr Melchior: A Defeated Enemy' begins again with the armistice conditions, explaining how Keynes was involved in them as the English financial representative on the Supreme Economic Council. (He had already had some experience in the use of diplomacy in financial negotiations with the United States.) Keynes outlines the differing positions of the Allies on the blockade of Germany. The irresolute English, who had perfected it, regarded the blockade almost as an end in itself. The Americans wanted the blockade lifted so they could unload their large pork reserves. The French insisted no potential reparations money or ships should be used for the needed food, while the Germans warned of imminent starvation and Bolshevism if the blockade were not lifted. At Trèves the negotiations over food and finance accomplished little: the Germans handed over some money in exchange for food and finally the surrender of the German ships was agreed upon. Then it was back to Paris and bed, for Keynes was ill with the flu. He convalesced with the Bussys in the south of France and then was summoned back for more inconclusive negotiations at Trèves. Keynes quotes from the German arguments (acknowledging but rejecting his own objections to the loan they wanted) that food, ships, and gold were all connected. He was convinced in spite of French objections that German gold had to be used to pay for food.

Time passed and the question of food became more urgent. The peace conference was preoccupied with the claims of various emerging religious nationalities (including Lawrence of Arabia supposedly translating his Emir's speech in support of Arab hegemony in the Middle East while the Emir recited a chapter from the Koran). Then Keynes was off to Spa on the frontier of Belgium with Rear-Admiral Hope and the Armistice Commission for more negotiations, where Dudley Ward, his chief of a staff and an old neo-pagan friend, obtained the reports on what was happening in Germany – reports that had previously gone only to the acting first secretary of the Foreign Office in Paris, one Sydney Waterlow, who had been keeping them to himself. Keynes' diplomatic efforts on behalf of the Treasury must have been irritating for the Foreign office. Waterlow was among Keynes' Memoir Club audience, but there is no record of his response to Keynes' memoir.

The impasse continued at Spa to which Keynes adds some mixed-metaphor relief on the interpreters' difficulties. Keynes' narrative is laced with irony and humour but it is not often quite so comic. Over French protests, the language of negotiation had been English, and at one point the translator was defeated when the presiding German paused before reaching his verb.

> Nor could the Frenchman, once wound up to oratory, his pregnancy consummated, and the motions of evacuation set in train, interrupt the processes of Nature half-way or restrain the stream half-cock, until he had far overpassed the retentiveness of the interpreter's vessel.

Finally Keynes, as frustrated as the pained Melchior appeared to be, at the empty formalities and triple translations of the conference, sought permission from a surprised Admiral Hope to overcome the restrictions on civilian interchange with the enemy and talk privately with Melchior, who spoke and understood English perfectly. It was granted and Keynes had his first private meeting with Dr Melchior, the memory of which was blurred by his excitement. 'In a sort of way', Keynes notes almost parenthetically,

'I was in love with him.' Both men were moved at the interview, during which Keynes tried to reassure him and his Weimar government of the English and American support for supplying food once the ships were handed over, and that the German negotiators at Trèves should have some latitude in the matter. Melchior tried to persuade his government but failed; when this was communicated, Keynes persuaded Hope to break off negotiations and leave for Paris without informing the Germans.

The matter was now taken over by the Supreme War Council led by Clemenceau and Lloyd George and Wilson's adviser Colonel House, the President being absent. While Keynes and Hope were advising him, Lloyd George used the trick of a staged telegram from the army about how the troops could not stand by while children starved. Clemenceau yielded on the issue of ships being turned over, and Lloyd George evaded his trap to have the matter handled by Foch by arguing that it was a naval matter, and the First Sea Lord Admiral Wemyss should manage it. The French finance minister Lucien Klotz still resisted using German gold for food rather than reparations, but Lloyd George dramatically crushed him with anti-Semitic gestures of a Jew clutching money bags and allusions to the threat of Lenin and Trotsky that led to conference whispers of 'Klotzky'. The Americans supported the English, the French cause was lost, and Keynes together with a French advisor were instructed to prepare a formula for the use of the gold for food. Never had Lloyd George's extraordinary powers been more admired by Keynes. It was the most melodramatic scene he had ever witnessed, he wrote Vanessa Bell at the time.

Now Keynes' narrative is off to Brussels where Wemyss was to settle the issue of the ships. The Admiral, having apparently learned something of what Keynes calls his 'escapade' with Melchior, summoned Keynes to tell him the Germans must surrender the ships without preliminary declarations or haggling, and could he see the Germans privately about this. Which he did, meeting Melchior again, this time accompanied by the Admiral's Chief of Staff, and reassuring him that if the Germans first declared freely that the ships would be turned over, the Allies would revictual Germany. And so it happened.

The plot summary of Keynes' memoir tells, then, how the English along with the Americans supported the Germans against the French in the negotiations over paying for food with German gold and their merchant marine.

There were other meetings with Melchior that Keynes does not detail, but in a brief coda to his memoir he describes an Amsterdam meeting with Melchior in October, without barriers, and after Melchior resigned his position at the betrayal of Germany by its negotiators, and Keynes his at Lloyd George's giving up on moderating the Peace Treaty. Their Paris negotiations now seeming like an absurd dream, they gossiped 'as two ordinary people' about the situation at Weimar, Keynes understanding now the German fear of Russia. He read to Melchior and his business associate, the 'German American Jew' Paul Warburg, the attack on President Wilson in *The Economic Consequences of the Peace*. Warburg giggled at it, but Melchior, almost in tears, felt 'The Tablets of the Law . . . had perished meanly.' Those are the last words of the memoir. Keynes does not use the letter Melchior wrote him after receiving the book in which he praised 'the refined and magnetising art of representation that gave me the feeling of reading a lugubrious, bewildering and lofty drama . . . '[8]

* * *

Any sketch of the involved plot of Keynes' memoir without its settings and especially characters leaves out its most unforgettable parts. As with *The Economic Consequences of the Peace*, where the arguments have been largely forgotten while the characterizations of the leaders that Keynes later reprinted separately remain, the places and people of 'Dr Melchior: A Defeated Enemy' are the most memorable aspects of Keynes' 'elaborate memoirs'.

The settings of Keynes' memoir are mostly rooms – that Bloomsbury motif made familiar in the titles and works of E. M. Forster and Virginia Woolf (and to which Keynes had devoted an

Apostle paper). The memoir opens with getting rooms in Paris which was the first priority and also, he says, defending the prerogatives of the Treasury represented by Keynes and his staff, including Dudley Ward. The atmosphere of Keynes' hotel and the officials there 'had already developed in full measure the peculiar flavour of smallness, cynicism, self-importance, and bored excitement that it was never to lose'. Later when he was ill the art nouveau wall-paper would prey on his sensibilities. At Trèves Keynes stayed on the cramped negotiating train rather than in a requisitioned German household as he first intended as a small kind of enjoyable wartime atrocity. Fifteen negotiators were crowded around a bridge table at the start of the negotiations; later the discussions were carried on in the back parlour of a public house.

The Teutonic setting of the semi-baronial villa at Spa –'hardly larger than Charleston' – had imitation medieval décor and melancholy pinewoods where the Kaiser, Hindenburg, and the militaristic Ludendorff (a name Keynes enjoyed applying to Vanessa Bell) owned villas. Keynes went on to speculate that the German leaders had been influenced by Wagner. 'What else', he wrote in a passage marked for cancellation, 'had planted them in their villas at Spa but that these were the likes the neighbourhood could furnish to third-rate operatic scenery?' With the English taking over however, Wagner was replaced by Jane Austen: 'Miss Bates had vanquished Brünnhilde, and Mr Weston's foot was firmly planted on the neck of Wotan.'

The setting for Keynes' first interview with Melchior, however, had to be in a small room because Melchior's arrogant German clerks at their leisure refused to move from a larger one. After that came the gorgeous scenery of the Supreme War Council in a great oak-panelled conference chamber hung with tapestry representations of Rubens, the leaders sitting in a steep horseshoe with advisers crowding behind. Then comes the second meeting with Melchior in a Brussels bedroom with the night detritus of a chemise on the bed and an unemptied chamber pot.

※   ※   ※

But it is the personalities in the 'magnetising art' of 'Dr Melchior: A Defeated Enemy' that make it most memorable. 'I cant say how much I envy you for describing characters in the way you do' (L II 456) Virginia Woolf wrote to Keynes the day after hearing the second part of his memoir. Keynes had already demonstrated his ability to describe characters in the depiction of the leaders in *The Economic Consequences of the Peace*. In the first part of his memoir alone there is the simple, peasant-minded, moustache-tugging Allied Commander-in-Chief Marshal Foch, dangerous but unimportant, according to Keynes. There is the empty-headed, surly seadog Admiral Browning with a meat-hook for a hand with which he filled his pipe. Admiral Hope was gentle and deaf, with pink cheeks and peculiar irises. Then there is an American lieutenant 'with charms' and what Keynes mysteriously calls a habit of 'internal expectoration' characteristic of the type, but which he has no time to explain. There is time for the fat, fur-coated Minister Erzberger, and his hunnish aides, one looking like the pig in *Alice in Wonderland*, whose personal appearance allows Keynes the Strachean exclamation, 'who knows but that it was the real cause of the war!' Accompanying them, however, was the small, exquisitely clean, sorrowful figure of Dr Melchior.

Part II brings in the immaculate, irresolute Lord Reading picking at his thumb and looking like his tie-pin, and Herbert Hoover dreaming of floating pigs in his concern with disposing of American bacon supplies, a description quoted from Keynes' official report and about the only time he let himself go in them. The French negotiator in the Trèves conference, Charles de Lasteyrie, identified only as 'Count de C——', leads Keynes into a personal digression for the Memoir Club. The Count would not admit that he could not understand English, which caused problems in the negotiations, as Keynes noted in his report. The Count, who later became finance minister, is dismissed in Keynes' memoir as 'a foolish creature! I wonder what has become of him. I don't believe that I have ever in the aggregate been so rude to anyone' (an awesome remark, thought one of his biographers, given Keynes' fabled rudeness to subordinates). A banquet lunch once with Count de C—— and wife in the graceless exactitude of their apartment, complete with hired waiters, exquisite conventional food and Madame's witticisms on Keynes' bachelorhood, leads Keynes to comment on 'the grasping sterility of France; or that part of France, which in spite of what Clive and Roger may say, is France'. Nowhere else in the memoir is Keynes' antipathy to the French made so explicit and so personal.

Keynes continues his vignettes in describing the Trèves talks: one German representative is compared to a broken umbrella, another with a face full of duelling scars is more cheerful. Then there is their spokesman Dr Melchior, with whom Keynes introduces the title theme of his memoir:

> This Jew, for such, though not by appearance, I afterwards learn him to be, and he only, upheld the dignity of defeat.

Later in his memoir, describing Lloyd George's ridicule of Klotz by gesturing with money bags, Keynes mentions 'the anti-Semitism, not far below the surface in such an assemblage'. It is not far below the surface in Keynes' memoir either, particularly the stereotype of the defeated Jew. Melchior may not have looked like a Jew as the short, plump, well-groomed Klotz did with his 'unsteady, roving eye, and his shoulders a little bent in an instinctive deprecation'. But in his private meetings with Keynes Melchior 'spoke with the passionate pessimism of a Jew'. And at the end of the memoir he is the sad German not the laughing American Jew, 'a strict and upright moralist, a worshipper of the Tablets of the Law, a Rabbi'.

Maynard Keynes' post-Dreyfus, pre-Holocaust anti-Semitism is a paradox. Dreyfus is unmentioned in his account of Europe before the war in *The Economic Consequences of the Peace* or anywhere else in his extensive writings. (Clemenceau, the most impressive of the leaders at the peace conference for Keynes was, together with his friend Zola, a Dreyfusard.) Two of Keynes' close economist friends at Cambridge were Jewish, not to mention

Leonard Woolf sitting among his auditors at the Memoir Club. In the Twenties Keynes wrote an admiring sketch of Einstein, a Jew like 'my dear Melchior' and some other German economist friends; yet he went on to say that if he lived in Germany he thought he might turn anti-Semite too preferring to be 'mixed up with Lloyd George than with the German political Jews'.[9] In the Thirties Keynes joined in a College protest against the Nazi treatment of Jews, yet during and after the Second World War he disparaged the 'gritty' Jewish types among the Americans he was negotiating with.

In 'Dr Melchior: A Defeated Enemy' the recurring allusion to Jews is an aspect of Keynes' national/racial stereotyping. French grasping sterility, empty-headed English eccentricity, methodical Huns, American brashness, even Lloyd George's Welsh wizardry are all a part of it. So too is the characterizing – caricaturing really – of Admiral Browning, Lord Reading, Marshall Foch, Minister Erzberger and others. One of the best examples is the description of Admiral 'Rosie' Wemyss, a descendant of one of William IV's illegitimate progeny, and a very different kind of admiral than Browning or Hope. With 'a comical, quizzical face and a single eye-glass', Wemyss was experienced, lazy, pleasure-loving, middle-aged, but with the instincts still of a flirtatious midshipman that Keynes found very agreeable. Wemyss's social self-confidence, indifference to appearances, and openly comical, despairing appeal to Keynes' expertise in conference difficulties (like the Provost of King's says Keynes, in an aside to the Memoir Club) were perplexing to the Germans:

> was he half-witted and imbecile? Or was he playing a game with them far cleverer than anything conceivable? They never made up their minds which; to the end of history, I expect, the character of the English Rosie of the day will confound the understanding of Central Europe.

Keynes' keen awareness of the physical appearance of the characters in his memoir (there are, apart from Count C——'s wife, practically no women in it) is part of his memoir's unconcealed homoeroticism which the Memoir Club familiar with Keynes' susceptibilities would appreciate. (At least one of his lovers was among the audience.) Quite different is the reticence of the later memoir on his Cambridge beliefs that accompanied the Melchior one in *Two Memoirs*.

All of which raises the question of what Keynes originally intended to do with 'Dr Melchior: A Defeated Enemy'. It is, above all, a memoir, a personal reminiscence in form, though of public events in its content. Several features of the printed text suggest he was intending to publish it. There is an extended foot-note describing the general who was Foch's 'attendant sprite' – was this an afterthought or also read to the Club? There is the concealment of identities with initials in describing a French negotiator and an American one, and there is the cancelled passage about Wagner. Nor would the personal references to Clive, Roger, Charleston, and the Bussys have been understood outside the Club. Then there was the 1924 controversy with Klotz who had written a book ironically attacking Keynes' 'monetary megalomania' and had to be reminded in the *Times* by Keynes of the onslaught he had received from Lloyd George at the peace conference, though without an allusion to its anti-Semitism.[10] Keynes might have included the memoir in *Essays in Biography* (1933) where he reprinted the striking portraits of the Peace Conference leaders from *The Economics Consequences of the Peace* and added a cancelled fragment describing Lloyd George. But that may have entailed some reconsideration of the homoerotic allusions in the memoir. Keynes did add an enigmatic footnote to his 1929 review of Churchill's history of the war, in which he referred to recording his impressions of the negotiations over the provisioning of Germany 'but the time to consign them to print is not yet'.[11] After its posthumous publication, the Melchior memoir was added to editions of *Essays in Biography*. When reprinted in the *Collected Writings*, it was illustrated with a photograph of Keynes and Melchior along with the wives they had both married later.

Lastly there is the odd irony of Keynes' title. Much of the memoir – the masterly narration, the vivid characterizations – has little to do with the dear enemy Melchior, who, incidentally, is never mentioned in *The Economic Consequences of the Peace*. Keynes' later meetings with Melchior, after he arranged to have the German delegation locked up in a French castle near Paris so he could visit and negotiate with them, are all passed over. Nor does Keynes include the story that he liked to repeat later of telling Melchior, who was being obstinate about some point, 'if you go on like that, Melchior, we shall think you are as difficult as an Ally'.[12]

As for the three meetings with Melchior that are detailed, do they really convey the notion of 'an escapade' with an enemy, or the 'curious intimacy' and 'strange passages of experience' that Keynes foretells at the end of the first part? But then it does not much matter that the memoir is really not about Dr Melchior. In the end, the relationship may have been for Keynes a way of expressing and relieving personally his own pessimism about the peace treaty and his involvement with it.

＊　＊　＊

For the Memoir Club, 'Dr Melchior: A Defeated Enemy' expanded the scope of what their memoirs were about, and with a daunting literary skill. In extending its subjects to contemporary public events with a narrative art that set a very high standard for all the memoirists, not just the professional writers among them, 'Dr Melchior: A Defeated Enemy' changed the Memoir Club. Keynes demonstrated that its memoirs could be about serious issues without forsaking humour or intimacy. As for himself, the Memoir Club gave Keynes an opportunity, an occasion with an audience of old friends, for the private elaboration of the protest he had made with such public success. Though he read only a few more memoirs, the Club remained important to him. Clive Bell remembered Keynes saying years later after one of the dinners preceding a meeting, 'if everyone at this table, except myself, were to die tonight, I do not think I should care to go on living'.[13]

The Woolfs had to leave before Keynes had finished reading his lengthy second part, so Virginia wrote in her letter next day that praised his character descriptions asking to borrow his manuscript, which they thought 'quite magnificent'. Leonard's account after its publication nearly thirty years later called the memoir not only a secret appendix to *The Economic Consequences of the Peace* but in its own right 'a masterpiece of subtle and dramatic description' that shed light on

> all his qualities as a thinker and man of action – his quickness of mind, romanticism, imagination, humour, humanity, puckishness, ruthlessness, unscrupulousness.

The claim, Leonard continued, that Keynes had sacrificed truth for literary purposes under the influence of Lytton Strachey was to misunderstand 'a brilliant, amusing thinker writing in his shirtsleeves for his intimate friends . . . '[14] Yet the praise is not unqualified: imaginative, humorous, humane, yes, but also ruthless, unscrupulous. And romantic? Perhaps that was part of the memoir's secrecy for Leonard Woolf.

David Garnett, not a member of the Memoir Club in the Twenties, which may be why he misdated it, thought the Melchior memoir 'the finest of Maynard's writing', deeply personal in feeling, passionate for humanity and justice, witty, uncanny in its detailed observation – 'a work of art', in short, like a chapter out of Tolstoy.[15]

Two Memoir Club members who did hear Keynes' 'elaborate memoirs' wrote of them in their diaries. Their reactions and summaries make an interesting comparison. Virginia Woolf noted that though the politics bored her a little, she was very impressed by the characterization, as she wrote to Keynes. (Keynes had returned the compliment not exactly to Virginia's liking when later in the year he said her memoir on George Duckworth was the best thing she had done and encouraged her 'to write about real people & make it all up' (D II 121), which of course depressed her: 'if George is my climax I'm a mere scribbler' she wrote in her diary. Keynes, she noted earlier, had read neither of her novels (D II 67).

In her 5 February diary entry on Keynes' memoir she mentioned the mock despair with which Wemyss relied on Keynes, Melchior's arrogant clerks whom she quotes, and Lloyd George overwhelming Klotz with his gestures of a miser clutching money bags. Virginia also conveys a little of the atmosphere of the Memoir Club when she says, apropos Keynes' remark that he was rather in love with Melchior, 'I think he meant it seriously, though we laughed' (D II 90). It was the laughter of friends familiar with Keynes' sexual preferences which, nevertheless, were about to change the next year as he fell in love with Lydia Lopokova. (Keynes' last male love affair was with Sebastian Sprott, who would in time join the Memoir Club.) The change would be felt most in the Club and in Bloomsbury by Vanessa and Duncan. Weeks later Virginia Woolf summed up her feelings about Keynes and the Memoir Club, telling Katherine Mansfield the Club was getting 'more and more brilliant and more and more unreal'.[16]

The other Memoir Club diarist was Morgan Forster, who knew something of Clemenceau's writings at least. Forster alluded to Keynes' polemic, it seems, in 1920 when reviewing a bad novel by Clemenceau, the man, says Forster, who 'outwitted humanitarians and economists and ruined Europe . . . '[17] At the time he heard Keynes read 'Dr Melchior: A Defeated Enemy' Forster was intermittently keeping one of his diaries. His recounting of the memoir, more detailed than Virginia Woolf's and with a rather surprising conclusion, throws a quite different light on how memoirs were received in the Memoir Club, and shows again Forster's sharp self-consciousness about his relationships there and in Bloomsbury. The memoir, Forster wrote to himself, was complicated, interesting, 'admirably written', telling how Keynes broke through the official atmosphere of Trèves to contact the Germans' Jewish leader Melchior and avoid disaster. Though he says he has neither the experience nor the memory to record the details of the fascinating intrigue, Forster mentions the partly false, partly honest actions of everyone including Keynes in the Trèves discussions; he recounts the Wagnerian description of Spa and the triumph of Jane Austen and Fielding (misremembering the characters named by Keynes); he refers to the telegram and Lloyd George' triumph over Klotz, to Wemyss, and to the second meeting with Melchior in the bedroom with the unemptied pot. Finally there is the later meeting of Keynes and Melchior as unfettered friends in Holland (Forster does not mention Keynes' remark about being in love) and Melchior's depression as 'The tablets of the Law had been broken meanly.' The memoir was, Forster sums up,

> a most wonderful paper. Privilege to listen to it, and even to Clive Bell on his copulations with Mrs Ravenhill, wife of the Punch artist, though this was repulsion also.

Yet after noting that he spent the night at 46 Gordon Square (London home of Keynes and the Bells) Forster concluded

> I don't think those people are little; but they belittle all who come into their power unless the comer is strong, which I am not. Great as is my admiration for the Club, I shall resign I think.[18]

'Morgan has started resigning from the Memoir Club again', Quentin Bell complained to Desmond MacCarthy in 1948 after the latest of his attempted withdrawals.[19] Once again he was dissuaded.

In the event he did not. A few weeks after thinking he might resign, Forster wrote archly to Molly MacCarthy to suggest a change in the Club's procedures, and revealing more of the source of his anxieties over belittling. Molly had hoped he would read a memoir the next month along with Leonard and Virginia, but he had other plans:

> Forster cannot come to the Memoir Club for a bit as he is going to India. He has however a motion to propose: that members shall not write about

other members. If his motion is carried, he will find the Club as flourishing as he leaves it. And if the motion be felt by the late Miss Stephens to too extensively cripple their output, some modification might be admitted to meet their particular case.

Blood relationships or events occurring in the members' teens are the kinds of modifications he had in mind.[20] It is unlikely the motion was put to a vote.

There is much amusing ridicule in Keynes' memoir, and it was not absent from the two that Forster had read to the Club on his uncle and on his introductions to Bloomsbury. But there was much else in Keynes' account, as Forster's own summary indicates, and in Forster's too. Bloomsbury belittling would continue to bother Forster over the years. He would continue protesting and sometimes talking of resigning but he kept coming to Memoir Club meetings and reading more than a dozen memoirs to it.

* * *

One of the most interesting of those memoirs for both Forster's art of fiction and for his relations with the Memoir Club is an undated early one written some time before his departure to serve as the temporary private secretary for a maharaja. It begins,

Every Memoir contains a chapter entitled 'My Books and I'. Please imagine that you have come to it. You have listened to my childhood, adolescence and undergraduation.[21]

With four published novels and a collection of stories behind him, Forster was the one Memoir Club member fully entitled to discuss 'my books'. The direct address of the short paper (under 3000 words) and its later allusions to Club members by their first names show once again that he was writing for the Memoir Club.

It is a remarkable memoir: confessional, apologetic, funny, as subjective as Virginia Woolf could wish, and as vulnerable and self-conscious as her first lost one. The title Forster suggests gives its ostensible subject: the relation of his books to himself, which turns out to be about the nature of his literary inspiration and its regretted loss. But the memoir is also very much about Morgan Forster's relation to the Memoir Club. The memoir begins with Forster's Cambridge tutor's revelatory remark that we know more than we think we do; next came the 'great good word' that his pupil had the 'special and unusual apparatus' of a writer. As for 'the great evil word' that was said years afterwards, Forster tells the Club he might explain it sometime if he has the inclination. He never did. The remark is part of the mystery surrounding creativity that Forster maintains in his memoir, and it also reveals how present the Club is in his memoir. The great evil word may have had to do with the unprintable homosexual fiction he wanted to write. (*Maurice* and its unusual inspiration is the only one of his completed novels unmentioned in the memoir; only a few of the Club's males had been allowed to read it.)

Forster goes on to describe how his writer's apparatus first worked, how inspiration came to him in several stories: 'The Road from Colonus', 'The Rock' (whose title he thinks he may have forgotten and whose moral complexity he certainly seems to have), and particularly 'The Story of a Panic' where for the first time he experienced the process 'of sitting down on a theme as if it was an ant-hill'. Not mentioned is 'The Story of the Siren', another early story of Italian transformation that the Woolfs had printed and bound as the ninth publication of the Hogarth Press in 1920. The initial inspiration for 'The Story of a Panic' had to be combined, Forster explains, with 'faking' to create the tale of how an English picnic in Italy briefly becomes a panic, with the resulting goatish transformation of an adolescent boy assisted by a young waiter. When published, the story was hilariously interpreted by a decadent Cambridge librarian and friend of Keynes' as a tale of bestiality and 'B---'. That is what the much revised manuscript of the memoir has, however Forster pronounced it in his reading.

'Of course Maynard flew chirruping with the news. It seemed to him great fun, and to me disgusting', Forster continued, realizing only later that 'in a stupid and unprofitable way' that is what the story was really about; hence his indignation. This leads Forster to talk about his dislike of explaining his work or hearing it explained, which brings him back to the Memoir Club and the observation that 'if you had invited me to read this chapter I should certainly have made some excuse. So make the most of it.' Forster's biographers and critics have certainly done so, sometimes without always recognizing how hedged about some of his explanations are and how conditioned by his listeners.

The difficulty of explaining any of this, Forster insists to writers such as Virginia Woolf, Maynard Keynes, and Lytton Strachey is that, saving their presence, 'the process of writing is something sacred and mysterious . . . ' Acknowledging and humorously dismissing the creative other half of the Memoir Club, he imagines it is the same with painting, and that 'painters talk so much because they know their explanations are unintelligible'. So much for aesthetics. Writers have to be more careful with their medium, hence the reticence and secrecy. If only books could be anonymous. As it is now, he will take refuge with Matthew Arnold and Joseph Conrad in mysterious, inexplicable inspiration, at least until Freud prevails.

For Forster as a novelist and a critic, character-creation remained the most important aspect of fiction. In 'My Books and I' he thinks he has failed in those books to create either himself or the people who irritate him. Therefore he resorts to mystery in talking of his writing. Now comes another appeal, moving and ambivalent, to the Memoir Club:

> So far as I tell you anything this evening it is because I respect and love you – and this although I know that I can hold the lot of you for a second in the hollow of my hand. Before you slip through my fingers, realize this.

In the remainder of his memoir Forster mentions people who inspired characters in *Where Angels Fear to Tread*, *Howards End*, and especially *The Longest Journey*. But so pervasive is his dislike of literary analysis, he will not go into the disingenuous techniques by which people are turned into characters and 'life is transmuted into a Forster novel'. Fortunately, he adds, the Memoir Club is not a craftsman's guild. Forster, struggling with his own infertility – he now had three unfinished novels on his hands – despised the productive, professional craftsmen-of-letters who demeaned the mystery of artistic inspiration.

Forster ends his memoir by relating the inspiring encounter with a Wiltshire shepherd that gave rise to *The Longest Journey*, 'the last of my books that has come upon me without my knowledge'. (The experience has already been mentioned in the context of the Apostles.) 'We write in order to do good work, but our reward is the extraordinary experiences that have accompanied it.' That is Forster's throw-away conclusion to a memoir that says nothing about good works, and not very much about inspiration, but quite a bit about how he felt when talking of his books with his friends.

Forster never published this or any other of his Club memoirs but he did return to some of its ideas and even phrasing in later published writings, such as the pamphlet *Anonymity: An Enquiry*, which the Hogarth Press brought out a few years later, or the introductions to his collected stories and *The Longest Journey* that Forster wrote toward the end of his career. But of his unfinished Indian novel there is no mention.

· * * *

The Memoir Club meeting that Forster on his way to India could not attend took place on 23 February when Duncan Grant and Vanessa Bell were the readers. Grant's early memoirs have disappeared along with all of Vanessa's except for the one that she probably read that day, and which displays her remarkable talent, in Leonard Woolf's words, for 'a fantastic narrative of a labyrinthine domestic crisis'.[22] Forster would not have found Vanessa's memoir belittling. Its implicit humour lies in the gullibility of Vanessa herself as well as her servants as the reported catastrophes accumulate.

Asked once by Naomi Black what his mother and aunt actually talked about, Quentin Bell answered 'servants'. The general theme of Vanessa's memoir – which is no memoir but a narrative of events occurring less than a year before – concerns Bloomsbury and the servant problem, although the Bloomsbury involved is not Virginia Woolf's but that of Gordon Square in 1920. (The Woolfs, living in Richmond, are unmentioned.) A central figure, however, is the Stephen family's old cook Sophie Farrell. Virginia would eventually write a memoir fantasy of Sophie called 'The Cook', and Vanessa would describe in a much later memoir how she had collaborated and connived with Sophie in managing the household of the financially neurotic Leslie Stephen. Sophie was now on loan from the Duckworths to cook and help with the children while Vanessa went to Italy in the Spring in 1920 with Duncan Grant and Maynard Keynes. Keynes is the only member of Bloomsbury really involved in the story, for it was he who threaded the domestic labyrinth to find a mad maid.

Vanessa's story begins at the end of February when she moved into the two upper floors at 50 Gordon Square, the lower ones being occupied by Adrian Stephen and his family, while Clive remained at 46, now a tenant of Keynes'. Early in March Vanessa employed a new maid named Mary Elizabeth Wilson to assist Sophie. Hers is 'the strange story' described in the title of Vanessa's published narrative.[23] The bones of the story, without all the complicating details given by Vanessa, are as follows.

Sophie was pleased with Mary, and she made friends with Blanche Payne and Jessie, servants at 46 Gordon Square, as well Nellie Brittain, Angelica Bell's nurse (not to be confused with the Woolfs' cook Nellie Boxall). So Vanessa went off to Italy with Duncan Grant and Maynard Keynes leaving she thought a contented household. (While in Italy they visited Bernard Berenson, where Grant and the Keynes were amusingly confused, which became the subject for a much later memoir by Grant.) Then bad news for Vanessa began to arrive from London where telegrams and phone calls (relayed from 46, until a phone was installed in Adrian's flat) had informed Mary, first of her mother's death from a fall, then of her young man's succumbing to scarlet fever, next of her father's death, and finally of her brother's serious illness. Mary cries and moans in her sleep so much that Sophie worries about the children; the servants at 46 Gordon Square take Mary in before Vanessa's doctor (Marie Moralt) is summoned and sends Mary to the St Pancras Infirmary. Blanche tries contacting the family of Mary's intended to help her; their baffled reply suggests Mary's family should be contacted, as they know nothing about the matter. At this point Keynes (who had returned earlier) was apparently consulted by the servants and expressed his disbelief in the whole business.

Vanessa arrived back in London on 15 May and is filled in by Sophie on the details of the deaths, the phone calls, the telegrams, the letters. For the next three weeks Mary's drama intensifies. Vanessa visits Mary in the mental ward of the infirmary, and as Mary talks of her family, Vanessa is impressed by her

as one of the most charming characters I had ever met and I was interested in her talk in the same kind of way in which I am interested in Defoe.

Arrangements are made for her release but then an illiterate letter arrives at the infirmary from Mary's supposedly dead mother asking that Mary be sent home! Mary says it is from her delusional brother; long consultations by Vanessa with the nurses and magistrates follow before Mary can be released. She returns with Vanessa who then attempts to find someone who knows of her brother's condition. Mary suggests two people, a man named 'Nigger' Bracenbury, whom she says is now her guardian, and a nurse named Gibson who is taking care of her brother. Next Bracenbury telephones and asks to see Vanessa, who writes inviting him after getting an address from Mary. The letter is returned; others arrive from Nurse Gibson, including one from Mary to Bracenbury saying he should not bother Mrs Bell. More phone calls and letters ensue, some of which Vanessa quotes. Mary is out of the house for some time, becomes more undependable in her work, and has bad nights again. Vanessa, despite her longing 'for immunity from kitchen life' becomes more and more involved (her studio was above the kitchen). After another bad scene with Mary sobbing and Sophie and Vanessa scolding, she is sent to bed.

On 2 June Sophie tells Vanessa either she or Mary must go. Next a letter comes from a friend of the Wilsons saying they are not dead; more phone calls from Bracenbury follow before it is finally arranged to send Mary by train, accompanied by Blanche, to a friend named Mr Page.

Now the denouement. Mary escapes when changing trains; Blanche pursues; she's caught and escapes again. Vanessa, accompanied by her doctor, arrives to find a Mr Page who knows nothing about Mary, nor apparently does Mr Bracenbury, who is a well-known solicitor, and others mentioned by Mary who have only remote connections to the Wilsons. And there is no Nurse Gibson. The police, now involved, are sent in pursuit of Mary. In the evening Keynes goes into the whole affair, notices that the various letters had not been sent through the post; telephone messages, it now seems, had arrived when Mary was out, and were not long distance calls. Finally a letter arrives from the Wilsons saying they and their large family were alive and well, and mentioning Mary had disappeared three times before.

Vanessa's conclusion: 'The servants now all agreed in thinking Mary an artful hussy and deceiver. It was terrible to have been taken in so.' Meanwhile with Mary still at large, more alleged messages arrive from Nurse Gibson and Bracenbury. Mary is finally found in London and brought to Gordon Square, where, waiting to be admitted by the infirmary, she becomes incoherent and recognizes nobody. She would probably be certified as insane, Vanessa adds in a note. A visit to Vanessa from Mary's father confirms that there was no truth to her story.

The family might have warned her, Vanessa grumbled to Keynes in an unpublished letter on 5 June thanking him for his brilliant detective work and regretting her own gullibility. The letter begins by saying 'the biography club' is put off for a week – a name for the Memoir Club that seems to fit her own performance better.

'The Strange Story of Mary Elizabeth Wilson', as a contemporary and relatively impersonal account of domestic affairs, has
none of the 'emotional depths' – in Virginia's words – of Vanessa's
first lost memoir, and is quite unlike any of her later memoirs
or indeed any other Club memoir. The pathetically pathologi-
cal story of a charming, imaginative, delusional, and anguished
domestic servant reflects something of the life of Bloomsbury
circa 1920. Vanessa's letters at the time, one to Roger Fry for
example, confirm the accuracy of her account of Mary's story as
it was unfolding.[24] Except for Keynes and the co-operating servants at 46 and 50, however, Vanessa seems almost isolated from
Bloomsbury. Her three children, including two-and-a-half year-
old Angelica, are unnamed; Clive Bell is nowhere to be found;
and Duncan Grant appears only once in a fragment when he
answers the telephone and recognizes Mary's disguised voice. But
then Vanessa's audience would have taken her relationships for
granted, as they would the absent centre of Vanessa's existence,
the reason she sought kitchen-immunity, which was her life and
work as an artist. Once again in trying to understand Vanessa's
'memoir', the context of her audience is crucial.

As a contribution to Bloomsbury and the servant problem,
Vanessa's story is a reminder of domestic conditions in 1920
England. Aside from class considerations – and they can never
be just set aside – if Vanessa Bell was going to exist as an artist and a mother, she had to have servants to cook, clean, and
help care for her children. What this could involve is what her
memoir is about. For all Vanessa's wish for immunity, her pains-
takingly detailed reconstruction of 'The Strange Story of Mary
Elizabeth Wilson' shows how infected she had become with
domestic affairs. The published story, edited by a later member
of the Memoir Club, Anne Olivier Bell, was shortened by almost
a third of a nine-thousand word typescript. (Cuts involved some
letters and phone calls concocted by Mary, details about her
family as well as the servants' relations with Mary.) In addition,
several hand-written pages have survived along with two letters
by Keynes and Vanessa on the subject. Yet for all its detail of

Vanessa's compassionate involvement in Mary's delusions, there is little attempted analysis or comprehension of Mary's condition. Keynes attributes it to 'domestic hysteria' in his letter to Vanessa, who later alludes to Mary's attacks of 'double personality' in her letter to Keynes.[25] That is about all. The next year the Hogarth Press would begin publishing translations of Freud, which might have been some help dealing with the psychopathology of everyday, pre-medicated domestic life of 1920.

At the end of May Vanessa engaged another maid to replace the unreliable Mary. Her name was Grace Germany, later Higgens. She was sixteen, stayed forty years to became the cook known as 'the angel of Charleston'.

*   *   *

Vanessa Bell's non-memoir on a very different kind of private affair from Clive Bell's may indicate the problems Molly MacCarthy was having in arranging meetings of the Memoir Club and extracting memoirs from the members. There was to be a meeting of the Club at the end of March then no more until Whit Sunday when all members were expected to meet at Charleston and read memoirs, but there are no records of this happening. An attempt was made by Leonard Woolf and others to record Desmond MacCarthy's table talk one evening, but the result was disappointing. At the end of the year Clive Bell reported to Mary Hutchinson that Molly had finished her memoirs and intended to write no more.

Of a March meeting of the Memoir Club the next year, no trace of papers remains. Then in April Molly MacCarthy wrote asking Lytton Strachey to read next time and expressing her doubts about the Club's continuation, influenced partly perhaps by her having finished her own memoirs, and also partly by her own sadly increasing deafness:

I suggest we meet quarterly & say for another year – then I think we might give up the club. It was very lively two or three times – the meetings

> I mean – at the beginning – but I think you have come in for some rather
> feeble evenings.

And, she continued, 'Everyone hitherto has shifted responsibility on to someone else – so now this is a new experiment . . . '[26] It was certainly a more realistic one than the frequency of meetings and memoirs originally planned. Strachey complied, telling Molly that he did not think he could say anything exciting. To Sebastian Sprott in a letter marked private he complained he was 'hag-ridden' while writing the memoir of his family home entitled 'Lancaster Gate' that he was to give on 19 June. Reading with him was Morgan Forster, back now from India. Strachey had encountered him in May and told Molly that Forster was anxious now to read a memoir to the Club.

The evidence for Lytton Strachey's involvement with the Memoir Club is scanty. Thus far he appears to have read no memoirs to the Club, though he had read chapters of *Queen Victoria* to the Woolfs before his biography (dedicated to Virginia) was published in April 1921. Yet he described well, in an early review of a book on Mlle. de Lespinasse's salon, what the Club may have been for him and other members:

> And, if one were privileged to go there often, one found there what one
> found nowhere else – a sense of freedom and intimacy which was the
> outcome of a real equality, a real understanding, a real friendship such as
> have existed, before or since, in few societies indeed.[27]

How often Lytton went to the Club is now unknown, and although 'Lancaster Gate' was the only memoir intended specifically for the Memoir Club, Strachey wrote at least two other short memoir-like recollections. One about a country visit to Vanessa Bell's family during the war was read at some time to the Memoir Club and will be described later. Another, on H. H. Asquith, written just before the publication of *Eminent Victorians* in May 1918, anticipates Keynes' disillusioning sketches of politicians in *The Economic Consequences of the Peace*. If, according to its editor, Strachey's sketch of Asquith was intended for posthumous publication – like Keynes' *Two Memoirs* perhaps – it took more than half a century before such matters as the former prime minister's erections could be mentioned in print.[28] There was also the awkward fact that just after Strachey had written his memoir, Asquith influentially praised *Eminent Victorians* in an Oxford lecture attended by Strachey in June.

'Asquith' is a pre-Memoir Club memoir; Strachey's historical remarks, as he calls them, were written for listeners or readers familiar with the first names of Ottoline Morrell, Henry Lamb, and Maynard Keynes. Strachey writes of being introduced to Asquith by Ottoline at Garsington in 1914, then seeing him again as Prime Minister there in 1916 when Strachey found him quite changed – larger, redder, like some emperor or pope, but with an infectious geniality. Finally a year later, again at Garsington, he appeared to be a diminished and deflated ex-Premier. Summing him up, Strachey notes the combination of a middle-class North countryman influenced by worldly Oxford culture (gratitude is expressed by the memoirist for having gone to Cambridge), next the Bar, and then his wife Margot's set: 'The middle-class legal Don became a *viveur*, who carried a lot of liquor and was lecherous with the ladies.' His published speeches lead to one of Strachey's favourite rhetorical devices: who would have guessed from them, he asks, that their author 'would take a lady's hand and make her feel his erected instrument under his trousers?'

Asquith lacked ideals, Strachey wrote; he mismanaged Ireland, led the country incompetently during the early years of the war, and was inexcusably inconsistent in the matter of conscription, according to Keynes. Yet Keynes, who had worked with him, admired Asquith, as did Desmond MacCarthy who had known him later as Lord Oxford and discussed his writing posthumously in *Portraits*. As for Strachey's attitude in his memoir-sketch, he applied to an eminent Georgian the method he had just announced at the end of his preface to *Eminent Victorians*: 'to quote the words of a Master – "Je n'impose rien; je ne propose rien; j'expose".' That the 'Master' has never been identified adds to the ironic self-consciousness of Strachey's biographies.

*   *   *

Lytton Strachey ends his exposé of Asquith quoting Henry Lamb, then breaking off with 'but this is becoming too personal'. 'Lancaster Gate', dated June 1922, and published only in 1971, is, if not exactly exciting, at least avowedly personal.[29] A memoir of private rather than public affairs, it is a carefully wrought Memoir-Club companion piece to Virginia Woolf's memoir of her Hyde Park Gate home on the other side of Kensington Gardens. Both memoirs describe the disconnections – Strachey's term is 'disintegration' – of the large Victorian family system. Again the accent is comic. Both memoirs end with amorous encounters with relatives in bedrooms: Virginia in George Duckworth's arms and Lytton gazing at the uncovered, sleeping Duncan Grant. Drawing room life, with its doors and odd visitors, figures in both memoirs. In Virginia's memoir it is described before her mother's death and George Duckworth's ascendancy. In Strachey's memoir the room, its grotesque mantle piece, eccentric relatives and visitors embodies 'the riddle of the Victorian age'. Strachey's mother vaguely dominates his family, but in 'Lancaster Gate' the significance of personal life lay not so much in human relations as in the atmosphere of the house in which that life was entangled. The impression of that atmosphere, although admittedly not wholly analysable, is what Lytton's memoir attempts to evoke with a mandarin style, the vocabulary of which includes words such 'elephantiasis', 'lugubrious', 'portentous', 'disintegration and *degringolade*', 'full incorrectitude', and 'filth-packets'. Sometimes the prose can rise into a written equivalent of the Strachean shriek.

There may be in Strachey's memoir an echo of Keynes' earlier Apostle paper on the influence of furniture on life and love, but it was also a theme of Queen Victoria's biography that Strachey published the year before his memoir. There the effect of the

Queen's vast possessions on her strange life is described as 'a collection not merely of things and of thoughts but of states of mind and ways of living as well'.[30] In 'Lancaster Gate' such Victorian accumulations are contrasted with our modern states of mind:

> We find satisfaction in curves and colours, and windows fascinate us, we are agitated by staircases, inspired by doors, disgusted by cornices, depressed by chairs, made wanton by ceilings, entranced by passages, and exacerbated by a rug.

Strachey details in his memoir how the colours, sounds, windows, staircases, and rooms of his home agitated and depressed him. For all its size, 69 Lancaster Gate afforded little privacy: the rooms were small, and there were not enough of them; one bathroom with a lavatory audible in the drawing room served some twelve family members, guests, and servants.

The quarter century that Lytton spent growing up at 69 Lancaster Gate shaped his biography and haunted his dreams. It was not an unhappy time, he writes, though it was a restricted and repressed one in a family whose finances were strained. In the preface to *Eminent Victorians* again Strachey said his aim was to illustrate not explain. 'Lancaster Gate' memorably and amusingly illustrates the atmosphere of the Stracheys' Victorian household life. That atmosphere is what Strachey says he wants to reconstruct. In doing so, nevertheless, he also offers an explanation of it. First there was the advanced decomposition (Lytton's metaphor) of the Strachey class from aristocracy to gentlefolk to middle-class professionals. Then there was

> the peculiar disintegrating force of the Strachey character. The solid bourgeois qualities were interpenetrated by intellectualism and eccentricity.

Meals were served by unpresentable butlers, the silverware came from the Army and Navy Stores, and the wines from the corner grocer.

The Victorian age was ending, however. Lytton's close older sister Dorothy courageously married a French painter – and later wrote the anonymous novel-memoir *Olivia* that begins by depicting, with some exaggeration of her own, Lady Strachey and Lancaster Gate life. Lytton's memoir closes in the twentieth century as he walks home at night, leaving Clive Bell at the Temple, and entering once again the vast pile with its seven layers of human habitation, climbing up and around 'the great dim ochre well' to his bedroom at the top, to find the exposed Duncan in one of the beds. The exciting opportunity is declined and the memoirist goes soundly to sleep.

Lytton's home was abandoned for financial reasons in 1907, the family moving to Hampstead and then in 1919, reduced in number, to 51 Gordon Square where, Strachey wrote to Virginia Woolf, 'Very soon I foresee that the whole square will become a sort of College. And the recontres in the garden I shudder to think of.'[31] Virginia's response to Lytton's memoir of his old Kensington Gardens home was a laconic comment on both Lytton's and Forster's memoirs in her diary (23 June). Unlike some of the earlier Club memoirs she had heard, there was little to read into these finished performances: 'Our standard is such that little is left out for me to hint & guess at. They say what they mean very brilliantly; & leave the dark as it was before' (D II 178). Whether the same could be said about the unpublished *The Waste Land* which T. S. Eliot had read to the Woolfs earlier in the week is not clear; it left her in her diary with a strong emotion, though she was not sure what held the beauty and intensity of the poem together.

*   *   *

The memoir that Morgan Forster told Strachey he was anxious to read to the Club may have been the one he later titled 'Kanaya'. From his ten months while acting as private secretary to His Highness, the Maharaja of the small Dewas State Senior in the middle of India, Forster brought back his still unfinished novel, some journals, and retrieved letters to family and friends, as well as notes that he turned into two memoirs of his public and private Indian affairs. The novel, Forster explained some thirty years later in *The Hill of Devi*, he had been unable to finish in India because

> the gap between India remembered and India experienced was too wide. When I got back to England the gap narrowed, and I was able to resume. But I still thought the book bad and probably should not have completed it without the encouragement of Leonard Woolf.[32]

Immediately after completing *A Passage to India* in 1923, Forster wrote to thank both Leonard and Virginia for their help.

In *The Hill of Devi*, subtitled *Being Letters from Dewas State Senior*, Forster included, along with letters and journals from his visits to India in 1912 and 1921, a memoir of his dispute with the Maharaja's permanent private secretary, one Colonel Leslie (called Wilson in the book). Based on notes Forster said he made at the time in 1921, the almost complete memoir was both cut and expanded in 1953 for publication in *The Hill of Devi*.[33] The other memoir of his affair with Kanaya is crucially absent from Forster's book. That 'unpublishable section . . . couldn't go in because it couldn't', Forster helplessly explained to an understanding friend who had reviewed the book.[34] (Forster did use Kanaya's name, giving it to a driver in the memoir of Colonel Leslie/Wilson; in Forster's authorized biography, however, the barber's name was reduced to 'K——'.) It took another thirty years before that memoir became part of *The Hill of Devi*, and then only as an appendix to a definitive edition of that book.

Whatever the sequence of Forster's two Indian memoirs, it is apparent that the one about his affair with Kanaya assumes the background given in his account of Colonel Leslie. The letters from and to Leslie are not included in the manuscript but simply marked as 'read' in it, indicating that the memoir was composed to be read out loud, probably to the Memoir Club. The deleted comic opening of the original manuscript memoir is closer in tone to the 'Kanaya' memoir. In it Forster tells the story of the unsuccessful first Englishman hired by the Maharaja of Dewas State Senior – called 'His Highness' or simply 'H. H.' in Forster's memoirs – as a private secretary for himself and a tutor to his young son. That secretary/tutor lasted four days because of his indiscriminate sexual needs, H. H. disallowing copulations in his palace and deploring homosexuality elsewhere. On the advice of Malcolm Darling, who had been guardian and tutor to the young Rajah himself, the position then went to Colonel Leslie, a friend of Darling's. Another friend was Morgan Forster, who had been at King's with Malcolm before Darling joined the Indian Civil Service in 1904 (the same year as Leonard Woolf entered the Ceylon Civil Service). Darling's friendship with Forster, the older Leslie, and the younger H. H. is the background of Forster's memoir. Indeed friendship is at the centre of Forster's Indian writings, fiction as well as non-fiction as was the essential background of imperialism in the early twentieth-century.

Forster describes Colonel Leslie as fearless, an adored raconteur and father-figure to His Highness. Leslie was also a 'vigorous penman' – the only quality he appears to have shared with his temporary replacement. They never met. Forster had mentioned to H. H. during his first visit to India in 1912–13 that he might come back; the opportunity arose in 1921 while the Colonel was recuperating in England from an Indian railway injury. Forster was eager to experience the hot season in India and become more familiar with Hindus – both important for his unfinished novel, though he does not say so.

At the Maharaja's chaotic court Forster discovers the Colonel's vast beloved garden works, for which water was unfortunately not planned. Other public works and their various functionaries were encountered, including one called 'Eighteen Offices'. Then the Colonel's letters began to arrive – and it is on letters that Forster's memoir turns. To Leslie, Forster wrote detailed replies, among them, he said, 'the longest letter I have ever written in my life'. Forster helped get the Colonel some owed money; he inquired about lack of water for the gardens, which the Colonel blamed on intrigue. To H. H., Leslie wrote complaining letters, wondering if he was wanted back, to which H. H., who realized he was always hypnotizing himself into believing situations bearable, replied only by cable, assuring him of his love. Forster, who had annoyed Leslie by dismissing a driver (named Kanaya in the revised published text), traces the stages of Colonel Leslie's declining reputation. The Colonel had quarrelled with everyone, as it became clear that H. H. did not really want him back. Then Leslie started to intrigue against his temporary replacement, whom he described as 'a weak minded literary man'. Whatever H. H. thought of Forster, he would not have him insulted. Forster believed H. H. was fond of him, 'though you never can tell with saints'. In this memoir and especially in the second one, Bapu Sahib, as Forster and Darling also used to call him, emerges as the most interesting figure, who, Forster to wrote Darling after leaving Dewas, 'remains one of the great spiritual experiences of my life . . . .'[35]

Colonel Leslie seems not to have understood that Forster was his temporary replacement. Just what the private secretary's duties were is never very clear in the memoirs or to the memoirist, but attending to mail seems to have been one of them. Inadvertently opening some of the Colonel's private correspondence earns Forster an insulting rebuke from Leslie ('I can only think the hypnotic power of your surroundings has affected you . . . ' etc.) H. H. – who had also opened the Colonel's mail, but deliberately as a joke and to spy on him – is as upset as Forster over the letter and sends him off on a ruined holiday, which Forster spends hurting and composing insulting replies to the Colonel. One is finally sent demanding a full apology or the cessation of relations, to which there was no reply.

Meanwhile Malcolm Darling, wife Jo, and children return to India, but without the Colonel. H. H.'s religious observances intervene as they frequently do, and Forster goes off to meet the Darlings. In a ludicrous scene, Forster arrives on board with garlands, having hired a boat to meet the ship, therefore disappointing a number of English brides expecting him to be their

prospective husband (and thus embittering their future marriages according to Jo). Malcolm is surprised, both annoyed with
Forster's mail indiscretions and amazed at Leslie, who had half
laughingly once inquired if 'your Morgan Forster's all square'.
H. H. impressively insists, despite Malcolm's regret, on sending a
cable, composed by Forster, saying he can no longer afford a private secretary; a refund for the Colonel's passage is enclosed. H.
H. blames his own weakness as Leslie, who has become engaged,
keeps inquiring about returning. There the memoir breaks off.
In the published version Forster concludes it was also his fault
for opening letters and Leslie's for being so disagreeable. As for
Malcolm Darling, he could 'have had no reason to feel proud of
his three friends'.[36] It was to Malcolm, nevertheless, that Forster
dedicated *The Hill of Devi*.

*   *   *

'A middle class-row' is how Morgan Forster later characterized
his Colonel Leslie memoir.[37] That could not be said of his second
memoir, involving as it does an affair with a barber aided and
abetted by royalty. Forster had enjoyed and yet was repelled by
hearing of Clive Bell's copulations; the degree to which the Club
enjoyed his own Indian ones is unknown. There is only Virginia
Woolf's remark that, though brilliant, it left little to guess at. Later
Lytton Strachey, who had probably heard the memoir, thought
'the increased bite and hardness of *A Passage to India* and its
lack of sentimentality' were the result of an Indian love affair.[38]
(More directly the experience influenced the posthumously published short story 'The Life to Come' that Forster wrote in 1922
in which a missionary and a native love disastrously for both.)
    The title 'Kanaya' that Forster later gave to his manuscript
does not really identify his memoir's centre of interest, which is
his relation not to the barber but to the Maharaja of Dewas State
Senior who facilitated the affair. Forster called his time at Dewas
'the great opportunity of my life' in the preface to *The Hill of
Devi*. With the publication of the omitted memoir, the strangeness

of the Dewas court and the saintliness of its ruler become more apparent. Public and private affairs merge when Forster's two Indian memoirs are read together, especially the unrevised form of the first one. Even in its published version, however, there is a hint of the second in Colonel Leslie's humorous inquiry about how 'square' Forster' was.

Forster's Memoir Club memoirs of India are quite unlike his own earlier performances. There are no allusions or appeals to the Club or its members; the foreign setting would not have been all that strange to the members from families familiar with India such as the Stephen sisters, Strachey, Molly MacCarthy, not to mention Leonard Woolf, whose Ceylon memoirs the Club would hear. Although not without humour, the 'Kanaya' memoir is more confessional than Forster's others, more openly concerned with self-respect and its loss. It was also a memoir Forster was prepared to have read outside the Club, for a little later he sent it to Siegfried Sassoon, noting that he had tried 'to write the thing without self-pity or swank'; he thought it had some value as result, 'though it is anxious work showing it to anyone else'. Later others would circulate less intimate Club memoirs with less anxiety.[39]

The unpublished memoir differs from those he had read or would read in its sexual candour. Not just copulations but masturbation, erections, involuntary emissions, and even some sadism are mentioned. The memoir begins this way:

> As the car took me into H. H.'s dominions, I reflected how severely I had once heard him censure homosexuality, and how little I could help in any way, and I said to myself 'The least I can do is to cause no trouble.'

But trouble is just what he causes, not unlike the Colonel's predecessor. 'An empty mind' and the hot weather Forster wanted to experience provoke him sexually. Frequent masturbation brings little relief; he arranges an assignation with a Hindu coolie; becomes convinced it is known and he is being mocked; confesses almost tearfully to H. H. who has heard nothing which makes Forster feel like an utter fool. H. H., upon learning his new private secretary has no feeling for women, arranges to get a boy for him – a barber named Kanaya who will shave him, etc. Forster is finally gratified; H. H. assists with locations, while urging Forster to avoid 'passivity', and then informs his court of Forster's advanced age of 42 at which 'any properly constructed Indian is impotent or nearly so and can dally no more with maiden or boy'. But rumours start anyway; Kanaya talks while Forster is away, even approaching an infuriated H. H. On his return Forster suffers impertinences from others in the court, and inflicts pain on his boy, which is bad for both of them, as he realizes there is no relation, no companionship that he craved, beyond carnality in this master/slave affair, which was so different from his Egyptian experience (about which he nevertheless felt he had to lie to H. H.).

Such an outline cannot convey the sympathetic, saintly, cynical, financially impractical, religious yet merry, intriguing (in both senses of the word) and above all affectionate personality of Forster's Maharaja, whose tragically messy life Forster would sketch at the conclusion to *The Hill of Devi*. The Kanaya memoir is a carefully crafted piece of writing. There are scenes with dialogue, at some of which Forster is not present. The memoir opens and closes with the explicit symbolism of a dead cow surrounded by vultures. 'That's how it will end', Forster tells himself at the beginning; 'thus it ended', he affirms it at the close of the memoir, seeing himself 'disintegrated and inert' like the cow. (Disintegration is a Forsterian as well as a Stracheyan memoir theme.) The vultures in H. H.'s court are unidentified, but one appears to have been Forster's assistant who undermines his position, as he had the Colonel's. Another victim is an Indian Forster was attracted to, despite 'that damnable quality of willowiness that makes an Indian's body as unsatisfactory to grapple with as his mind' – an illuminating comment for *A Passage to India*. But again, what exactly Forster's position was at Dewas is also unclear. 'Little is clear-cut in India', Forster states in *The Hill of Devi*, and his memoir bears this out.[40] He did not know how to be a private secretary and the Maharaja did not know how to employ one, he says earlier in the book. There exists a one-page fragment, however, in which Forster describes a religious ceremony in which he participated; it included consecrating a shrine of the elements of his profession – account books, pen, paper, ink, and a wastepaper basket.[41]

The memoir ends rather bleakly with Forster asking H. H. how to 'dominate lust' and is told 'when you are dissatisfied with your present state of existence you will enter another – that's all'. In a review of the Emperor Babur's memoirs written after his return but before he read his Indian memoir to the Club, Forster remarked that in most cases (not Babur's but perhaps Forster's) the inmost confidence that a writer invites us to enter is 'an enervating chamber'.[42] Forster also wrote two articles on the political context of his Indian memoirs for *The Nation and Athenaeum*, whose literary editor was Leonard Woolf. (In an early letter from India Virginia remarked in her diary 'He seems as critical of the East as of Bloomsbury, & sits dressed in a turban watching his Prince dance, quite unimpressed.') He was also unimpressed by Strachey's just published *Queen Victoria* which he thought flimsy and Virginia agreed (D II 138–9). Forster had some misgivings about his articles and wondered to Darling if the articles had bothered H. H. whom he had not heard from. In 'The Mind of the Indian Native State', Forster noted how the British imperialists were encouraging the princely native states as a counter-weight to Gandhi's nationalism, then commented on, among others, the Dewas court's lack of experience of the modern world, its rivalries and jealousies, and the absurdities of its new constitution. But he left the future up in the air – to others who could see it and who knew 'in what human happiness consists'.[43]

Years later E. M. Forster returned to his Dewas memories in an essay on reading Hardy's novel *Woodlanders* while there. He describes the unfinished grandiose waterless dying gardens, compares them with tidy English 'cleanups and cruelty', and ends contemplating the burnt-up Hill of Devi, at the summit of which 'I could detect the cave which contained an unobtrusive god.'[44]

Goddess, actually – Devi is a generic name for the divine female principle whose name and setting Forster invokes in his title – with what irony? – to preside over his male Indian memories.

*   *   *

No more meetings are recorded in 1922. For three years now the Memoir Club had met a dozen times or more to hear from thirty to forty memoirs, of which some fifteen still exist in various published and unpublished forms.

Then the Memoir Club stopped.

Hiatus: 1922–1928

5

For some six years the Memoir Club appears dormant: no allusions by members to the Club are recorded, no accounts of meetings are to be found, no Club memoirs of the period exist. It was, however, a prolific period of writing by Club members, including fiction, criticism, and a variety of published and unpublished autobiographical work that is germane to the Memoir Club's history. There were autobiographical novels and critical essays on autobiography by Virginia Woolf, who had moved back to Bloomsbury with Leonard in 1924. Private memoirs of grief were written by both Roger Fry and E. M. Forster. Forster's memoir belongs with his Egyptian writings, but is not unconnected to the Indian novel he finally finished in 1924. A book of Forster's Egyptian pieces was published in 1923 by the Hogarth Press, which also, during this period, published books by Roger Fry, Clive Bell, Mary Hutchinson, Maynard Keynes, and Molly MacCarthy as well as works by two ancestors: Leslie Stephen's late *Some Early Impressions* and Julia Margaret Cameron's *Victorian Photographs of Famous Men and Fair Women*, introduced by both Virginia Woolf and Roger Fry.

At Charleston a series of family newspapers by Julian and Quentin Bell, aided and abetted by their aunt, mother, and father, mocked the doings of various Memoir Club members including aunt, mother, father, and the recently married Keyneses. And installments of Molly MacCarthy's reminiscences – the first Memoir Club memoirs to be printed – were published by Leonard Woolf after he had become the literary editor in 1923 of the *Nation*, whose chairman was Keynes.

Also worth mentioning are installments of Lady Strachey's memoirs in the *Nation* as well as a series of brief portraits by

Lytton that he would collect later. Leonard himself wrote a number of reviews of autobiography, in competition to some extent with those of Desmond MacCarthy, the literary editor of the *New Statesman*. Leonard's 1927 Hogarth Press *Essays on Literature, History, Politics, Etc.*, taken from his journalism, included brief discussions of nineteenth- and early twentieth-century autobiographers, along with short essays on egoism, aristocrats, and old age in autobiography. And among Clive Bell's essays during this time was the self-referencing 'Creed of an Aesthete', an attack on George Bernard Shaw's values which, of course, produced a controversy with him as well as Desmond MacCarthy who tried to moderate. In another essay on eclecticism Bell qualified his earlier formalism, urging the enjoyment of life and asking, among other things, 'must we deny ourselves the delights of memoir-reading for fear of blunting our appetite for lyrics?'[1]

However, the most familiar autobiographical writings by members during the time of the Memoir Club's suspension were three works of fiction by Virginia Woolf that need to be briefly described.

*   *   *

Virginia Woolf's *Jacob's Room*, her first novel to be published by the Hogarth Press, appeared in 1922, four months after the Club meeting at which Strachey and Forster had read their memoirs. Virginia's notebooks indicate that the novel was begun a month after the Memoir Club's first meeting. Following *Night and Day* (1919) with its depiction of contemporary friends and relatives and after the stories and sketches collected in *Monday or Tuesday* (1921), *Jacob's Room* returns to the Edwardian past, perhaps under the stimulus of the Memoir Club. Autobiographical in subject, like her previous novels, but not in form, *Jacob's Room* is an anti-novel whose title identifies a room rather than an occupant. It is a quest, novelistically reflexive, and epistemological. The novel is a fictive demonstration, as it were, of what the creation of character might mean in a modern novel, following Virginia

Woolf's critical attacks in the essay 'Modern Fiction' and the later pamphlet *Mr Bennett and Mrs Brown* on the psychologically unrealistic characters of materialistic Edwardian novelists such as Arnold Bennett.

But *Jacob's Room* is also very much an elegiac quest, for Jacob Flanders is based on Virginia's brother, whose young death in 1906 brought the early members of the Bloomsbury Group closer together. In the novel, however, his death is transposed to the First World War. At the start and end of the work Jacob's family and friends call for him. 'It's no use trying to sum people up' the narrator announces twice in the novel; they are not sums but complex wholes whose sometimes startling reality is nevertheless transient. But if Jacob is not consistently knowable, he is at least killable in the war that his surname suggests while also alluding to Defoe's *Moll Flanders*. With its discontinuous story, its sporadically absent central character, and his undescribed death, *Jacob's Room* is also an anti-memoir, treating in its experimentally oblique way death, grief, and loss – topics that the memoirs of Memoir Club had thus far avoided for the most part. Death is central to all three of the extended works of fiction Virginia Woolf wrote between 1922 and 1928.

In *Mrs Dalloway* (1925) Clarissa Dalloway's room is not where the novelist searches for a character but where Clarissa recognizes in mystical moments of perception the miracle of other people's existence in other rooms. Rooms and windows are symbols of consciousness in this novel as in *Jacob's Room*, *A Room of One's Own* and elsewhere in Virginia Woolf's, as well as Forster's work. Septimus Smith, for example, throws himself out of a window as his room is invaded by the soul-forcing doctor in *Mrs Dalloway*. Timeless writing moments, ecstatic mystical experience, madness and mortality were not, however, the kinds of memories to be shared among friends in Virginia's memoirs or anyone else's. Clarissa's transcendental theory that one's 'apparitions' survived after death among the friends and places one had known might be seen as a kind of Memoir-Club fantasy.

Mrs Dalloway focuses on both the character of Clarissa Dalloway (the last line of the novel is 'For there she was') and on the critically depicted social system in which she lives and Septimus dies. The working title for the novel was 'The Hours', the entire action of the novel taking place on one clock-chiming, post-war London day in June. The characters' past experiences appear in present memories, which are rendered through interior monologues as their current lives connect web-like to one another.

Clarissa Dalloway is more autobiographically ambiguous than the principal characters of the two novels that preceded and followed it. Virginia reported in her diary in June 1925 the criticism of another Memoir Club member, Lytton Strachey, who thought 'that I alternately laugh at her & cover her, very remarkably, with myself', and she agreed there was something 'tinselly' about her, as in *The Voyage Out* where she first appeared (D III 32). Then Virginia began to invent memories for Mrs Dalloway; thus the novel as well as a series of stories around Mrs Dalloway developed. With her next novel, however, it was not necessary to invent memories.

To the Lighthouse moves from the Joycean present of *Mrs Dalloway* to a Proustian ancestral past. Years rather than hours pass, while the setting of a house by the sea with its lighthouse remains. The most memoiristic of her novels, it was to have, she told herself in her diary as she began writing (14 May 1925), 'father's character done complete in it; & mothers; & St. Ives; & childhood; & all the usual things I try to put in – life, death etc.' (D III 18–20). The Stephen models of the Ramseys were immediately recognized by Vanessa Bell with her Cornwall childhood memories. Later in 'Sketch of the Past' Virginia Woolf recalled that with the writing of *To the Lighthouse*, her mother's presence ceased to obsess her. *Jacob's Room* was elegiac; *To the Lighthouse* is an elegy, as Virginia Woolf had called it during the writing. Instead of a urban post-war social system there is a seaside family, one in which the novel's pre- then post-war settings are barely indicated. Again, as in *Jacob's Room*, however, the novel is not chronologically autobiographical.

The three separate sections of the novel move from the past to the present, connected by a lyrical meditation on the passing time and the relation of consciousness to external nature, symbolized by light and water. The loving opposites of the Ramseys are balanced in the painting of the Vanessa-like painter Lily Briscoe in the third section of *To the Lighthouse*. Time and space, appearance and reality are reconciled in her post-impressionist painting: an apparition of the dead Mrs Ramsey appears at a window as Mr Ramsey reaches the lighthouse with his children at the end, and Lily achieves her artistic vision, as does her creator, at the novel's end. Again death figures with understated prominence (Mrs Ramsey dies in a parenthesis, as does her son in the war). Bringing the past into the present was what Memoir Club memoirs sought to do, yet without all the sadness of remembered loss.[2]

Except for *Orlando*, Virginia Woolf did not dedicate any of her novels after the first two. She wished, as she wrote to Roger Fry, that she had dedicated *To the Lighthouse* to him, but thought it so bad she could not, and planned, if her friends advised against her novel, to write historical memoirs (D II 129).

*   *   *

Virginia Woolf's autobiographical fiction of the Twenties was accompanied with a series of published commentaries on various forms of autobiography but as close as she actually got herself to non-fictive autobiography was the essay 'On Being Ill' (E III 317–29) ' . . . Illness is the great confessional' she confesses in a parentheses, but there is little or no confessing in the rather abstract descriptions of bodily illness as the essay modulates into a description of what one reads when ill. As for Virginia Woolf's commentaries on autobiography, they range from the famous through the forgotten to the forgettable: Montaigne, Evelyn, Stendhal, De Quincey, Ruskin, George Moore, then the aristocrats, the anecdotalists, and the obscure.[3] The first *Common Reader*, published the same year as *Mrs Dalloway* and dedicated to Lytton Strachey, collected some of these. Though she did some as reviews or for other occasions, her critical point of view in these pieces is not of a critic or a scholar, but of a reading writer who is guided by, as the opening of *The Common Reader* says (in now obsolete gendered language),

> an instinct to create for himself, out of whatever odds and ends he can come by, some kind of whole – a portrait of a man, a sketch of an age, a theory of the art of writing. (E IV 19)

Only Montaigne, Pepys, and Rousseau really succeeded, she thought, in self-portrayal – more so than, for example, Browne and Boswell. Montaigne's efforts at self-expression, at observation, at questioning life's meanings continue to absorb us, and among the reasons for this is the originality of his autobiographical form.

The essay-memoir is the form practiced in the Memoir Club, and Montaigne was more of a model than longer forms of self-revelation. The *Common Reader* essay on the modern essay suggests some of the significance of the essay for the Club; there Virginia Woolf castigates modern essayists with their nauseating 'trivial personalities decomposing in the eternity of print'. Their attempts are now remote from the Victorian 'extravagant beauty of Walter Pater' or 'intemperate candour of Leslie Stephen' (E IV 221, 233).

As for 'the lives of the obscure', Virginia Woolf sees herself rescuing stranded ghosts as she retells, with various asides, the memoirs, letters, diaries she delighted in reading all her life, as she does those of less obscure people such as the inhabitants of those padded lunatic asylums called stately homes. There are some speculations on patrons, including the remark already quoted, that knowing whom to write for is knowing how to write. In the last essay in *The Common Reader* Virginia Woolf becomes again a post-war contemporary, with some regret:

> We are sharply cut off from our predecessors. A shift in the scale – the war, the sudden slip of masses held in position for ages – has shaken the fabric from top to bottom, alienated us from the past and made us perhaps too vividly conscious of the present.

As she had said in the essay on modern fiction, the accent of 'the life of Monday or Tuesday' now falls differently than in the past. The difference is ultimately a matter of values. And she goes on to remark as a contemporary that with writing 'to believe your impressions hold for others is to be released from the cramp and confinement of personality' (E IV 238, 240). In the Memoir Club the alienation, the changed accentuation of values and the release from limits of personality had been possible.

A number of other collected and uncollected reviews of life-writing that followed *The Common Reader* also reflect Virginia Woolf's attitudes towards autobiography and to some of its contemporary practitioners whom she knew, such as Margot Asquith and George Moore. Two great nineteenth-century auto-biographers, De Quincey and Ruskin, were also reviewed and admired above all for their style.

Finally, neither famous nor obscure, was the memoirist of *A Nineteenth-Century Childhood* which appeared as a book in 1924. Leonard Woolf had edited Molly MacCarthy's memoirs when they appeared in the *Nation*: 'a little comb and brush is all that's needed', Virginia wrote to Molly; 'you know how Clive conceals his bald patch? Well, that's how to treat your memoirs' (L III 44).Then Virginia wrote a short, anonymous review of the book for the *TLS*. It was the first occasion but not the last in which a member of the Memoir Club would review the published contributions of another. Style again attracts the reviewer's atten-tion: Mrs MacCarthy is a phrase- rather than a sentence-maker, not an orderly but a flitting autobiographer trying to catch the queer Victorian insect-celebrities observed from the child's schoolroom point of view of her Memoir Club memoirs, without the ironic influence of *Eminent Victorians*. The Eton setting is now faintly disguised and the family names altered – Virginia mocks the changes a little – but the elusive warden and his eccen-tric, dominating wife are the same, as is Molly MacCarthy's 'whimsical radiance'. A hurried, wretched review, Virginia Woolf wrote deprecatingly to the author of a book she read with envy and delight at its tone of 'slight audacity'.[4] Such was the public and private reception of its founder's memoirs by the Memoir Club's most articulate critic.

* * *

If Virginia Woolf's three novels are, along with Forster's *A Passage to India*, the most familiar writings by the Memoir Club members during the dormant years of the Club, the least familiar are her still unpublished contributions to the Charleston family newspaper. Vanessa Bell, remembering Virginia's childhood for the Memoir Club after the Second World War, recalled how in the 1890s Virginia had written most of the *Hyde Park Gate News*, the Stephen family newspaper. *The Charleston*, later called the *New Bulletin* was again a children's family newspaper, edited sporadically by fifteen-year-old Julian, with thirteen-year-old Quentin as assistant editor, illustrator, and also co-author of a number of pieces with his aunt. The *Bulletin* was a more substantial undertaking than *The Hyde Park Gate News*, appearing sometimes daily over a period of five years until Julian went to Cambridge – a period that coincides with the inactive years of the Memoir Club. In addition to jokey family and servant news items and even an animal fable by Virginia, the *Bulletin* also issued a number of 'Supplements' that reflect a teenage view of the lives and relationships.[5]

The supplements consist of scenes illustrated by Quentin Bell accompanied by descriptive commentary in Virginia's hand. Their subjects are mostly about the lives of Vanessa Bell, Duncan Grant, Clive Bell, and Maynard Keynes. Virginia acknowledged the partnership in the preface to *Orlando*, published the year after the last issue of the *Bulletin*, in describing Quentin as 'an old and valued collaborator in fiction'. The acknowledgement has often been noted but seldom with an indication of what Virginia was alluding to. In the earlier supplements Virginia's commentary appears in the margins of Quentin's drawings. In others her descriptions are on separate pages.

For the Christmas 1923 supplement of the *Bulletin* Virginia 'invented' – Vanessa's word – a series of comic 'adventures', illustrated by Quentin, from Vanessa's childhood, travels, and married life. Another series of incidents, illustrated by Quentin with marginal descriptions by Virginia are entitled 'Eminent Charlestonians' and included Vanessa, Clive, Mary Hutchinson, Duncan, and Roger. A visit by the eminent novelist E. M. Forster is also mentioned in the *Bulletin*. For Christmas 1924, Quentin and Virginia produced 'The Dunciad': scenes in the life of Duncan that demonstrated the subject's imperturbable folly. Next Quentin and Virginia presented 'The Life and Death History of a Studio' which Quentin explained more than sixty years later was about the collapse of an old studio and the planning of a new one at Charleston, the principal actors being Duncan again, Vanessa, a deploring Clive, and an arranging Roger with a 'formidable, gristly, grumpy, grousely, ill-temper (Hah, hah!)', according to Mrs Woolf.[6]

In 1925 Virginia and Quentin collaborated on a life of Clive Bell, dubbed 'The Messiah' (of Bloomsbury). In Quentin's improbable illustration of a dinner party at 46 Gordon Square, Clive and Vanessa's guests were Caroline Emelia Stephen, Lord Robert Cecil, Mrs Humphry Ward, Lytton Strachey and William Butler Yeats. Virginia's description includes their conversation:

> 'Ha' said Mrs Ward.
> 'Hum' said the Quaker.
> 'Huh!' said Lord Robert.
> 'Tosh!' said Lytton.

A description follows of Yeats's stamping feet and grinding teeth 'expressive of considerable mental equipment in a congealed condition'. Quentin used Virginia's description – without explanation – as the frontispiece for the second volume of his aunt's biography. The operative word in Virginia's *Orlando* acknowledgment of Quentin would seem to be 'fiction'.

Then for 1927 Virginia wrote a calendar of Quentin-illustrated events, including events such as a visit from the Woolfs themselves to the Bells at Cassis, then Clive's deserting Bloomsbury for the civilization he was writing a book about. Other incidents that year concerned the competitive advent of automobiles in Bloomsbury, with Vanessa's car supposedly decapitating a young bicyclist in Hyde Park. A different kind of article in Clive Bell's handwriting was contributed by the *Bulletin*'s scientific correspondent on the alarming infestation of pig-mentish painters around Charleston.

The Keyneses, of course, came in for much attention from the *Bulletin*. Their life and adventures (they were married in 1925) were described in a saga called 'The Tiltoniad' by Virginia with Quentin's illustrations. Virginia confessed in a letter to Vanessa late in August 1927, that it was written in a hurry, and 'a good many indiscretions, not to say indecencies, may have crept in'. It was also very vulgar, she thought, and should be kept for the Bells unless Vanessa could censor it. Among the jokes was one that had Keynes buying the nation (rather than the *Nation*) – a crisis which the King then averted. During the hiatus of the Memoir Club and later the Keyneses themselves engaged in the self-mockery of Bloomsbury parties that brought Club members together, including one by the Keyneses in 1927, entitled 'Interpretations', which concluded with 'The Economic Consequences of the Piece', according to the invitation printed by the Hogarth Press.[7]

A diary entry by Virginia Woolf after the *Bulletin* ended suggests the relevance of her contributions to it for both her writing and the history of the Memoir Club. From time to time she thought of her diaries as material for the memoirs she would write when of a memoir-writing age, and on 20 September 1927, she wrote:

> One of these days, though, I shall sketch here, like a grand historical picture, the outlines of all my friends . . . . There may be something in this idea. It might be a way of writing the memoirs of one's own times during peoples lifetimes.

The memoirs of one's own times and friends is what the Memoir Club was about and also, in their mocking way, the *Bulletin* biographies. But the Club and the *Bulletin* lives had a further significance for Virginia's writings. She went on in her diary:

> It might be an amusing book. The question is how to do it. Vita should be Orlando, a young nobleman. There should be Lytton. & it should be truthful; but fantastic. (D III 156–7)

Among the lives to be related were those of Roger, Clive, and Duncan as well as others outside the Memoir Club such as Gerald Brenan and Adrian Stephen. 'Truthful but fantastic' is a good description of Virginia's life-writing with Quentin. How it would lead to *Orlando* is not often recognized.

* * *

Among the biographies in the *Charleston* and the *New Bulletin* was one entitled 'La Vie Amoureuse de Monsieur Fry by Virginia Woolf', which, however, consists entirely of illustrations by Quentin Bell. In the dozen pages illustrating the love life of Roger Fry there are clearly scenes from a memoir Fry began in April 1924. The year before the Hogarth Press had published his handsome *A Sampler from Castile*, which sampled, for his own pleasure he insisted, his sensations while travelling in Spain, expressed verbally and graphically (there are sixteen drawings of places). It was the only instance of the autobiographical travel genre from the Memoir Club. The same year the Hogarth Press also started a 'Living Painters' series on Duncan Grant, introduced by Fry, but no other volumes followed.

Roger Fry's memoir 'L'Histoire de Josette', though never read to the Memoir Club, would perhaps not have been written without the examples provided by the Club. The memoir of love and madness was read by Vanessa and others at Charleston; later Virginia would quote from it in her biography of Fry. Two overlapping states of it exist: a rough, disorganized holograph draft of some 15,000 words and a slightly shorter reorganized but still disordered version typed apparently by someone other than Fry.[8]

Neither manuscript nor typescript presents a completely coherent narrative. Both start, stop, and begin again, sometimes on different pages; events and settings in the memoir are interspersed with letters, poems, musings, and grieving. The incomplete condition of the two versions may explain why the memoir has never been published. Yet from one or the other a sequence of events emerges.

As with the Memoir Club, the audience being addressed in Fry's memoir provides the context for its tone, settings, incidents, and even its language. Fry's memoir is addressed initially to a woman who would never read it, and it is written in French, Fry explains while starting his manuscript account again, because he is trying to create the illusion for himself that Josette is listening to him, as he did in his long letters to her which she had destroyed. The story 'is of a idyll of nine months and of a tragedy of fifteen days which ended with a revolver shot'. Of the three experiences of love that life has offered him, Fry continues in his manuscript,

> all were turned into tragedy by mental illness. The first by incurable madness and the so sadly prolonged life of my wife, the second by the fact that the woman abruptly stopped loving me at the moment when she was completely cured, and the third by the suicide of one whose whole story I am going to tell.

After more than a dozen years of marriage and two children, Fry's wife, who was to outlive him, was institutionalized with schizophrenia (a fate that Fry later says is worse than suicide). The second love was of course Vanessa Bell, whom he is addressing in his memoir as well, and who is also probably the woman wise in love that he mentions consulting. Their brief affair following Vanessa's breakdown in 1912 ended with her attachment to Duncan Grant.

In his memoir Fry maintains that he is pursued by madness because reason is so strong in him and imagination so sympathetic that he can understand insanity without in the least sharing it. That was not how it would be seen by others, because what Fry thought of as an open-minded scientific rationality could seem at times a notorious gullibility. For the Bells and the Woolfs there was something, if not comic, at least grotesque in 'La Vie Amoureuse de Monsieur Fry'. Their responses in particular to Fry's story of Josette are revealing about the reception that memoirists might expect from their Club. Hearing the story of Josette from Fry in June, Virginia remarked in her diary how she and Vanessa could not help being cynical and merry over it, heartless as they might appear to someone like Ottoline Morrell:

> But how long can Roger love a woman without driving her mad? This creature thought he laughed at her, seeing that he dyed vests yellow & sent them to her, telling her to turn to the East & put them on, as a cure for tuberculosis. And he sent her pictures of negro sculpture. For some reason, against my habit, I feel as if I should like to write a story of this. (D II 303)

And she did, briefly, in her biography of Fry when she alludes to the 'legend' of the saffron vests and an anonymous tubercular lady. Her source now was one of the anecdotes Clive Bell compiled for the Memoir Club in 1939, where Josette is named, and her suicide attributed to what Fry thought was a cure. Fry's memoir does allude to an X-ray of her lungs she gave to him for medical advice and which he returned in a broken state; that, along with the African mask he had given her, increased her suspicions that he was mocking her. She then bought a revolver and shot herself on a cliff facing England, 'with her last look towards me still on her pupils'.

In his memoir Fry's credulity is shown by his belief in Coué's kind of self-hypnosis. His relationship with Josette Coatmellec originated symbolically at Coué's Nancy clinic. Fry was impressed with Coué's success with patients and he admired the materialist basis of his therapy. Josette was thirty-four when they met, Fry twenty years older. At Nancy, in Paris where Fry was testifying effectively about a fake Leonardo da Vinci painting, then at Josette's home with her sister in Harfleur, and later in other meetings in France, their affair proceeded, but mostly it was by letter when they were apart, which more easily allowed for Josette's 'omnivorous suspicion'. But once together, they did attain 'jouis-sance'. Fry tried, he says, for emotional honesty – the only sexual morality for him (as well as for Bloomsbury) – but it clearly was not a sufficient response to paranoia.

'L'Histoire de Josette' is not a tragic memoir. Fry says of himself that he is poorly suited for a tragic life. There is more pathos than tragedy as Fry tries to heal himself by revisiting the happiness of the loving affair with Josette as well as its agonizing end. There is little about Josette herself or her background, just that she was small, not pretty; could be fantastic, whimsical, mischievous; and lived with her schoolteacher sister at Harfleur. Fry says he can-not analyse her; all that remains is a scent. For Josette the formi-dable Fry was a great man, and this increased her conviction that he was ridiculing her. Fry became possessed by her love, though he was aware of something unhealthy in it. Reviewing the story of their brief relationship, Fry appears to be talking more to Vanessa rather than to Josette, though the need for self-justification seems relevant to both Roger and Josette.

Fry concludes the manuscript memoir of his love with a medi-tation on life's contradictory principles of absolute, eternal love and relative perpetual change. Women and men embody these differently. The only way to live with the contradiction for Fry is to avoid the vanity of egoism, as the Taoists he cites knew, while madness consists of being imprisoned by it. These reflections are quoted by Virginia Woolf in Fry's biography at the end of her short account of Josette.

The manuscript ends by connecting love and madness again through Stendhal's theory of how love crystallizes in the mind without correspondence to external facts. 'Is it the same with Madness?', Fry asks himself, and cries out, 'it is the only truth'. But the last word is of love. Included with Fry's memoir is a mock-up of the unused tombstone Fry wanted for Josette (also illustrated among the scenes by Quentin). Its simple epitaph from a Mallarmé sonnet was 'O Sɪ Déʟɪcɪeusement Toɪ'.

*   *   *

Two years earlier E. M. Forster had begun a grieving, disjointed memoir, also addressed to a dead lover and not read to the Memoir Club. Forster never wrote of his Egyptian experiences for the Memoir Club. His memoir of Mohammed el Adl, his later memories of Constantine Cavafy, the quasi-autobiographical sketches of Alexandria he did at the time, the reminiscence concerning his Alexandrian guide written more than thirty years later, and even the memoir of swimming in Egypt – none, it appears, were ever read to the Club. The differences from his Club memoirs can be revealing.

Briefer and more private than Fry's memoir to Josette, the memoir-letter for and of Mohammed el Adl was continued off and on for seven years, remaining unpublished until 2004, though Forster thought it could be shown to others. To the twenty-page memoir itself Forster appended another fifty or so pages of copied letters from Mohammed and also some of his 'words spoken'.[9] After an epigraph on loss and time beginning 'Good-night, my lad, for nought's eternal . . . ' from A. E. Housman's just published *Last Poems*, the memoir, which Forster first thought of as a book, begins

> **To Mohammed el Adl who died at Mansourah shortly after the 8th of May, 1922, aged about twenty three of consumption . . . and to my love for him.**

The memoir ends in 1929 with Forster, now nearly 51, writing 'tomorrow you must join my dead . . . '. Though he no longer cares for love as he did, his needs now being lust and friendship, Forster adds that he did love Mohammed and might again if love is eternal (which he disbelieves). He probably will not think of Mohammed when he comes to die, but for now Mohammed has his love, though Forster also has his doubts about how deeply Mohammed really cared for him.

Forster knew Mohammed was dying, and learned of his death a week after reading to the Memoir Club what most likely was the account of his affair with Kanaya in India. The memoir, begun a month or so later, is an attempt to commemorate a love rather than a lust affair, and while there are frank sexual details, the purpose and the tone of his Egyptian memoir is very different from the Indian one. There is no swank in it either, as Forster said of the memoir 'Kanaya' but self-pity is not absent from the grief of the memoir.

Forster's experience of Alexandria, where he worked for the Red Cross interviewing wounded soldiers during the war, was also, of course, quite different from his experience of India both before and after the war. A theme the Kanaya and Mohammed memoirs share, however, is the degrading effects of British imperialism on human relations, which were exacerbated by the racial tensions, social incompatibilities, and economic disparities between Forster and his lovers. Disparities of different kinds also separated Forster from two other quite extraordinary men in India and Egypt, the Maharaja of Dewas State Senior, who facilitated Forster's affair with Kanaya, and the great Alexandrian poet Constantine Cavafy.

It was Cavafy whose poetry Forster was instrumental in having translated into the canon of modern English literature. One of his triumphs, Forster would call it, though the triumph was delayed by Cavafy's compulsive revising and his translators' various difficulties. It took the persistent Leonard Woolf nearly twenty years before the Hogarth Press finally brought out in 1951 *The Poems of C. P. Cavafy*, a posthumous translated collection of his poems – which Leonard called one of his triumphs. Cavafy does not figure explicitly in Forster's Mohammed memoir, which reflects the distinction Forster sometimes drew between Egyptians and Alexandrians. Much later Forster wrote of his association with Cavafy in a review of his poems (reprinted in the English edition of *Two Cheers for Democracy*): Cavafy was amazed that Forster could make some sense out of 'The God Abandons Antony' in Greek, which seems to have been the beginning of his modern English reputation. Forster describes the Alexandrian context of Cavafy, but the homosexual aspects of his life and art could still not be mentioned, though they are implicit in some of Forster's quotations. Eclectic, exilic, erotic, and ironic, Cavafy's poetic voice is very different from Forster's prose one, though they shared in their different ways these characteristics.

In the course of the memoir for Mohammed el Adl, Forster says he hoped to describe 'every moment of our intercourse' but as the months passed Mohammed grew dimmer. What he records are their first encounters in Alexandria while Forster was working for the Red Cross and Mohammed was a tram conductor. Their meetings in Mohammed's room, their riding together outside of Alexandria, and then their later meetings after a friend of Forster's found Mohammed a better job with the government in Cairo follow, as Forster was able to help him and his family with money. At one point Forster says he must write sensually and describes kisses, caresses, thigh-fondling, erections, their hurting each other; and later he mentions his apprehensive resolve to let himself be penetrated. The letters that follow describe Mohammed trying to sell cotton, his marriage, his arrest and unjust imprisonment for allegedly trying to buy a gun, and the damage prison did to his consumption. Forster left Egypt in 1919 but saw Mohammed again en route to India and when he came back. More details of the relationship are to be found in Forster's letters at the time to his confidante Florence Barger in England.

At the opening and throughout the memoir, Forster emphasizes, as in his dedication, that the memoir is for both Mohammed and himself, difficult as it is to distinguish between Mohammed, now 'a putrid scrap', and himself trying to keep his words from getting in the way of his memories. Forster gives three reasons for writing the memoir of Mohammed: his own comfort, to recall the past, and because as a professional writer he wants to pay Mohammed the last honour of a memoir. But Forster worries that he is evoking not Mohammed but only his own memories through self-stained words. Memories and words – Forster's anxieties about them and what death does to them are central to memoir-writing, and the articulation of them may be the most enduring part of Forster's memoir of Mohammed el Adl.

Rereading the memoir-letter much later, Forster noted in his journal (14 July 1958) that his grief had made it 'stagey and hysterical'. He was inclined to destroy it and write of Mohammed with dignity but his attempt to finish his uncompleted novel 'The Other Boat' interfered. Forster was nevertheless surprised to find Mohammed influencing the story in the characterization of the charming, mixed-race Cocoa, who ends up being strangled by his suicidal English lover. Earlier in his memoir Forster stated that he had written another story because of Mohammed and also dedicated a book to him. The story is 'The Life to Come', again a tale of love between a missionary and a native, that ends in murder and suicide. What impact his experience with Kanaya may have had on these fictions, Forster never says. It is not easy, on the basis of his memoirs, to separate distinctly the significance of the two affairs in Forster's life or writing.

The book Forster says he dedicated to Mohammed was *Pharos and Pharillon*, published to considerable acclaim by the Woolfs in 1923. Earlier Forster, at Leonard Woolf's urging, had used his memories of Alexandria to state the facts, compiled from imperialist and nationalist books about the British occupation of Egypt, for a 1920 Fabian research pamphlet entitled *Notes on Egypt*. In it Forster is highly critical of efforts to maintain imperial control. He wrote the pamphlet, Forster told Florence Barger, 'for the sake of Mohammed and his sufferings' (*Letters*, 10 Nov. 1920). In it Forster observes that 'the mild and cheerful Egyptians seemed (especially to one who had known Indians) an easy people to live with', adding, however, that evil influences were changing that political situation. Except for the Sudan, which Forster in the language of his time described as inhabited by a 'a backward race recently delivered from barbarism' and that should still be imperially controlled, Forster appears to favour a League of Nations Mandate for Britain to help Egypt manage its own affairs.

Pharos and Pharillon – the names of the great Alexandrian lighthouse of antiquity and its diminished successor – is a very different book about lighthouses than the one Virginia would complete a few years later. Still, one wonders if Forster's Alexandrian descriptions stimulated Virginia's Cornwall memories. The dedication to Mohammed el Adl, once a conductor himself, is oblique and in Greek, which translated reads 'To Hermes Conductor of Souls' (to the underworld). The contents of *Pharos and Pharillon* were largely selected from the articles, a number of them called 'Alexandria Vignettes', that Forster wrote under the penname 'Pharos' for Alexandrian newspapers and then revised, with additional pieces from the *Athenaeum* after his return to England. The tone especially in the historic Pharos half of the book is ironic, as is the penname; 'pert' was the term Forster's used to describe *Alexandria: A History and a Guide* but it is even more suitable for *Pharos and Pharillon*. Forster had not read Lytton Strachey's book when he wrote most of his portraits, but there are some resemblances between his eminent Alexandrians and Strachey's Victorians. And of course there is the acknowledged influence of Gibbon, so important also for Cavafy, and his detached historic tone, which is quite different from Forster's rather intimately personal one.

The more contemporary Pharillon section includes autobiographical visits to the cotton market and a drug den, and ends with a reprinted essay on Cavafy's poetry. It is the Alexandrian spirit of Cavafy, 'standing absolutely motionless at a slight angle to the universe', not Mohammed's, that pervades the book. Cavafy's 'The God Abandons Antony' separates the two parts of the book. Yet the poem also evokes something of the fading memory of Mohammed when it urges Antony to listen to the music of the departing God with emotion, and 'bid farewell to her, farewell to Alexandria, whom you are losing' without deluding himself that it was a dream.

*   *   *

It was to Constantine Cavafy, who had died five years earlier, that Forster dedicated the 1938 second edition of the book that he had published – or tried to – in Alexandria in 1922. Much of the reading and some of the writing that he used in *Pharos and Pharillon* was done for *Alexandria: A History and a Guide*. The complicated history of that book became the subject much later of a very different Egyptian memoir – a humorous one written by Forster to be read aloud, though not apparently read to the Memoir Club. 'Reminiscing', he says for his own pleasure, in 1956 to an audience at the Aldeburgh music festival, Forster begins the memoir he called 'The Lost Guide' in London during the First World War. He was interviewed there for the Red Cross by the formidable Gertrude Bell who told him that as an interviewer of wounded soldiers in Alexandria, he will have no time for Alexandrians other than passing them on the streets. But he does. In Alexandria he looks at passing people who sometimes looked back 'with extensive results' including 'an Egyptian tram conductor' and 'most important of all' the now famous but then obscure Cavafy. He was typically Alexandrian, and by that Forster means 'a mixture, a bastardy' which he finds attractive in contrast to 100 per cent nationalisms of then and now. An eclectic but harmonized mixture, if not a bastardy, informs the guidebook too that Forster decided to write. His memoir tells the story of its publication.

A branch of a well-known British stationer and printer, located in Alexandria, agreed to publish the guide, but Forster's dealing with the director – whose name Forster conceals – drove him nearly dotty. From proofs to royalties, the publisher apparently had little idea of how to do a book. Back in London Forster complained to the head office, and the book was finally printed in 1922, only to disappear in a fire at the printers (exactly when this happened has been questioned). What followed as described in Forster's later memoir has to be one of the most ludicrous incidents in the history of modern publishing. The loss was covered by insurance, and Forster received a substantial cheque, only to learn that the books had not actually burned after all:

> They were in a cellar which had escaped the flames, and this as the publishers pointed out, placed us in a difficult position, for we had taken the insurance money. They had given some thought, and had decided that the only thing to do was to burn the books artificially, and this they had done. *Alexandria: A History and a Guide* perished in personal flames. I don't

know whether this was the right course. I only know that this fantastic enterprise is all of a piece.

End of the first edition. The second was the result of Forster the guide-maker humiliatingly losing his way in Alexandria when passing through the city in the Thirties. Friends helped update the guide part of the *Guide*, Forster leaving the history section as is, except for some corrections (of which more than a few were needed, it seems). The second edition then appeared in 1938, but did poorly with the coming of the Second World War. As for a third edition, in his memoir Forster thought not; it would have to be revised, friends pointed out, so as not to offend Egyptian susceptibilities. 'Indeed I don't know whose national susceptibilities this pert little work does not offend.' Yet half a dozen years later a third edition did appear, with a preface acknowledging the offending of susceptibilities and briefly recounting the circumstances of its writing as Forster walked around Alexandria with visions of the city's history coming to him. The destruction of the edition, however, is confined to a single burning in this public version of the guide's history.

Forster concluded 'The Lost Guide' by reading an excerpt from 'The Spiritual City'. In the *Guide*'s preface he described the chapter as a meditation on Alexandrian philosophy and religion, inserted between the earlier and later periods of the city's history, that would not interest many readers. The thread of Forster's meditation is the problem of the relation – the connection – of the divine and the human in Alexandrian religious philosophy. Intermediary solutions are surveyed in Egyptian paganism, the Jewish Philo's *logos*, the Greek Plotinus's mystical visions, and the various disputes about Christ's nature among Gnostic, Arian, and Orthodox Christians. Forster's own sympathies are clearly with the Neo-Platonists, whose thought approaches that of the East: 'The Christian promise is that man shall see God, the Neo-Platonic – like the Indian – that he shall be God.' The least sympathetic solution was Islam's, which needs no mediator other than its Prophet. Encounters with Islamic and Hindu thought were part of Forster's Indian experience before and after Alexandria and influenced the novel he finally published in 1924. As for Islam, Forster remained ambivalent about it, admiring its severities but regretting the absence of human–divine relations in it. From India later, however, Forster wrote that he had to come through Hinduism to appreciate Islam.

The chief utility of *Alexandria: A History and a Guide*, Forster insists in italics, lies in the references to places that are given in the history of Alexandria because the sights of the city are no longer interesting in themselves. In linking the historical and guiding halves of the *Guide* – separated, as in *Pharos and Pharillon*, by Cavafy's poem on Antony – Forster connects the City's present with its past. 'Only connect . . . ' could be the *Guide*'s motto as it was in different contexts for *Howards End* in 1910. Connecting the past with the present was what the Memoir Club was all about too.

Guidebooks follow their own laws, Forster said in his 'Lost Guide' memoir, and in his, history is less important than literature. History is 'too much an affair of armies and kings', he writes, 'only through literature can the past be recovered . . . '. But one of the consolations of history was the snubbing of the dead, Forster suggested, in an essay written on his return to England. This, it has been pointed out, he certainly does in *Alexandria*. As for the guide part of his book, Forster once remarked how Roger Fry enjoyed going around galleries with him because of his amusingly irrelevant comments,[10] and there are some of these to be found in *Alexandria: A History and a Guide*, which is part autobiography as well as history and guide.

Lastly, a brief Egyptian memoir written around 1921 takes us from wandering the streets and squares of the Alexandrian guide to swimming in the Mediterranean. It is unusual among Forster's memoirs in not often involving other people after an opening memory of not learning to swim as a boy. Entitled 'Swimming in the Sea', the memoir is about Forster's having taught himself in middle-age to swim incompetently but joyfully in Egypt.[11] There are digressions on literary swimmers such as Swinburne and

Jefferies, but mostly Forster writes about swimming as a silent, lonely, almost mystical, somewhat fearful thing. It is the only time one has both feet off the ground, he thinks (he would soon have his first experience flying in an airplane). And it is in the sea rather than imprisoning lakes or ponds that one should swim. Nudity is also desirable, as the hard-thinking Scandinavians and thoughtless Egyptians have both decided. Some of Forster's observations are a little odd, such as that the caress of brine should not be washed off by sea-lovers. Nor does Forster comprehend how swimmers can take the sea into their mouths without drowning. Meanwhile the Mediterranean watched from a cliff rather than the beach appears beautiful, friendly, and grave as it pushes a current in and out of a little Egyptian cove.

*   *   *

Forster wrote no fiction about Egypt. In Egypt, back in England, and again in India he carried around his unfinished novel about India. With Leonard Woolf's encouragement, as was noted, he finally finished it, writing the last words with Mohammed el Adl's pencil in January 1924, as he noted in his diary (21 January 1924), then writing to Leonard, as Virginia recorded in her diary on 23 January, 'to whom first but you & Virginia should I tell the fact that I've put the last words to my novel' (D II 289).

The last words and the novel as a whole describe, Forster told his closest Anglo-Indian friend Malcolm Darling, a necessary parting of human relationships because 'individuals progress alternately by loneliness and intimacy . . . ' (*Letters*, 15 Sept. 1924). *A Passage to India* was originally dedicated to the seventeen years of Forster's friendship with Syed Ross Masood; later he added the name of the Maharaja of Dewas State Senior. Forster wrote not a memoir but a tribute to Masood, a distinguished educator and Forster's most significant Indian friend. There Forster spoke of his love for Masood who had roused him from his suburban and academic existence, showing him a new civilization.[12] Masood's relevance to the character of Dr Aziz seems more plausible than that of the Egyptian tram conductor and the Indian barber who influenced the quite different fictions of 'The Life to Come' and 'The Other Boat'. Yet Gerald Brenan recalled Lytton Strachey's remarking that he thought 'the increased bite and hardness of *A Passage to India* and its lack of sentimentality are due to [Forster's] having meanwhile had a love affair with an Indian'.[13] Masood, Mohammed, and Kanaya were all involved in the parting of relationships for Forster. Aside from such generalities, however, the sources for Forster's characters are indeterminately complex. The character Fielding, for example, takes his name from a Cairo acquaintance and has something of Malcolm Darling in him and not a little of Forster himself.

Also important for the finishing of his novel in ways difficult to identify very specifically were, according to Forster, two very different kinds of autobiographical works. *Seven Pillars of Wisdom*, which Forster read in an early version as he was writing the last chapters of his novel, delighted him with its Eastern setting and characters. A friendship developed with T. E. Lawrence, which led eventually to an abortive attempt to edit his letters, that Forster would later tell the Memoir Club about. And returning from India in February 1922, Forster bought Proust's *Du coté de chez Swann*, and thought its use of memories would influence the composition of his novel, as Virginia Woolf felt Proust would influence *To the Lighthouse*. (Proust died in November and early next year the *TLS* published a tribute to him signed by Forster, Virginia Woolf, Clive Bell and others.) Yet *A Passage to India* could not be described as an autobiographical novel in the way that Virginia's novels of the Twenties are, or Proust's for that matter. The exact historical time of the novel remains deliberately indefinite; Forster wanted to avoid contemporary politics in *A Passage to India*, and there are no explicit allusions to the Amritsar massacre of 1919 or Gandhi's non-cooperation movement. Unlike Virginia Woolf's three novels, where the First World War figures significantly, Forster remains deliberately indefinite about the War in the novel he started before it and completed afterwards.

Three years after the publication of *A Passage to India*, Forster began a series of lectures on the novel in Cambridge by announcing that 'Time, all the way through, is to be our enemy'; life by time was contrasted unfavourably with life by values, yet in the novel there was always the story and always a clock.[14] In *A Passage to India*, however, one cannot tell what time it is. Elsewhere Forster wrote that he was more interested in space than time, in infinity than eternity. Expansion not completion was what he aimed at in *A Passage to India*, a novel whose spatial setting dominates its temporal one from Whitman's title onwards. The unifying idea of the *Aspects of the Novel*, Forster announced in his lectures, was that in the novel there are two forces, human beings and other things which the novelist must conciliate, namely plot, fantasy, prophecy, pattern, and rhythm. And Forster worried while writing his *A Passage to India* that its people were not as interesting as their Indian atmosphere – an anxiety he had expressed earlier in his memoirs. (This did not bother readers like Cavafy who loved the novel's characters.) As for a unifying idea in the novel, it might be found paradoxically in the unresolvable conflict between India's multiplicity and various failed attempts at unity through imperialism, religion, or love. But any adequate account of the novel should also mention, as Forster did to his publishers, Edward Arnold Ltd., the humorous aspect of his passage to India.

Forster never committed himself to discussing *A Passage to India* for the Memoir Club the way he had his early novels. His two Indian memoirs – the public one revised for *The Hill of Devi* – were written before he had finished the novel (see Chapter 4). Afterwards he made various scattered published and unpublished remarks about the novel but devoted no memoir directly to it. A note in the Everyman edition of 1957 explained that the India of the novel no longer exists, that the novel dates, but its main purpose was not political or even sociological. Then in a late autobiographical talk on three countries of his fiction – Italy, England, India (Egypt was not one of his fictive countries) – he explained how his connection with India rested on personal relationships, initially with Masood, who had showed him how Moslems like

Aziz lived, but also with the English and Hindus. Denying again that the now famous novel was about politics, he did refer to racial tension and incompatibility, but the emphasis remains on Indian scenery, and the spiritual cum philosophical sequence from mosque through caves to the Hindu temple in the novel. The novel, Forster added in his talk, was, among other things, 'a search of the human race for a more lasting home . . . '[15] That sounds a little like *Howards End*, but in India connecting was not enough. Forster did not go as far as Fielding had in finding after India the Mediterranean – Italy, that is, but also Egypt a little – to be 'the human norm' (Chapter XXXII).

The year after *A Passage to India* was published Forster articulated his view of autobiography's relevance to fiction in a characteristically modernist theory of impersonality. In the Hogarth pamphlet *Anonymity: An Enquiry*, he maintained a dichotomy between information, which is relative, and creative work which is absolute. Fiction partakes of both, but its study can be dangerous, especially for the immature, where it can become 'only a serious form of gossip'.[16] What would he have thought of the study of memoirs – his and his friends' in their club? A mature form of gossip perhaps.

As for the Memoir Club itself, their opinions of *A Passage to India* were mixed. Strachey, as was mentioned, found it less sentimental than Forster's earlier novels for autobiographical reasons. Leonard Woolf, who had encouraged Forster to stop reviewing and finish the novel, praised it highly in the *Nation*, complaining about the difficulty of reviewing it in 1200 words. Yet he appreciated the subtlety of its humour, the reality of the characters (Aziz was the only living Indian Leonard had met in a book), the effectiveness of the dialogue and description – all without the lapses into silliness that had marred Forster's earlier novels. The review, entitled 'Arch Beyond Arch' saw the themes of the book as a series of arches within arches: there was the arch of two women who wanted to see India, the arches of Anglo-Indian society and politics, of friendship, mystery, muddle, and the 'terrible arch of "personal relations"'.

Desmond MacCarthy appears to have avoided reviewing
A Passage to India for the *New Statesman*; the review there pro-
voked letters from Anglo-Indians criticizing the depiction of their
class. And from H. W. Masssingham, former editor of the *Nation*,
came a rare complaint that Leonard Woolf was too formalist a
critic in attending to the novel's spiritual form, and ignoring its
Indian content.[17]

Virginia was less enthusiastic than Leonard. Privately she
wrote in her diary Forster was too restrained by facts in his
new novel (D II 304). Later in 1924 she was cheered by an article Forster would publish praising her early novels, especially
Jacob's Room and *Mrs Dalloway*.[18] Three years later in 'The
Novels of E. M. Forster', she clarifies some of the differences
between her conception of fiction and his. She notes the characters in *A Passage to India* were less important than the land,
although Aziz was Forster's most imaginative creation; relieved
'for a time to be beyond the influence of Cambridge', she found
the double vision or method of poetry and satire, of comedy
and moralizing that had bothered her in Forster's earlier novels
becoming one. Still there were ambiguities, incomplete symbols,
and, again, too many facts to be coped with imaginatively (E IV
491–500). Forster responded in a letter protesting his method
was not wrong, he just could not make it work.[19] Then in her
biography of Roger Fry, Virginia quoted a letter of Fry's on the
marvellous texture and beautiful writing of *A Passage to India*,
'but Oh lord I wish he weren't a mystic, or that he would keep his
mysticism out of his books', because only the meanings an artist
knows nothing about are worthwhile in art.[20] The criticism was
similar to those he made of 'Time Passes' in *To the Lighthouse*.

*   *   *

Virginia Woolf and Roger Fry were also involved during the hiatus of the Memoir Club with recovering not ancestral voices but
ancestral visions. In 1926 the Hogarth Press brought out the first
major book of Julia Margaret Cameron's photographs. Entitled,

a little provocatively, *Victorian Photographs of Famous Men & Fair Women*, the volume was introduced by Virginia on her great aunt's life and by Roger on her art. Bloomsbury had been using Victorian photographs in books since *Eminent Victorians* (where Strachey insisted on their importance), and they were continued through *Queen Victoria*, *Orlando*, and *Flush* to the satirical photographs of *Three Guineas*.

Victorian Photographs of Famous Men & Fair Women consists of fourteen plates of intense, slightly unfocused and uncoiffed men of art and science, followed by ten beautiful dreamy ones of posed women and children, including three portraits of Julia Cameron's niece, Julia Duckworth – Virginia's mother-to-be.[21] Lytton Strachey remarked that he did not like her character in the photographs, her mouth seeming to complain – '& a shaft of white light fell across my dusky rich red past', said her daughter recording the remark in her diary (D II 239). The book's juxtaposition of the Victorian sexes is rather undermined, however, by the introductions on the famous woman artist – the only one of the Pattle sisters not beautiful – who made the photographs. The two introductions also depict or discuss the mid-Victorian milieu in which Julia Margaret Cameron's eccentrically energetic personality and creativity flourished.

As early as 1919 while finishing *Night and Day*, Virginia Woolf had been thinking of writing something on the scene near Freshwater Bay on the Isle of Wight where Cameron thrived with her retired and retiring Indian-administrator husband, together with Tennyson as well as G. F. Watts and his young wife Ellen Terry. (Anne Thackeray Ritchie's memoirs of Freshwater were an important source, as were the memories of Virginia's mother.) In 1923 Virginia wrote a skit on the subject, to be stage-managed by Desmond MacCarthy, with Cameron's photographs used as props, and this may have led to the volume of photographs three years later, though the play was not actually performed then. The photographer (played by Vanessa Bell), the poet, and the painter are all mocked for their artistic fervour and pretentiousness. Then in 1935 *Freshwater: A Comedy* was rewritten and expanded considerably. It was performed in Vanessa's studio with Bloomsbury members playing Freshwater characters and making Bloomsbury jokes. The effect is something like a literary double exposure.[22]

Virginia's biographical introduction to Cameron's *Victorian Photographs* could also be subtitled 'a comedy'. The aggressive, affectionate enthusiasm of her great aunt manifested itself in her voluminous correspondence ('the Victorian age killed the art of letter writing by kindness: it was too easy to catch the post') and then in photography at Freshwater before she finally returned with her husband and their coffins to Ceylon to die. The props, the costumes, the composed scenes, the lengthy poses and difficulties of exposure, the harried models from the poet laureate to the serving maid are all part of the comic biography. Roger Fry's discussion, entitled 'Mrs Cameron's Photographs', also fixes on the Victorian setting of her art but less satirically. In her portraits rather than her imitative pre-Raphaelite scenes, Julia Margaret Cameron was a great artist, Fry maintains, recording Victorians who were unafraid of their own personalities. She demonstrated that photography was an art whose end was composition not virtuosity – a familiar theme of Fry's with implications spelled out for the National Portrait Gallery with its acres of painted portraits that had not yet really accepted the art of photography. It is a theme with the same concluding polemic twenty years later in another introduction to Julia Margaret Cameron's photographs by Clive Bell, who called her a Giottoesque primitive; and twenty years after that Quentin Bell praised the psychological insight of Cameron's chiaroscuro portraits.[23]

How the selection and arrangement of Julia Margaret Cameron's photographs was made is unknown but they must have involved Vanessa Bell who had hung a number of them at Gordon Square and at Charleston. 'You are urgently needed', Virginia wrote to her in 1926, 'to start a Club: to get up a book of Aunt Julia's photographs among other things' (L III 276).

'To start a Club . . . ' – it seems that the Memoir Club's apparent demise was being felt. One plan in 1926 was to start another secret one called 'The Bloomsbury Bar' at which eight Bloomsbury hosts would be allowed three guests each at meetings, the hosts being the Bells, the Woolfs, Duncan Grant, Roger Fry, E. M. Forster, and Lytton Strachey. But nothing came of it. Finally in the late spring of 1928 Molly MacCarthy wrote to members that Virginia had agreed to read a paper on the beginnings of Bloomsbury at what Molly thought, perhaps with her increasing deafness, might well be the last meeting of their ancient Memoir Club.

Old Bloomsbury

6

[unfinished]

'Are you coming to town to hear Virginia read on Old Bloomsbury on Wednesday?' E. M. Forster wrote to Lytton Strachey 2 July 1928.[1] Two days later Virginia read to the Club a memoir that has become, along with '22 Hyde Park Gate', which she read to the Memoir Club in 1920, a prime source for the biography of Virginia Stephen. Perhaps because the memoir opens with a continuation of the life at Hyde Park Gate, Quentin Bell dated it – parenthetically within a footnote – as having been read to the Club 'in about 1922'. Subsequent biographers and editors have followed him in this misdating.[2] Memoir Club correspondence of Forster, Molly MacCarthy, and Lytton Strachey confirms, however, that 'Old Bloomsbury' was read to the Memoir Club years later on 4 July 1928.

Curiously, there is no mention of the paper in either Virginia Woolf's diary, which is blank between 22 June and 7 July, or her letters. Aside from the Memoir Club correspondence, evidence for the date of 1928 comes, first, from the opening that recapitulates her previous memoir and which would hardly have been needed if the memoir had followed a year or two after the first. Secondly, Vita Sackville-West reported that Virginia read 'Old Bloomsbury' to her and then to friends of theirs while travelling in France the following September.[3] Except for her much later *Dreadnought* Hoax talk, it is the only known occasion on which Virginia Woolf read her memoirs outside the Club (though she later copied out one for Ethel Smyth).

The 1928 date is significant for the history of Virginia's career because of its place between *Orlando*, the book she had just finished, and *A Room of One's Own*, which she was beginning to write. That the historical sequence of Virginia Woolf's writing should still be unknown at this stage of her fame is surprising and suggests the usefulness of the Memoir Club's history. The 1928 date is important for the history of the Memoir Club as well because, rather than ending the Memoir Club as Molly MacCarthy had hoped, Virginia's 'Old Bloomsbury' renewed it. Memoirs on the beginnings of Bloomsbury by Desmond MacCarthy and then Clive Bell followed, and the subject became a recurrent theme for later memoirs by Vanessa Bell, Leonard Woolf, Duncan Grant and others. The theme of encounters with Bloomsbury had been the subject of a memoir by E. M. Forster the first year of the Club, but the later memoirs by Virginia, Desmond, Clive and eventually Vanessa shifted the direction of their reminiscences from private memories of childhood, youth, and relatives, as Clive would note, to memoirs of collective remembering. Unrecoverable Club discussions that followed the reading of memoirs had certainly involved collective remembering, but now it became the subject of memoirs themselves. The growing fame of individual Bloomsbury members and the result- ant publicity and misinformation about the Group as well as the growing hostility toward it also stimulated the memoirs, as remarks in them indicate.

And with the revival of the Memoir Club came the recurrent concerns about its continuation and its membership. To Molly's announcement in May of one more Memoir Club meeting Maynard Keynes had replied hoping it would not be the final meeting because it seemed the right psychological moment for reviving the Club. He did not explain why he thought so, but it may have had something to do with the productivity of members that year. Clive Bell and Leonard Woolf published very different books on civilization, Forster brought out a second collection of stories, Strachey completed his biography of Elizabeth, Virginia finished her fantasy biography of Vita Sackville-West, and Clive wrote for the Hogarth Press the first book in English on Marcel Proust. Forster, who also had wanted another meeting, expressed again his recurrent anxieties about the Club, cautioning Molly to be severe about no guests, for 'if Nell this or Gwynne that are brought, all the readers will discover at the last moment they have mislaid their papers'.[4] In arranging the July meeting, Molly had therefore to explain to Keynes that they would have to stay with their old rule of members only, no guests, which meant no Lydia Lopokova. How and when Lydia become a member remains obscure, for she read no memoirs to the Club.

Afterword

James M. Haule

S. P. Rosenbaum did not live to complete Chapter 6. While his notes and drafts on remaining chapters are preliminary, they allow a glimpse into the complete book he envisioned. He planned to write four additional chapters. 'Beyond Bloomsbury' would have included a discussions of Leonard Woolf's Ceylon memoirs, Forster's Indian letters, Virginia Woolf on the Women's Co-operative Guild, and memoirs by Desmond MacCarthy, John Maynard Keynes, and Mary MacCarthy. Later chapters were provisionally entitled 'The War', 'Later Bloomsbury', 'Posthumous Bloomsbury' (memoirs devoted to Club members and others, like Julian Bell, who had died) and 'Post Bloomsbury' (featuring the papers of later members of the Memoir Club including Quentin Bell, Jane Bussy, Julia Strachey, Frances Partridge, and Angelica Garnett among others).

Rosenbaum had already done a substantial amount of research and organizational work, allowing us to see that he continued to focus not just on what papers were read at meetings but also on what the members wrote and published on their own. He sought not just a recitation of facts or a successful hunt for manuscripts and typescripts. He wanted to understand the influence each had on the other, how ideas could spark and ignite them all.

One of the best examples of the value of this approach is a paper that S. P. Rosenbaum wrote shortly before he died for an international conference in Paris: 'Virginia Woolf parmi les philosophes' (Du 22 mars 2012 au 24 mars 2012, Lycée Henri IV, Paris). Entitled 'Virginia Woolf among the Apostles', the paper discusses the influence of philosophers on Woolf's life and work and focuses special attention on the Cambridge Conversazione Society, the 'Apostles', who formed the core of the Memoir Club and influenced its membership and conduct throughout its existence. Along with 'The Philosophical Realism of Virginia Woolf', the first chapter of *Aspects of Bloomsbury: Studies in Modern English Literary and Intellectual History* (1998), it provides a philosophical and historical foundation for our understanding of Virginia Woolf and, most especially, the Memoir Club. An edited version of that paper is presented here with permission.

Appendix 1:
Virginia Woolf among the Apostles

S. P. Rosenbaum

A conference on the topic of 'Virginia Woolf among the Philosophers' might well begin, if not end, with a consideration of the philosophers she knew. All of them were from Cambridge and all but one were associated with a remarkable, secret society known formally as the Cambridge Conversazione Society, and informally as the Apostles, the Brethren, or simply the Society. In her late memoir 'Sketch of the Past' Virginia Woolf includes the Apostles among the 'invisible presences' in her life. They impinged on her writing as well and need to be recognized in the philosophical interpretation of her work. Before we speak of Woolf's work, however, it is necessary to say something about the philosophers she knew.

The one Cambridge philosopher not an Apostle was her father. Few writers whose fiction and essays attract philosophical interest have had philosophers for fathers. Leslie Stephen, well-known as an agnostic, attempted in his family-centred *The Science of Ethics* (1882) to reconcile the nineteenth-century ethical philosophies of intuitionism and utilitarianism. The reconciliation was based on a Darwinian notion of evolving duty within that primitive relation that Stephen thought held people together: namely the family. The prominent Cambridge philosopher Henry Sidgwick found, however, that *The Science of Ethics* had not really reconciled intuitionism with the modified liberal utilitarianism Stephen actually favoured. Sidgwick, whom Stephen admired, was known to Virginia Woolf. She probably did not read his famous *The Methods of Ethics*, but she must have been aware of his efforts on behalf of women's education at Cambridge, since he helped found and continued to support Newham. I will come back to Sidgwick.

'Read Mill' was Leslie Stephen's cry at Cambridge, and his daughter had certainly read John Stuart's autobiography along with his writings on liberty and on the subjection of women. She may have read the conservative critique of *On Liberty* by her uncle James Fitzjames Stephen, also an Apostle. But the cry of Virginia Stephen's Cambridge contemporaries was 'Read Moore'. G. E. Moore's *Principia Ethica* dismissed evolution as moral concept in Herbert Spencer's philosophy, and thus Stephen does not mention it. Even without knowing Moore's criticism, Virginia would not have found a family-based ethics very satisfactory in theory or practice, though she remained an agnostic and committed to the freethinking and plain speaking that Leslie Stephen proclaimed in the title of a collection of essays.

Among the philosophers Virginia Woolf knew, G. E. Moore, the man as well as the thinker, was the most impressive and influential. She read his celebrated *Principia Ethica* carefully and later came to know him well when he stayed with her and Leonard on various occasions. *Principia Ethica* is quoted in Virginia's first novel and a philosopher like Moore is alluded to (under the charming name of Bennett – no first name given) in both *The Voyage Out* and her next novel, *Night and Day*. The analytic, common-sense tone of Moore's philosophy was described by Leonard Woolf as astringent; he thought, as he wrote in his autobiography, that its purifying effect could be found 'in the clarity, light, and absence of humbug in Virginia's literary style' – qualities also to be found among her father's stylistic aims, it should be noted.

The influence of G. E. Moore's epistemology of philosophical realism on Virginia Woolf's assumptions in her fiction about the nature of consciousness was the subject of a long paper that I wrote some forty years ago – and included in a collection of essays on English literature and British philosophy by various critics. I tried to show there how Moore's dualistic emphasis on subjective immaterial consciousness and its objective, independent material contents underlie Virginia Woolf's fictive accounts of perception and what is perceived. Most familiarly this is expressed in *To the Lighthouse* when Mr Ramsey's philosophy is described to the painter Lily Briscoe by his son as 'Subject and object and the nature of reality'; and when she says she did not understand, he adds, 'Think of the kitchen table . . . when you're not there.' Virginia Woolf's epistemological dualism is assumed in her novels in different ways – in *The Waves*, for instance, with its pageant of soliloquizing consciousnesses set against the sea of time.

To the relevance of Moore's philosophy of sense perception needs to be added the significance of his principles for ethical presuppositions of Virginia Woolf's work. The character of Moore's influence has been much discussed by his disciples and others. John Maynard Keynes thought he and his friends adopted Moore's religion, as he called it, but ignored his morals: 'nothing mattered except . . . timeless passionate states of contemplation and communions. . .'. But Leonard Woolf disagreed, insisting their contemporaries were fascinated by questions of right and wrong and argued endlessly about the moral consequences of actions. Others have maintained Moore's impact was chiefly a matter of personality, but Moore's tough-minded Cambridge followers such as Keynes, Lytton Strachey, and Leonard Woolf cared deeply about ideas as well as personalities.

The ethical principles of *Principia Ethica* were fundamental to Moore's influence. These have sometimes been reductively described, under Keynes' influence, as ideals of personal relationships and aesthetic pleasures. These ideals are fundamental to his moral philosophy, but their significance needs to be understood in the context of a basic ethical distinction that underlies the values not only in Virginia Woolf's work, but also in Leonard's and in the writings by their friends Keynes, Strachey, E. M. Forster, Desmond MacCarthy, Roger Fry – all Apostles – as well as Clive Bell, who was a devoted follower of Moore.

Moore's fundamental distinction is expressed in the preface to *Principia Ethica*. He explains there that he has attempted to distinguish two kinds of questions which moral philosophers claimed to answer but are mostly confused. In Moore's words, 'These two questions may be expressed, the first in the form: What kind of things ought to exist for their own sakes? the second in the form: What kind of actions ought we to perform?' These are questions about ends and about means, about intrinsic and instrumental values, and they reverberate throughout the work of Virginia Woolf and her Bloomsbury friends. They are implicit in her fiction and explicit in non-fiction works such as *A Room of One's Own*, with its means of £500 and its ends of rooms where women writers can think of things in themselves, or in the introduction to working women's memoirs where Virginia Woolf wrote of ladies desiring 'things that are ends, not things that are means'. Once she said to Vita Sackville-West, for whom Moore was the name of a novelist not a philosopher, that she, Virginia, had been 'educated in the old Cambridge School', and concluded, 'My dear Vita, we start at different ends', meaning 'ends' in more than one sense.

Distinguishing ends and means is a common enough practice in ethics, but what made the distinction revelatory for Moore's followers was his conception of intrinsic value. At the centre of Moore's ethic, for all its rigorous analytic rationalism, is a notion (derived from Henry Sidgwick) of good that is ultimate, intuitive, and indefinable. With it Moore undermined hedonistic, vitalistic, and evolutionary ethics. Also basic was Moore's conception (not in Sidgwick) of organic or complex wholes that were not merely the sum of their parts: as wholes their value might be more or less than their value as totalities. Aspects of these concepts of indefinable good and organic wholes are reflected in Virginia Woolf's fictive moments of vision, as are Moore's ideal states of mind involving personal relations, aesthetic objects, and the pursuit of truth for its own sake.

Though Moore's influence on Virginia Woolf was most important, his was certainly not the only philosophy she knew. She read Plato in Greek, and perhaps Plotinus, but Platonic influences are not easily disentangled, for they were also central to Moore's philosophy, as was Kant. Virginia Woolf did not, as far we know, read Kant, but she could hardly have escaped his significance. Moore's ethical emphasis on things in themselves is Kantian, and Kant's exposition of disinterestedness in aesthetics was central to Roger Fry's and Clive Bell's aesthetics, as Desmond MacCarthy pointed out after the first post-impressionist exhibition. Virginia Woolf also read Montaigne (on whom she wrote) and Rousseau, but not Bergson, as has been supposed. Virginia's closest approach to Bergson's thought would have been through the writings by her sister-in-law Karen Costelloe Stephen before she became a psychoanalyst. Later, if not earlier, Virginia read Freud whom the Hogarth Press was publishing. Besides Mill, she may have read others in the English tradition including Hobbes and Locke, probably Berkeley, and certainly Hume, perhaps his empiricism and his history, as well as his remarks on suicide.

Initially, the best-known philosopher connected with Virginia Woolf was Bertrand Russell; his significance for Woolf's work has been well argued by several commentators. It was not Russell the mathematical philosopher – though she knew his collaborator Alfred North Whitehead and his wife – but the author of *The Problems of Philosophy* and popularizing works of social and moral philosophy with whom Virginia Woolf was familiar, including some wartime lectures she attended. Russell's personality interested Woolf as much as Moore's, but in very different ways, as she indicated in her diary in 1924:

His luminous, vigorous mind seems attached to a flimsy little car, like that on a glinting balloon. His adventures with his lives diminish his importance. He has no chin, & he is dapper. Nevertheless, I should like the run of his headpiece.

Russell came to reject Moore's common-sense epistemology and his ethics, but he remained friends with the Woolfs, and in the Thirties they would publish two large volumes of his parents' letters and diaries, edited by Russell and his wife.

A third Cambridge philosopher known to Virginia Woolf has become the object of much attention and analysis. She did not read

Ludwig Wittgenstein, though he read her. Even if she had not met him, Virginia would have known of Wittgenstein from Leonard, from Keynes, and particularly from her nephew Julian Bell, and Julian's satirical poem 'An Epistle on the Subject of the Ethical and Aesthetic Beliefs of Herr Ludwig Wittgenstein (Doctor of Philosophy)'. Despite the distance between Wittgenstein's misogyny and Virginia Woolf's feminism, one could speculate on the applicability to her fiction of some of Wittgenstein's ideas in both his earlier and later thought – his later conception of philosophy as description rather than explanation, for example. It is an idea he applied to aesthetics and criticism and is useful for an account of the philosophers Virginia Woolf knew.

Among the other Cambridge philosophers of Virginia Woolf's acquaintance was the older Idealist J. M. E. McTaggart who influenced Russell and Moore before their revolution of philosophical realism. Virginia would probably not have read any of McTaggart's mystical Hegelianism but may have known his more popular critique of religious dogma. McTaggart's contemporary the political philosopher Goldsworthy Lowes Dickinson was a friend of the Woolfs. Virginia became impatient with Goldie's smooth prose abstractions, but he influenced Leonard's ideas about the League of Nations.

Not all the philosophers Virginia Woolf knew can be described as her elders. Two were contemporaries of Julian Bell's at King's College: Richard Braithwaite and the brilliant Frank Ramsey. Julian Bell's poem on Wittgenstein was originally addressed to Ramsey before he changed the dedication to Braithwaite after Ramsey's tragic early death. Virginia had met Ramsey, thought him a true Apostle, and would have heard more about him in the course of Julian's affair with his widow Lettice.

※　※　※

It is striking how all the Cambridge philosophers that Virginia Woolf knew or knew of at one time or another were connected with the Apostles – all, that is, except Leslie Stephen. His brother,

Fitzjames, was a member, as was Fitzjames's son, the well-known comic poet J. K., who disturbed the Stephen household in his madness and died young. Virginia may have first read about the Apostles in Leslie's biography of Fitzjames, where the Society was described as a group cultivating 'the freest discussion of all the great topics', except perhaps current political ones, and whose members were contemptuous of humbug and looked out for others with intellectual originality.

Founded in the early nineteenth century by twelve Cambridge evangelicals, the Apostles met weekly to discuss a paper by one of them usually on a topic with sceptical philosophic, religious, or moral implications. Sidgwick, McTaggart, Dickinson, Whitehead, Russell, Moore, Wittgenstein, Braithwaite, and Ramsey were all Apostles. (Wittgenstein quit the Society as an undergraduate, and was ritually cursed, but Keynes brought him back so that he could properly resign after his return to Cambridge in 1929.) And the influence of the Apostolic philosophers was extended and renewed for Virginia Woolf by her husband, her nephew, and her close Apostle friends Lytton Strachey, Maynard Keynes, Desmond MacCarthy, Roger Fry, E. M. Forster, and Saxon Sydney-Turner. (Duncan Grant, who did not go to Cambridge, was considered something like an adopted brother by some of them and later wrote an unpublished memoir on his amusing experiences among the Apostles.)

The Society was not just an undergraduate affair. An important feature of its discussions was the participation not just of under-graduate Apostles but others who had graduated and were either visiting or in residence, like Sidgwick, McTaggart, Dickinson, Moore, and for a time Russell. Annual Society dinners in London brought the Apostles together again, and Leonard's accounts of some of these are mentioned in Virginia's diaries. None of the Apostles – be they philosophers or friends – were, of course, women, though some now are.

The character of the Cambridge Conversazione Society in the late nineteenth and early twentieth centuries appears in a famous account of the Apostles by Henry Sidgwick. As quoted by Leonard Woolf in his autobiography, Sidgwick described in a memoir the spirit of the Apostles

> as the pursuit of truth with absolute devotion and unreserve by a group of intimate friends, who were perfectly frank with each other and indulged in any amount of humorous sarcasm and playful banter, and yet each respects the other, and when he discourses tried to learn from him and see what he sees. Absolute candour was the only duty that the tradition of the society enforced.... It was rather a point of the apostolic mind to understand how much suggestion and instruction may be derived from what is in form a jest – even in dealing with the gravest matters.... It came to seem to me that no part of my life in Cambridge was so real to me as the Saturday evenings on which the apostolic debates were held; and the tie of attachment to the society is much the strongest corporate bond which I have known in life.

So wrote one of the university's leading philosophers and educational reformers whose whole career was spent in Cambridge. Sidgwick went on in his memoir, in a passage not quoted by Leonard Woolf, to note that it was his experience as an Apostle that led him years later to devote himself to philosophy.

Leonard Woolf observed autobiographically that all the Apostles of his generation would have agreed with every word of the quotation from Sidgwick. Leonard also noted that from time to time various Apostles came to dominate the society; Sidgwick was one, G. E. Moore another, and Lytton Strachey a third. Strachey and Keynes were critical of Sidgwick's endless Victorian religious doubts and his inhibited friendships as expressed in his memoir, but they were in accord with him about the spirit of the Apostles. And they continued to use Apostolic jargon to distinguish, in a Platonic cum Kantian way, reality from mere phenomenal appearance: real people understood things valuable in themselves whereas inauthentic ones were preoccupied with appearances, with means rather than ends. Echoes of these distinctions are to be heard in Virginia Woolf's various uses of the word *real* and its cognates.

The influence of the philosophy and the philosophers of the Cambridge Apostles began in earnest for Virginia when Thoby Stephen invited his college friends to evenings in Bloomsbury where they met his sisters. Neither of Virginia's brothers nor her brother-in-law to be were Apostles, but a number of their Cambridge friends were. (Leonard, Lytton, and Saxon would regret not having elected Thoby to the Apostles.) The early death of Thoby Stephen intensified the friendships, with Vanessa and later Virginia marrying Thoby's college friends.

Following the dispersal of the First World War, the influence of Cambridge and the Apostles became manifest again in the Memoir Club started by Molly MacCarthy in 1920 to bring her old Bloomsbury friends together again and incidentally help her dilatory husband Desmond to write his memoirs. It is evident from her invitations to various prospective members that Molly – daughter and wife of Apostles – thought of the Club as a kind of continuation of the Society in London where their pursuit of truth could now to be carried on through memoirs and their ensuing discussions. Women would now be present as well as the brethren and men such as Clive or Duncan who were not Apostles. The intimate friendship, truthful candour, and humour recalled by Sidgwick, were Apostolic characteristics of the Memoir Club, in addition to a feature not mentioned by him, namely its secret exclusiveness.

Meditating on the influence of what she called 'invisible presences' in biography and autobiography while writing 'Sketch of the Past', Virginia Woolf wonders why these were never analysed in memoirs. By 'invisible presences' she means

> the consciousness of other groups impinging upon ourselves, public opinion; what other people say and think; all those magnets which attract us this way to be like that, or repel us the other and make us different from that ...

The influence of her mother (who did not want the vote) is her primary example but also referred to, though capable of less definite description, are

> the influence on me of the Cambridge Apostles, or the influence of the Galsworthy, Bennett, Wells school of fiction, or the influence of the Vote, or of the War ...

In her criticism Virginia discusses the limitations of Galsworthy, Bennett, and Wells as well as the impact of the war. As for the Cambridge Apostles, Virginia describes their felt presence in various writings, early and late, most specifically perhaps in her 'Old Bloomsbury' memoir that she wrote for the the Memoir Club and other friends but never published.

Virginia Woolf read 'Old Bloomsbury' to the Club in 1928 (it has been misdated earlier by biographers and editors). Among the audience were Apostolic friends and relatives. It was her first memoir to the Club about life with her father and her step-brother George Duckworth at Hyde Park Gate. After Leslie Stephen's death in 1904 and the move to Bloomsbury, Virginia's memoir brings in the Apostles. In 'A Sketch of the Past' Virginia wondered if scene-making was the origin of her writing impulse, and it is in three scenes of 'Old Bloomsbury' that she most vividly describes her recollection of the effect of Apostles on her life and Vanessa's. The first scene is about the Thursday evenings when Thoby's Cambridge friends joined his sisters in Bloomsbury. Out of these gatherings Virginia thought the Bloomsbury Group developed. At first Thoby's friends Lytton Strachey, Saxon Sydney-Turner, and Ralph Hawtrey were silent, though Clive was not. Then a remark, perhaps by Vanessa about beauty, started a discussion which, culminating at two or three in the morning, resulted in a very important edifice that proved beauty was, or was not, part of a picture, Virginia was not quite sure which. Atmosphere in fiction was another topic, maintained successfully by Virginia against the scepticism of Cambridge.

Noting in her humorous account how she and Vanessa thought they derived the same kind of pleasure that undergraduates had with their friends at Cambridge, Virginia goes on,

part of the charm of those Thursday evenings was that they were astonishingly abstract. It was not only Moore's book had set us all discussing philosophy, art, religion; it was that the atmosphere . . . was abstract in the extreme.

The philosophical origins of the Bloomsbury Group are being described here in the Apostolic discussions that *Principia Ethica* stimulated and in which Virginia now participated. Her memoir continues:

> It had been very austere, very exciting, of immense importance. A small concentrated world dwelling inside the much larger and looser world of dances and dinners had come into existence. It had already begun to colour the world and still I think colours the much more gregarious Bloomsbury which succeeded it.

The progression from the first to the second chapter of Old Bloomsbury, as Virginia calls them, was divided by Thoby's death, followed by Vanessa's marriage to Clive. The 'immense importance' of the discussions remained, if not the excitement and the abstract atmosphere. This is worth remembering in Virginia's subsequent accounts of the Apostles.

The early talk in Bloomsbury was about philosophy, art, literature, religion, but not love and friendship – yet. That talk involved Apostolic discussions of reality as distinguished from phenomenal appearance. In a rather different sense, it was the absence of appearance that Virginia Woolf found odd. Thoby's friends criticized Virginia's and Vanessa's arguments but never seemed to notice the way the sisters looked, something that had so obsessed their half-brother George Duckworth in Hyde Park Gate days. Not only that, but the friends themselves appeared shabby, even dingy. Henry James, for one, seeing Strachey and Sydney-Turner, wondered how Sir Leslie's daughters could have taken up with such deplorable-looking young men. The answer was, among other things, a philosophic one.

Appearance and reality figure in the next scene of Virginia's 'Old Bloomsbury' memoir. Although the austere, exciting, immensely important first chapter of Bloomsbury had ended with Vanessa's marriage, its atmosphere and ideals remained influential in the second chapter, but within a larger, looser social world. The time is five years later, the setting of the second scene the Cambridge college rooms of Lytton's younger brother James and his friends including Rupert Brooke. Virginia quotes from a recently recovered old dairy. The young men's views were honest and simple, Virginia wrote there; they had no padding, and yet had nothing to say in response to her laborious talk. She then realizes not only her talk but her presence was being criticized, for though the young men wished for truth, 'they doubted if I [her diary actually says 'a woman'] could speak it'. And the later Edwardian Thursday evenings that Virginia and Adrian had tried to continue were boring failures, she was convinced, because there was no physical attraction between the sexes.

Then shifting her language for the post-war Georgians of the Memoir Club, Virginia tells her auditors that she had known there were buggers in Plato's Greece and suspected there were in Cambridge, but never realized they were also present at the Thursday evenings hosted by Thoby (it was not a question he could be asked). The abstract simplicity of the immensely important discussions about art or about truth, but never about love, was a consequence; the young men, it seems, discussed personal relations endlessly among themselves, but not in the presence of women.

The third scene of Virginia's memoir is the famous one in which Lytton Strachey, pointing to a stain on Vanessa's dress, inquires 'semen?'

> With that word all barriers of reticence and reserve went down. A flood of the sacred fluid seemed to overwhelm us. Sex permeated our conversation.

Nevertheless in 1912, writing to Lytton Strachey at Cambridge, Virginia still began 'How difficult it is to write to you! It's all Cambridge – that detestable place; and the ap-s-les are so unreal, and their loves are so unreal . . . '

The advent of the older Apostle Roger Fry and the young Duncan Grant now fleshed out Bloomsbury conversations about art and beauty. No longer as austere and exalted, Virginia, her relatives, and Apostle friends like Maynard Keynes encountered

Ottoline Morrell's world of 'lustre and illusion', which also included another Apostle philosopher, namely Bertrand Russell. Russell in his autobiography claimed that with Strachey and Keynes the Apostles became a mutual admiration clique, among whom homosexual relations became common, though they were unknown in his time. Unknown to Russell, perhaps, but hardly to his Society brethren like Goldsworthy Lowes Dickinson.

Their sexuality was not the only aspect of the Apostles about which Virginia Woolf had misgivings, despite her immense admiration for them. She could tease Vita Sackville-West that she – Virginia – had been educated in the old Cambridge school, but she was acutely aware of how indirect that education had been. The differences in male and female education are noted throughout her writing. As early as 1906 she was mocking the anonymous versifiers of *Euphrosyne* – an anthology by Thoby's friends, most of whom were Apostles. She found there ironic evidence of the advantages women had in being educated at home and thus protected from 'the omniscience, the early satiety, the melancholy self satisfaction' of men like the young poets who had been educated at Oxbridge. And as late as 1940 in her essay on the 'leaning-tower' writers of the Thirties, as she calls them, Virginia contrasts the education in which they learned their art with the teaching received by women and other outsiders such as those of the workers' education association she was addressing. As an example of male education she quotes from a recent column of Desmond MacCarthy's in which he wrote of his old Moorean philosophical education:

> We were not very much interested in politics. Abstract speculation was much more absorbing; philosophy was more interesting to us than public causes. . . . What we chiefly discussed were those 'goods' which were ends in themselves . . . the search for truth, aesthetic emotions, and personal relations.

Then, when MacCarthy complained in a later column, that Virginia should not have included herself among an audience of

workers, she wrote him privately that her wretched little education was closer to her audience's than was his or Lytton's or
Leonard's – a mere toadstool beside their towers. Yet it was by
his Apostolic ideals that she measured her disadvantage. Years
earlier Virginia Woolf had quarrelled in print with MacCarthy
over the supposed intellectual inferiority of women, an opinion
that Arnold Bennett had maintained in a book and with which
MacCarthy had agreed in a favourable review.

The attitudes of Bennett and MacCarthy may well have
been behind Virginia Woolf's only published comment on the
Apostles: an oblique satire on the Society entitled 'A Society' that
she included among the stories she brought out in 1921 but later
decided against republishing. In 'A Society' a group of young
women form themselves into a society for asking questions, like
the Apostles, except that they seek answers not in discussion but
by examining the occupations of men. Some go disguised on a
warship like the *Dreadnought* that Virginia had helped hoax
before the war; others proceed to scholars' studies or business-
men's meetings; still others go to libraries, concerts, galleries; and
one (dressed as a man) reviews books by Bennett, Wells, etc. The
women have all agreed that the ends of life 'were to produce
good people and good books' (the Apostles presumably being
limited to the latter). Their inquiries try to determine how far
men have achieved these aims, and the women of the Society
vow, Lysistrata-like, to bear no children until they are satisfied
with the answers. The war intervenes with questions of why men
fight, then the members finish by discussing chastity and the
great fallacy of male intellect. Finally the Society's papers are all
presented to the tearful child that one of the members had borne
in spite of the Society's resolve. Eventually they would be useful
to the author of *Three Guineas*.

While writing the scattered satire of 'A Society', Virginia Woolf
was also composing her first modernist novel. The Cambridge of
Jacob's Room is taken seriously and also amusingly. The characters, present and absent, are wholes and cannot, the narrator
insists, simply be summed up. The discussions that Jacob has with

his friends resemble in their generality those among the Apostles in London that Virginia would recount in her memoir. The light Cambridge sheds is symbolic as well:

> So that if at night far out at sea over the tumbling waves one saw a haze on the waters, a city illuminated, a whiteness even in the sky, such as that now over the Hall of Trinity where there are still dining, or washing up plates, that would be the light burning there – the light of Cambridge.

The words were quoted in 1941 by another Apostle writing about Cambridge: 'How splendidly these words express our faith!' exclaimed E. M. Forster, who added laughingly, 'How unlucky that they should have been written by a woman!' The same year Forster paid his Cambridge memorial tribute to Virginia Woolf in the lecture where, referring again to the light of Cambridge, he cherishes a fantasy that she had taken a degree disguised as Orlando. (Despite the efforts of reformers such as Henry Sidgwick, who died in 1900, women were not granted full Cambridge degrees until 1948.)

Ambivalence then characterizes the Apostles' visible and invisible presence in Virginia Woolf's work. She was forthright in *A Room of One's Own* on the meaning of reality about which they were so much concerned. She concluded there that young women should 'live in the presence of reality' yet could not justify her belief in this, 'for philosophic words, if one has not been educated at a university, are apt to play one false'. So she turns away from philosophical abstractions like those of the Apostles to writers who may live more than others in the presence of a reality that is 'very erratic, very undependable' as it fixes and makes permanent random physical events, groups in rooms, casual sayings, stars, omnibuses, shapes – whatever remains 'when the skin of the day has been cast into the hedge'. Then comes the peroration which returns to Apostolic values:

> Do not dream of influencing other people, I would say if I knew how to make it sound exalted. Think of things in themselves.

At the end of the Twenties Virginia Woolf's interest in the Apostles was renewed when Julian Bell became caught in their web – the image is his aunt's. By then the topics of conversation in the Society had to do more with political issues. Julian did have a brief affair with the Apostle Antony Blunt, later renowned as an art critic and – along with Guy Burgess, another contemporary Apostle of Julian's – as a spy.

Becoming an Apostle, Julian felt, was the most tremendous thing that had happened to him. For Virginia he mixed their 'bleak integrity' with his own goodwill, but she felt, as she wrote to him later in China, that societies like the Apostles did more harm than good with their jealousies, vanities, and exclusions; it was wrong to draw chalk circles and keep people like Clive outside. Then writing *The Years*, she set its college scenes not in Cambridge but in the Oxford where her cousin Herbert Fisher was master of a college.

Virginia Woolf's last published remarks on the Apostles are in her biography of Roger Fry. From a outsider's view of them at the time as careworn youths discussing the ethics of determinism, she shifts to Fry's writing to his mother of 'the priding thing' of being elected to the 'very select, very famous and very secret society' (Virginia's adjectives) for 'the discussion of things in general' (Roger's words). It became the centre of his Cambridge life, as it had for Sidgwick and others. No other election meant as much to him, says his knowledgeable biographer, for the Apostles turned out not to be quite so careworn after all. They talked chiefly of politics and philosophy; art for them was literature with its prophetic messages by Shelley and Whitman, which is why they may have appeared to outsiders as 'eyeless, abstract, and austere in their doctrines'. Roger Fry's aesthetic development from his Cambridge brethren is prefigured in these descriptions.

Cambridge and the Apostles remained a standard of value for Virginia Woolf, however. Lives like those of Rebecca West and her husband, she remarked in her diary, were filled with appearances 'as the Apostles would say'. And those of Harold Nicolson or Hugh Walpole, while more colourful than those of Cambridge intellectuals, did not command her respect the way Moore's did, as she noted in 'Sketch of the Past'. And it was there, where she referred to the Apostles as invisible presences that she also formulated a 'philosophy', as she called it, but without troublesome philosophic words. Her idea was that, behind the cotton wool of daily non-being, in reality there is a pattern connecting human beings. It is revealed in moments of being which can be shocks of ecstasy or desolation. Turning shocks into words, she deprives them of their power to hurt her by making them real. It is a writer's philosophy which delights in the creation of Moorean organic or complex wholes out of the fragments of experience.

Fragments and wholes, unity and dispersity, are concerns in Virginia Woolf's final novel – the 'un . . . dis' of *Between the Acts*.

*   *   *

Appearance and reality, like means and ends, are philosophical commonplaces. The particular forms they assumed in Virginia Woolf's writing philosophy are connected in various ways to the influence – the invisible presences – of the philosopher Apostles and their followers, among whom she passed her life. The communion of love and friendship, the aesthetic contemplation of art and literature, and the pursuit of truth for its own sake were their ideal values. That these were originally confined to the prerogatives of masculine sexuality and education limited the appeal of the Apostles for Virginia Woolf.

Little that I have been rehearsing is new, but it is not merely historical either. Recently Henry Sidgwick – whose influence Lytton Strachey thought brought the discussions of the Apostles out of medieval Victorian theology – has been hailed again as the most significant English moral philosopher of modern times. Sidgwick's *The Methods of Ethics*, eventually written, he noted, out of his experience as an Apostle, attempted to combine two broad kinds of moral theory which Leslie Stephen and others including G. E. Moore also attempted to reconcile. One of these kinds of theory, to oversimplify, maintained teleologically that actions are good or bad according to their results; the other asserted deontologically that certain acts are right or wrong in themselves, regardless of their consequences. Among the issues debated in these theories are questions of good versus right actions and of instrumental versus intrinsic values. These types or groups of moral theory have been variously named, the current terms for them apparently being consequentialism and Kantianism.

A recent exhaustive attempt to bring these theories together by the Oxford philosopher Derek Parfit has been called the most important English ethical work since *The Methods of Ethics*. Parfit's acknowledged philosophical masters are Henry Sidgwick and Immanuel Kant. Sidgwick with his pluralistic commonsense and lucidity, and Kant with his dense, insightful metaphysics were (along with Plato) G. E. Moore's principal sources as well, and their influence is pervasive in Apostolic ethics. Without approaching the analytic intricacies of current consequentialist/Kantian debates, it may be worthwhile to suggest that future philosophical analyses of Virginia Woolf should consider how elements of these theories converge in her writing as they did in the Apostolic assumptions that influenced her. These might involve descriptions of how moments of being and non-being, of reality and the skin of appearance, come together in her work, and how thinking of things in themselves and the means to these thoughts are involved in the ways she combines common-sense clarity and lack of humbug with intuitive insight, ultimately and creatively combining in her writing feminist conviction and mystical experience.

Such interpretations should always keep in mind, however, the words Virginia Woolf gives to Bernard at the end of *The Waves*, and that is 'the sense of the complexity and the reality and the struggle' of her art.

Acknowledgement

Le Tour critique [online], 2 (2013). (http://letourcritique.u.parislo. fr). *Le Tour critique* is the original publisher.

Bibliographical Note

This paper is based on and developed from my early literary history of the Bloomsbury Group: *Victorian Bloomsbury* (1987), *Edwardian Bloomsbury* (1994) and *Georgian Bloomsbury* (2003) as well as on essays reprinted in *Aspects of Bloomsbury* (1998). Henry Sidgwick's *The Methods of Ethics* was first published first in 1874; his *Memoir* by Arthur and Eleanor Mildred Sidgwick appeared in 1906. G. E. Moore's *Principia Ethica* was published in 1903. For Leonard Woolf on the Apostles, see his autobiographies *Sowing* (1960) and *Beginning Again* (1964). Virginia Woolf's memoirs were published in *Moments of Being*, ed. Jeanne Schulkind and Hermione Lee (2002), and *Virginia Woolf, The Platform of Time: Memoirs of Family and Friends*, ed. S. P. Rosenbaum (2008); information on them is also taken from my work in progress on the history of the Memoir Club. Virginia Woolf's essays were edited by Andrew McNeillie and Stuart N. Clarke (1986–2011); her letters, by Nigel Nicolson and Joanne Trautmann Banks (1971–80); her diary, by Anne Olivier Bell (1977–84); her shorter fiction by Susan Dick (1989). Virginia Woolf's novels and book-length non-fiction have been meticulously edited for Blackwell's Shakespeare Head Press Edition (1995–2004). For biographies see those by Quentin Bell (1972) and Hermione Lee (1996). On her feminism see Naomi Black's *Virginia Woolf as Feminist* (2004). J. M. Keynes' 'My Early Beliefs' (1938) was published in his expanded *Essays in Biography* (1951). For Bertrand Russell, see his *Autobiography* (1967) and Ann Banfield, *The Phantom Table* (2000). E. M. Forster on Cambridge is reprinted in *Two Cheers for Democracy* (1951). W. C. Lubenow's *The Cambridge Apostles* (1998) is a detailed account. For Julian Bell see the revised biography by Peter Stansky and William Abrahams (2012). Derek Parfit's *On What Matters* appeared in 2011.

Appendix 2:
A List of Memoir Club Papers

S. P. Rosenbaum and James M. Haule

At the time of his death, S. P. Rosenbaum was working on a comprehensive list of the memoirs presented at Club meetings. He had two things in mind: completing his book on its history and preparing a companion volume that would publish a large collection of the most important memoirs, some for the first time. An edited, annotated version of this list is presented below.

Many factors make an authoritative memoir list difficult. As Rosenbaum notes in his book, there was no list of papers kept by the members and all took their drafts and notes with them when they left the meetings. Heavily edited versions of some papers appeared in print some time later, and others were incorporated into biographies and autobiographies of the participants. When possible, these instances are noted here. In addition, the source of Rosenbaum's information is not always obvious. The archives, therefore, were examined and the contents verified, identifying the location and condition of some documents for the first time. Any errors or omissions are the editor's. Rosenbaum was at the beginning of the process to record the disposition of all papers presented. This list contributes to that larger investigation.

Sources Referenced

The code in [brackets] following each entry identifies its use in describing or locating a memoir. Unpublished memoirs are noted with an asterisk (*) following their titles or descriptions.

Avery, Todd. *Close and Affectionate Friends: Desmond and Molly MacCarthy and the Bloomsbury Group*. Bloomington: Lilly Library of Indiana U, 1999. [CAF]

Bell, Clive. *Old Friends: Personal Recollections*. New York: Harcourt Brace, 1957. [OF]

——. *Roger Fry: Anecdotes, for the Use of a Future Biographer, Illustrating Certain Peculiarities of the Late Roger Fry*. Volume 14 of Bloomsbury Heritage. Diane F. Gillespie, ed. London: Cecil Woolf, 1997. [RFA]

Bell, Vanessa. *The Letters of Vanessa Bell*. Regina Marler, ed. Introduction by Quentin Bell. London: Bloomsbury, 1994. [DVB]

——. *Sketches In Pen And Ink: A Bloomsbury Notebook*. New York: Random House, 2010. [SPI]

Forster, E. M. *The Creator as Critic and Other Writings by E. M. Forster*. Jeffrey M. Heath, ed. Toronto: Dundurn, 2008. [CAC]

——. *The Hill of Devi and Other Indian Writings*. Elizabeth Heine, ed. London: Edward Arnold, 1983. [DEVI]

——. *The Longest Journey*. Elizabeth Heine, ed. Harmondsworth: Penguin, 1989. [L J]

——. *The Prince's Tale: And Other Uncollected Writings*. London: Deutsch, 1998. [TPT]

Garnett, David. *The Familiar Faces*. New York: Harcourt, Brace & World, 1963. [FF]

——. *The Flowers of the Forest*. London: Chatto & Windus, 1955. [FOF]

——. *The Golden Echo*. London: Chatto & Windus, 1970. [GE]

Glendenning, Gloria. *Leonard Woolf: A Biography*. New York: Free Press, 2006. [LWB]

Keynes, John Maynard. *The Collected Writings*. Donald Moggeridge and Elizabeth Johnson. 30 vols. London: Macmillan, 1971–89. [KCW]

——. *Two Memoirs*. New York: Kelley, 1949. [KTM]

MacCarthy, Desmond. *Desmond MacCarthy, the Man and His Writings*. David Cecil, ed. London: Constable, 1984. [MHW]

——. *Memories*. Oxford: OUP, 1953. [MM]

MacCarthy, Molly. *A Nineteenth-Century Childhood*. New York: New Adelphi Library, 1931. [19C]

Moggeridge, Donald. *Maynard Keynes: An Economist's Biography*. London: Routledge, 1992. [JMKB]

Partridge, Frances. *Everything to Lose: Diaries 1945–1960*. London: Gollancz, 1985. [EL]

——. *Hanging On: Diaries, 1960–63*. San Diego: Phoenix Publishing, 1999. [HO]

——. *A Pacifist's War: Diaries 1939–1945*. Orion Publishing Group, 1999. [PW]

Rosenbaum, S. P. *The Bloomsbury Group: A Collection of Memoirs, Commentary, and Criticism*. Toronto: U Toronto P, 1975, revd. edn. 1995. [BG]

——. *Virginia Woolf, The Platform of Time: Memoirs of Family and Friends*, edited and introduced by S. P. Rosenbaum. Expanded edn. London: Hesperus Press, 2008. [PT]

Skidelsky, Robert. *John Maynard Keynes: 1883–1946: Economist, Philosopher, Statesman*. New York: Penguin, 2005. [SJMK]

Stape, J. H. *Virginia Woolf: Interviews and Recollections*. U of Iowa P, 1995. [VWIR]

Strachey, Julia. *Julia: A Portrait of Julia Strachey*. With Francis Partridge. New York: Little, Brown, 1983. [PJS]

Strachey, Lytton. *Lytton Strachey by Himself*. Michael Holroyd, ed. New York: Abacus/Little, Brown, 2005. [LSH]

Woolf, Leonard. *The Autobiography of Leonard Woolf*. 5 vols. New York: Harcourt, 1975. [LWA]

——. *Memoirs of an Elderly Man*. London: Orion, 1945. [MEM]

Woolf, Virginia. *The Diary of Virginia Woolf*. Anne Olivier Bell, ed. 5 vols. London: Hogarth Press, 1977–84. [VWD]

——. *Moments of Being*. Jeanne Schulkind, ed. 2nd edn. New York: Harcourt Brace Jovanovich, 1976. [MB]

——. *Roger Fry: A Biography*. Diane F. Gillespie, ed. The Shakespeare Head Press Edition of Virginia Woolf. Oxford: Blackwell, 1995. [RF]

By Original Members

Clive Bell
(Papers of Clive Bell, Trinity College Library, Cambridge)

Recollections of Lytton Strachey [see OF]
Ottoline* (two versions listed)
Origins of Bloomsbury [BG 114–21]
Paris 1904 [OF]
Mrs Raven Hill* (untitled 15-page typescript with holograph additions dated 1921 and 1930)

Anecdotes for the use of a future biographer, illustrating certain peculiarities of the late Roger Fry (May 1937) read June 1939 [RFA]

Vanessa Bell
(The Charleston Papers, King's College Archive Centre, Cambridge; Tate Britain, Vanessa Bell Manuscripts and Typescripts)

Memoir on choosing a coffin for her father at Harrod's (lost)
'Memoir Relating to Mrs Jackson' [SPI; Tate: TGA 20096/1/11]
'Notes on Virginia's Childhood' [VWIR 3–8; Tate: TGA 20096/1/4–5]
'Life at Hyde Park Gate after 1897' [SPI; Tate: TGA 20096/1/1–2]
'My Sister-in-Law' [SPI]
'Memories of Roger Fry' [SPI, Tate: TGA: 20096/1/8–9]
'The Strange Story of Mary Elizabeth Wilson' (LVB & *Charleston Magazine*, No. 3, 1991)
'A Brother as a Chaperone: a visit to the Chamberlains' (fragment)*
'Introduction to Letters from Leslie Stephen to Mary Fisher'*
'Notes on the Death of Lytton Strachey' (Tate: TGA 20096/1/12–13)

E. M. Forster
(Papers of E. M. Forster, King's College Archive Centre, Cambridge)

Housman memoir [See CAC 484]
West Hackhurst: A Surrey Ramble [See CAC 107]
Meeting Old Bloomsbury [CAD 51–8, missing a page about Lytton Strachey]
Memory
Nassenheide [TPT]
Uncle Willy [L J 294–300]
My Books and I [See CAC 624]
Madame Myslakowska [CAC]
Charlie Day [See CAC 17]
Colonel Leslie [Devi]
Kanaya [Devi]
T. E. Lawrence condemned introduction to letters at Oxford* (see VW D 5.82)

Roger Fry
'I lived the first six years of my life . . . ' [RF 12–13]
Skating episode [RF 16–17]
Pierpont Morgan in Italy [RF 112–15]

'I must have been between 10 and 11 . . . ' judge and school memoir, censored 2nd version [RF 23–9]

'My first conscious Impressions' (Fry Papers at the King's College Library, Cambridge)

'It was one of the grand principles' labelled Memoir Club and 'First draft of Sunninghill' (Fry Papers at the King's College Library, Cambridge)

David Garnett

'My mother was five years older . . . ' (1920, lost or embedded in published material)

Lawrence memoir*

A Window in Hammersmith* (Robert Graves and Laura Riding memoir, 1962)

Meeting Lytton Again* (Possible copy at Texas A & M Cushing Library Manuscripts, Item 210)

Bugs in the Studio of D. Grant (lost or embedded in published material)

Getting to know Indians at school (perhaps embedded in Ch. VII GE)

Dorothy Edwards (embedded in FF)

Duncan Grant

Queer Ancestral Stories* (1920 lost)

A Curious Incident* ms. Beginning 'My heart cheeped like a sparrow', (described as about boyhood, swimming, ambitions to be a painter)

Intimations of Immortality* – variant of 'Where Angels Fear to Tread: A Memoir of the Apostles' also subtitled 'An Outsider's View of the Apostles' perhaps – notes only (1947)

Paris memoir- 2 parts (Hyman Kreitman Research Centre for the Tate Library)

I Tatti (*Charleston Magazine* No. 10, Autumn/Winter, 1994, 5–12)

Memoir of Working with Jacques Copeau on *12th Night**

Simon Bussy memoirs: biography and speech (lost)*

Childhood in India (1950, lost)*

J. M. Keynes

Melchior: A Defeated Enemy [KTM]

My Early Beliefs [KTM & BG 82–97]

Einstein titled 'My Visit to Berlin, 22 June 1926' [KCW X, 382–4].

Newton the Man (see SJMK)

Desmond MacCarthy

(Desmond & Mary MacCarthy Papers, Lilly Library, Indiana U, Bloomington)

Bloomsbury: An Unfinished Memoir [BG 65–74]
G. A. Paley memoir* (37 pages incomplete)
Memoir of Youth [MM]
Shooting with Wilfred Blunt [MHW]
Mark on the Shutter (*Life and Letters To-day*, Vol. 3, 1929)

Molly MacCarthy

(Desmond & Mary MacCarthy Papers, Lilly Library, Indiana U, Bloomington)

Parts of *19th Century Childhood* (19C)
Some Time Soon Again, for Certain: A Retrospect, 1939–1941* (Blitz experiences)
The Bird Is on the Wing* (fragmentary: 4th chapter to be *Nervous Breakdown 30 Years Ago. An Account circa 1934, lost)

Lytton Strachey

Lancaster Gate [LSH]
Monday June 26th 1916 [LSH]
Asquith Sketch 1918 [LSH]

Leonard Woolf

'Many of Leonard's papers for the Memoir Club were incorporated word for word, with minimal editing in the interests of clarity or discretion, in the autobiographies which he wrote in the 1960's . . .' (LWB 216)

Memoirs of an Elderly Man [MEM]
Dutton and tennis
Continuation of Dutton and Ceylon
Mrs Hopfengartner – Ceylon
Difficulty of writing for the Memoir Club
Ceylon: flannel collars
Spiders
Saxon & the Method

Virginia Woolf
22 High Park Gate [MB]
Old Bloomsbury [MB]
Am I a Snob? [MB]
Dreadnought Hoax notes [PT]
Early memoir (lost)
Proposals memoir (lost)

By Later Members

Olivier Bell
(A. O. Bell Papers, University of Sussex Special Collection SxMs70)

A Month in Paris* (summarized in *Canvas*, No. 1)

Quentin Bell
(Quentin Bell Papers, University of Sussex Special Collection)

Les Pinault* (lost or embedded)
Bugs in the Rue Montessuey*
The Vermillion Door*
The Squire of Tilton*

Jane Bussy
A Village Wedding* (Catherine Gide's wedding, lost)
A Great Man (Matisse) *The Burlington Magazine*, Vol. 128, No. 995,
     Feb. 1986

Angelica Garnett
The Walters*
Actress memoir (lost or embedded)*

Dermod MacCarthy
How I Came to Be a Doctor*
J. R. Eccles and the Honour System*
Memories of his father*

Frances Partridge
(Papers of Frances C. Partridge, King's College, Cambridge)

First memoir on a scandal concerning Hayley Morris

'If memoirs could always be written . . . ' Perhaps the memoir foundation for first two chapters of [EL]

Pacifist beliefs memoir [PW]

Dennis Proctor

'Brave Day, Hideous Night: Some Comments by the then Chairman of the Trustees'* (on John Rothenstein's *Brave Day, Hideous Night* and the Tate)

W. J. H. (Sebastian/Jack) Sprott

Memoir on Sprott's friendship with the public hangman in the 50s recalled by Quentin Bell* (lost)

Julia Strachey

The Bathrooms in My Life (PJS 99–103 'Harum-Scarum Life with Hester')

'Can't You Get Me out of Here' (*The New Yorker,* 23 Jan. 1960, originally 'Animalia')

Oliver Strachey

When I was 8 years old . . . (Eton memoir)*

Sydney Waterlow

A Dream* (lost)

Notes

Introduction

1. S. P. Rosenbaum. Typescript of his keynote address at the exhibit 'A Room of Their Own: The Bloomsbury Artists in American Collections' held at Cornell University, Ithaca, New York. October 2009. All Rosenbaum citations are from this source.
2. John Maynard Keynes, *Two Memoirs: Dr Melchior, a Defeated Enemy, And, My Early Beliefs*. Intro. David Garnett. London: Rupert Hart-Davis, 1949. 7.
3. Virginia Woolf, *Roger Fry: A Biography*. Diane F. Gillespie, ed. The Shakespeare Head Press Edition of Virginia Woolf. Oxford: Blackwell, 1995, 17.
4. S. P. Rosenbaum, ed. *The Bloomsbury Group: A Collection of Memoirs, Commentary, and Criticism*, revd edn. Toronto: U of Toronto P, 1995. 153.
5. See the reproduction in the National Portrait Gallery at http://www.npg.org.uk/collections/search/portraitLarge/mw85227/The-Memoir-Club
6. '22 Hyde Park Gate' in Virginia Woolf, *Moments of Being*. Jeanne Schulkind, ed. 2nd edn. New York: Harcourt, Brace, Jovanovich, 1976. 166.

1 Outlines

1. Virginia Woolf, *Roger Fry*. Diane F. Gillespie, ed. The Shakespeare Head Press Edition of Virginia Woolf. Oxford: Blackwell, 1995. 22.
2. 'The Beliefs of Keynes'. *The Listener* (9 June 1949) 993.
3. Leonard Woolf, *Downhill All the Way: An Autobiography of the Years 1919 to 1939*, in *The Autobiography of Leonard Woolf*. 5 vols. New York: Harcourt, 1975. 114.
4. Virginia Woolf once noted the pleasant custom in the *Dictionary of National Biography* (whose first editor was her father) 'of summing up a life, before they write it, in one word, thus – Stanhope, Lady

Hester Lucy (1770–1839), eccentric'. (Virginia Woolf, 'Lady Hester Stanhope', *The Essays of Virginia Woolf*, I. Andrew McNeillie, ed., vols. 1–4; Stuart N. Clarke, ed., vol. 5. London: Hogarth Press, 1986–. 325. The *DNB* actually gives 1776 as the year of her birth.)

In the list that follows, the custom will be continued, as all eleven original continuing members have had their lives recorded in the *DNB*, and ten of them have been the subjects of full-length biographies. Of the twelve later Memoir Club members (one of whom is still living) seven appear in the *DNB*. The dates of their joining are sometimes uncertain.

Members
Original Continuing Members

Clive Bell, 1881–1964, art critic and writer
Vanessa Bell, 1879–1961, painter and decorative artist
E. M. Forster, 1879–1970, novelist and essayist
Roger Fry, 1866–1934, art historian, critic, painter
Duncan Grant, 1885–1978, painter and decorative artist
John Maynard Keynes, 1883–1946, economist
Desmond MacCarthy, 1877–1952, literary and drama critic
Mary (Molly) MacCarthy, 1882–1953, writer
Lytton Strachey, 1880–1932, biographer and literary critic
Leonard Woolf, 1880–1969, writer and publisher
Virginia Woolf, 1882–1941, novelist, essayist, and publisher

Original Transient Members

Mary Hutchinson, 1889–1977, writer
Sydney Waterlow, 1878–1944, diplomat

Later Members and Dates of Membership

Anne Olivier Bell, 1916–, editor: 1954
Quentin Bell, 1910–1996, art historian and potter: 1938
Jane Simone Bussy, 1903–1960, painter: 1938–1946?
Angelica Bell Garnett, 1918–2012, painter and writer: 1949?
David Garnett, 1892–1981, writer: 1932–3
Lydia Lopokova Keynes, 1892–1981, ballet dancer: 1938?
Dermod MacCarthy, 1911–1986, pediatrician: 1947

Frances Partridge, 1900–2004, diarist: 1947
Dennis Proctor, 1905–1983, civil servant: 1959
W. J. H. Sprott (Sebastian), 1897–1971, sociologist: 1947?
Julia Strachey, 1901–1979, writer: 1952
Oliver Strachey, 1874–1960, cryptanalyst: 1951?

Married couples (MacCarthys, Woolfs, Bells) as well as relatives with the same last name (Bells, Stracheys) will often be referred to by both their names or just by the given ones they used; others will customarily be identified by their last names.

5. Leonard Woolf, *Downhill All the Way*, 114.
6. Galen Strawson, 'Against Narrativity'. *Ratio* XVII (December 2004), 430.
7. Francis R. Hart, 'Notes for an Anatomy of Modern Autobiography', *New Literary History*, I (1969–70), 485–511.
8. Lytton Strachey, 'Monday June 26th 1916', 'Asquith', *The Shorter Strachey*. Michael Holroyd and Paul Levy, eds. Oxford: OUP, 1980. 21–42.
9. E. M. Forster ['Incidents of War'], *The Creator as Critic and Other Writings*. Jeffrey M. Heath, ed. Toronto: Dundurn, 2008. 197.
10. Lytton Strachey, 'A Statesman: Lord Morley', in *Characters and Commentaries*. Westport, CT: Praeger, 1979. 231.
11. John Maynard Keynes, *The Economic Consequences of the Peace*, II. New York: Harcourt, Brace, and Howe, Inc., 1920. 23, 189.
12. Keynes, *Economic Consequences*, 20, 26.
13. John Maynard Keynes, *Essays in Biography*, *The Collected Writings*, Vol. X. Donald Moggeridge and Elizabeth Johnson. 30 vols. London: Macmillan, 1971–89. 20–6.
14. Virginia Woolf, 'The Mark on the Wall' in *The Complete Shorter Fiction of Virginia Woolf*. Susan Dick, ed. London: Hogarth Press, 1989. 89.

2 Ancestral Voices, Cambridge Conversations

1. For a discussion of the intellectual backgrounds of the Memoir Club see my *Victorian Bloomsbury: The Early Literary History of the Bloomsbury Group*, Vol. 1. London: Macmillan, 1987, and *Edwardian Bloomsbury: The Early Literary History of the*

Bloomsbury Group, Vols. I and II. Basingstoke and New York: Macmillan and St. Martin's Press – now Palgrave Macmillan, 1987, 1994.

2. S. P. Rosenbaum, *Virginia Woolf, The Platform of Time: Memoirs of Family and Friends*, edited and introduced. Expanded edn. London: Hesperus Press, 2008. 78, 76.

3. Rosenbaum, *Platform of Time*, 69.

4. Anne Thackeray (Lady) Ritchie, *Blackstick Papers*. New York, London: G. P. Putnam's Sons, 1908. 268. The essay was first published by Desmond MacCarthy in his *New Quarterly*.

5. Logan Pearsall Smith and J. A. Gere, eds. *Bensoniana and Cornishiana*, by Arthur Christopher Benson and Blanche Warre-Cornish. York, UK: Stone Trough, 1999. 3, 7, 11.

6. Molly MacCarthy, *A Nineteenth-Century Childhood*. New York: New Adelphi Library, 1931. 75.

7. Leslie Stephen, *Hours in a Library*, III. London: Smith Elder, 1894. 251.

8. Leslie Stephen, *Hours in a Library*, III, 242.

9. Leslie Stephen, *The Mausoleum Book*. Oxford: Clarendon Press, 1977. 4.

10. Leslie Stephen, *Mausoleum Book*, 58; S. P. Rosenbaum, *Victorian Bloomsbury*, 39.

11. Quentin Bell, *Bad Art*. London: Chatto & Windus, 1989. 216.

12. 'The Mausoleum Book', *Review of English Literature* VI (Jan. 1965), 9, 18. Virginia Woolf ['Reminiscences'], *Moments of Being*, Jeanne Schulkind, ed., revd. Hermione Lee. New York: Harcourt, Brace, Jovanovich, 1976. 8.

13. [Pearsall Smith], *Cornishiana*, 10.

14. See Rosenbaum, *Platform of Time*, 50–1, 66–7 and *Edwardian Bloomsbury*, 382.

15. James Stephen, 'The Clapham Sect', *Essays in Ecclesiastical Biography*, II. Oxford: Longmans, Green, Reader, and Dyer, 1867. 307.

16. E. M. Forster, 'Henry Thornton', *Two Cheers for Democracy*. New York: Harcourt Brace, 1951. 186.

17. Quoted in *E. M. Forster: The Critical Heritage*. Philip Gardner, ed. London: Routledge & Kegan Paul, 1973. 185.

18. Forster, *Two Cheers*, 188.

19. Agnes Fry, *A memoir of the Right Honourable Sir Edward Fry*. Ann Arbor: University of Michigan Library, 1921. 56.

20. Denys Sutton, ed., *Letters of Roger Fry*, II, 2 vols. New York: Chatto & Windus, 1972. 515–16.

21. *Memoirs of a Highland Lady*, by Elizabeth Grant of Rothiemurchus. Newton Abbot, 1988. iv.

22. Quoted by Andrew Todd, ed., in *Memoirs of a Highland Lady*, 127–8.

23. Elizabeth Raper Grant, *The Receipt Book of Elizabeth Raper and a Portion of Her Cipher Journal*. London: The Nonesuch Press, 1924. 9, 12, 21, 36–7.

24. Vanessa Bell, *Selected Letters of Vanessa Bell*. Regina Marler, ed. New York: Pantheon (Knopf Doubleday), 1993. 265.

25. Virginia Woolf, *Night and Day*. J. H. Stape, ed. The Shakespeare Head Press Edition of Virginia Woolf. Oxford: Blackwell, 1994. 43.

26. Leonard Woolf, *Sowing: An Autobiography of the Years 1880 to 1904* in *The Autobiography of Leonard Woolf*. 5 vols. New York: Harcourt, 1975. 129–30.

27. John Maynard Keynes, *Two Memoirs*. New York: Kelley, 1949. 82–3.

28. Leonard Woolf, *Sowing,* 148–9.

29. Leonard Woolf, *Beginning Again: An Autobiography of the Years 1911 to 1918* in *The Autobiography of Leonard Woolf*. 5 vols. New York: Harcourt, 1975. 25.

30. G. E. Moore, *Principia Ethica*. Cambridge: CUP, 1903. viii. See also S. P. Rosenbaum, 'Bloomsbury Group', *The Continuum Encyclopedia of British Philosophy* (2006), I, 361.

31. Desmond MacCarthy, *Portraits*. London: MacGibbon & Kee, 1949. 164–5.

32. E. M. Forster and Ronald Edmond Balfour, *Goldsworthy Lowes Dickinson*. New York: Harcourt Brace, 1934. 54–5.

33. E. M. Forster, 'Introduction', *The Longest Journey*. Elizabeth Heine, ed. Harmondsworth: Penguin, 1989. lxviii.

34. Forster ['My Books and I'], *The Longest Journey,* 306.

35. Rosenbaum, *Edwardian Bloomsbury*, 252.

36. Rosenbaum, *Victorian Bloomsbury*, 262.

37. Virginia Woolf, *Moments of Being*. Jeanne Schulkind, ed. 2nd edn. New York: Harcourt, Brace, Jovanovich, 1976. 92.

3   Beginnings

1. Keynes Papers, King's College, Cambridge. The card has been edited slightly.
2. Quentin Bell papers. Special Collections. University of Sussex Library.
3. Virginia Woolf, *The Diary of Virginia Woolf*. Anne Olivier Bell, ed. 5 vols. London: Hogarth Press, 1977–84. Further references in the text will appear as 'D' with volume and page numbers indicated (i.e. D II 24).
4. Molly MacCarthy, *A Nineteenth-Century Childhood*. New York: New Adelphi Library, 1931. 3.
5. The quotation is ambiguous, but given Molly's apologetic title, a literal translation could read 'The I and the Me are always present. But finally what knowledge can one have if there is only the I and the Me?'
6. 'Tributes to Sir Desmond MacCarthy' *Listener* (26 June 1952), 1031.
7. Memoirs. Roger Fry papers, King's College Cambridge.
8. Virginia Woolf, 'A Talk About Memoirs', *The Essays of Virginia Woolf*, III. Andrew McNeillie, ed., vols. 1–4; Stuart N. Clarke, ed., vol. 5. London: Hogarth Press, 1986–. 180–4.
9. Virginia Woolf, 'Money and Love', *Essays* III, 186–92.
10. Hermione Lee, *Virginia Woolf*. New York: Knopf, 1997. 18.
11. Forster's letters to Leonard Woolf are among the Charleston Papers at the University Sussex and King's College, Cambridge.
12. Letter dated 15 March. Mary Hutchinson papers, University of Texas at Austin.
13. The untitled memoir has been published as 'Uncle Willie', Appendix B, *The Longest Journey*, Elizabeth Heine, ed., Harmondsworth: Penguin, 1989. 294–300.
14. Hugh and Mirabel Cecil, *Clever Hearts: Desmond and Molly MacCarthy: A Biography*. London: Victor Gollancz, 1990. 202.
15. 8 July 1920 MacCarthy papers. Lilly Library, Indiana University.
16. Molly MacCarthy, *A Nineteenth-Century Childhood*, 18 & 24.
17. The memoir with the archival title 'Meeting Old Bloomsbury' has now been published, minus a missing page about Lytton Strachey, in E. M. Forster, *The Creator as Critic and Other Writings*, ed. Jeffrey M. Heath. Toronto: Dundurn, 2008. 51–4.
18. E. M. Forster, *Journals and Diaries and Letters of E. M. Forster, II*. Philip Gardner, ed. London: Pickering & Chatto, 2011. 32.

19. Virginia Woolf, *Roger Fry: A Biography*. Diane F. Gillespie, ed. The Shakespeare Head Press Edition of Virginia Woolf. Oxford: Blackwell, 1995. 12–13.

20. Memoirs, Fry Papers, King's College. The sketch is reproduced and described by Panthea Reid in *Art and Affection: A Life of Virginia Woolf*. Oxford: OUP, 1996. Plt 44.

21. Virginia Woolf, *Roger Fry*, 128.

22. Virginia Woolf, 'Moments of Vision', *Essays* II. 250–1. Further references to the *Essays of Virginia Woolf* (5 vols. Harcourt Brace Jovanovich/ Hogarth Press) will appear as in the text as 'E' followed by volume and page numbers.

23. Virginia Woolf, 'The Patron and the Crocus'; 'The Letters of Henry James' (E III. 202).

24. The typescripts are in the Monks House Collection, University of Sussex; the memoir was first published in *Moments of Being*, Jeanne Schulkind, ed., 1976, enlarged 1985, revised, 2002 (the edition used here).

25. *The Letters of Virginia Woolf*. Nigel Nicolson and Joanne Trautmann eds. 6 vols. London: Hogarth Press, 1975–80. Further references in the text will appear as 'L' followed by volume and page numbers (L V 13).

26. Virginia Woolf's untitled letter-biography to Vanessa's infant son Julian, mistitled 'Reminiscences', *Moments of Being*, 27.

27. See Rosenbaum, *Edwardian Bloomsbury*, 141–2.

28. Virginia Woolf, *Moments of Being*, 145.

29. Leonard Woolf, *Beginning Again: An Autobiography of the Years 1911 to 1918* in *The Autobiography of Leonard Woolf*. 5 vols. New York: Harcourt, 1975. 248.

30. Virginia Woolf, 'Gorky on Tolstoy' (E III. 254).

4   Private and Public Affairs: 1921–1922

1. Clive Bell, 'Maynard Keynes', in *Old Friends: Personal Recollections*. New York: Harcourt Brace, 1957. 42.

2. Memoir on Mrs Raven Hill: untitled 15–page typescript with holograph additions dated 1921 and 1930, Clive Bell papers, Trinity College, Cambridge. I have followed Bell's practice of omitting the hyphen in her name.

3. Quentin Bell, *Elders and Betters*. London: John Murray, 1995. 29.

4. John Maynard Keynes, *The Collected Writings*, XVI. Donald Moggeridge and Elizabeth Johnson. 30 vols. London: Macmillan, 1971–89. 416.

5. See Keynes, *Collected Writings*, XVII, 4.

6. Vanessa Bell's unpublished memoir of Keynes' letters is at King's College, Cambridge; Keynes' letters to Vanessa Bell are now at Northwestern University; her letters to him are at the Pierpont Morgan Library.

7. 'The Beliefs of Keynes', *The Listener* (9 June 1949) 993; (D II 33).

8. Keynes, *Collected Writings*, XVII, 10.

9. Keynes, *Collected Writings*, X, 383–4.

10. See Keynes, *Collected Writings*, XVI, 407–13.

11. Keynes, *Collected Writings*, X, 55.

12. Quoted in R. F. Harrod, *The Life of John Maynard Keynes*. New York: W. W. Norton Inc., 1982. 234.

13. Clive Bell, *Old Friends*, 52.

14. 'Beliefs of Keynes', 993.

15. 'Maynard Keynes as Biographer', in Milo Keynes, ed. *Essays on John Maynard Keynes*. Cambridge: CUP, 1980. 259.

16. Virginia Woolf, *Congenial Spirits: The Selected Letters of Virginia Woolf*. Joanne Trautmann Banks, ed. London: Random House, 2003. 129.

17. E. M. Forster, 'Where There Is Nothing', *The Prince's Tale: And Other Uncollected Writings*. London: Deutsch, 1998. 49.

18. E. M. Forster, *Journals and Diaries and Letters of E. M. Forster, III*. Philip Gardner, ed. London: Pickering & Chatto, 2011. 62–3.

19. Letter to MacCarthy, 2 January 1948, Quentin Bell papers of A. O. Bell.

22. Quoted in Todd Avery, *Close and Affectionate Friends: Desmond and Molly MacCarthy and the Bloomsbury Group*. Bloomington: Lilly Library of Indiana U, 1999. 29.

21. The untitled manuscript has been published as 'My Books and I', Appendix B, *The Longest Journey*. Elizabeth Heine, ed. Harmondsworth: Penguin, 1989. 300–6.

22. Leonard Woolf, *Downhill All the Way: An Autobiography of the Years 1919 to 1939* in *The Autobiography of Leonard Woolf*. 5 vols. New York: Harcourt, 1975. 115.

23. 'The Strange Story of Mary Elizabeth Wilson' was published in *The Charleston Magazine*, Issue 3, Summer/Autumn, 1991, 5–15, but not included among the writings collected in Vanessa Bell's

Sketches in Pen and Ink: A Bloomsbury Notebook. New York: Random House, 2010.

24. See *Selected Letters of Vanessa Bell*. Regina Marler, ed. New York: Pantheon (Knopf Doubleday), 1993. 246.

25. Vanessa's edited typescript is in the possession of Mrs Bell; the holograph additions and letters from and to Keynes, dated 15 May and June 5, are with Angelica Garnett's papers in the King's College, Cambridge archives.

26. Molly MacCarthy to Lytton Strachey, 25 April 1922, Strachey Papers, British Library.

27. 'Mademoiselle de Lespinasse', in Lytton Strachey, *Characters and Commentaries*. Westport, CT: Praeger, 1979. 106.

28. Lytton Strachey, 'Asquith', Michael Holroyd, ed., London *Times*, 15 January 1972, 7; reprinted in *The Shorter Strachey*. Michael Holroyd and Paul Levy, eds. Oxford: Oxford UP, 1980. 38–42.

29. Lytton Strachey, 'Lancaster Gate', *Lytton Strachey by Himself: a Self Portrait*, 16–28; reprinted in *The Shorter Strachey*.

30. Lytton Strachey, *Queen Victoria*. New York: Harcourt, Brace, 1921. 294.

31. Lytton Strachey, *The Letters of Lytton Strachey*. Paul Levy, ed. New York: Farrar, Straus and Giroux, 2005. 452–3.

32. E. M. Forster, *The Hill of Devi and Other Indian Writings*. Elizabeth Heine, ed. London: Edward Arnold, 1983. 99.

33. An incomplete mss. Memoir of Colonel Leslie is now at King's College archives. Forster published a cut version in *The Hill of Devi being Letters from Dewas State Senior* in 1953; this version along with notes giving the deletions was republished in Elizabeth Heine's edition, 89–97, 373–7. I am much indebted to Heine's account and careful editing; references are to this edition.

34. Quoted in Forster, *Hill of Devi*, ix. The mss. entitled 'Kanaya' is now at King's; it was finally published in appendix D in 1983 edition of *The Hill of Devi*.

35. Quoted in Forster, *Hill of Devi*, liii.

36. Forster, *Hill of Devi*, 97.

37. Forster, *Hill of Devi*, 94.

38. *E. M. Forster: Interviews and Recollections*. J. H. Stape, ed. Iowa City: U of Iowa Press, 1993. 53.

39. E. M. Forster, *Selected Letters*, II, 45.

40. Forster, *Hill of Devi*, 18.

41. Forster, *Hill of Devi*, 308–9.

42. 'The Emperor Babur', *Nation and Athenaeum* (1 April 1922), reprinted in E. M. Forster, *Abinger Harvest: And England's Pleasant Land. Elizabeth Heine*, ed. London: Trafalgar Square Publishing, 1997. 292.

43. 'The Mind of the Indian Native State', *Nation and Athenaeum*, 29 April, 13 May 1922), reprinted in Forster, *Abinger Harvest*, 329.

44. 'Woodlanders on Devi', *New Statesman and Nation*, 6 May 1939, reprinted in E. M. Forster, *The Prince's Tale: And Other Uncollected Writings*. London: Deutsch, 1998. 252–5.

5 Hiatus: 1922–1928

1. 'The Bran-pie and Eclecticism' (1924), reprinted in William G. Bywater, *Clive Bell's Eye*, unabridged edn. Detroit: Wayne State UP, 1975. 200.

2. The discussion of Virginia Woolf's novels is based on my 'The Philosophical Realism of Virginia Woolf' reprinted in *Aspects of Bloomsbury: Studies in the Literary and Intellectual History of the Bloomsbury Group*, Basingstoke: Macmillan; New York: St. Martin's Press – now Palgrave Macmillan, 1998. 1–36.

3. See *The Essays of Virginia Woolf*, III and IV, ed. Andrew McNeillie, 5 vols. Harcourt Brace Jovanovich/Hogarth Press, 1986; and James Haule's ' "Le Temps passe" and the Original Typescript: An Earlier Version of the "Time Passes" section of *To The Lighthouse*.' *Twentieth Century Literature*, 29, No. 3 (Fall 1983), 267–311.

4. See E III 443–4 and L III 135.

5. Surviving copies of the *Charleston* and *New Bulletin* with supplements are now in the British Library. An account of the *Bulletin* is given in Peter Stansky and William Abrahams, *Journey to the Frontier* (1966) 24–7.

6. Printed in the *Charleston Newsletter*, No. 21 (June 1988) 12.

7. The invitation is reproduced in J. Howard Woolmer's *A Checklist of the Hogarth Press, 1917–1946*, 2nd edn. New Castle, DE: Oak Knoll Press, 1986. 50.

8. The manuscript is among Fry's papers at King's College Cambridge; the typescript with holograph corrections in another hand than Fry's is among the Charleston Papers at the University of Sussex; a photocopy of the typescript is also with the Cambridge Fry papers. Quotations from the manuscript have been translated by Susanna Eve.

9. The memoir, preserved among Forster's papers at King's, was edited by Miriam Allott and included with Forster's other Egyptian writings in *Alexandria: A History and a Guide*. Gloucester, MA: Peter Smith Inc., 1974; and *Pharos and Pharillon*, vol. 16, 329–46, Abinger Edition of Forster. References to Forster's Egyptian texts (except for the swimming memoir and the late essay on Cavafy) are all to this edition. I am much indebted to Allott's informative introductions, editing, and notes. References to the diaries are to the *Journals and Diaries and Letters of E. M. Forster*, 3 vols. Philip Gardner, ed. London: Pickering & Chatto, 2011. References to the letters are to *Selected Letters*.

10. E. M. Forster, *Two Cheers for Democracy*. New York: Harcourt Brace, 1951. 126–7.

11. 'Swimming in the Sea' is printed in E. M. Forster, *The Creator as Critic and Other Writings*. Jeffrey M. Heath, ed. Toronto: Dundurn, 2008. 197–200, 601–5.

12. Forster, *Two Cheers for Democracy*, 285.

13. E. M. Forster, *E. M. Forster: Interviews and Recollections*. J. H. Stape, ed. Iowa City: U of Iowa Press, 1993. 53. The editor presumes that this was a mistake for Mohammed el Adl but Strachey had quite probably heard Forster's Memoir Club paper on Kanaya.

14. E. M. Forster, *Aspects of the Novel*. New York: Houghton Mifflin, 1947. 5, 20. I have discussed Forster's *Aspects of the Novel* under the aspect of literary history in my *Aspects of Bloomsbury*, 84–109.

15. The talk is reprinted in E. M. Forster, *The Hill of Devi and Other Indian Writings*. Elizabeth Heine, ed. London: Edward Arnold, 1983. 289–99.

16. Forster, *Two Cheers for Democracy*, 84.

17. The published reviews and letters are collected in *E. M. Forster: The Critical Heritage*. Philip Gardner, ed. London: Routledge & Kegan Paul, 1973. 204–10, 221–5, 246–53.

18. Virginia Woolf, *Essays*, IV 491–500; Forster, *Selected Letters* II, 79; Vanessa Bell, *Selected Letters of Vanessa Bell*. Regina Marler, ed. New York: Pantheon (Knopf Doubleday), 1993. 279.

19. Reprinted in E. M. Forster's *Abinger Harvest: And England's Pleasant Land*. Elizabeth Heine, ed. London: Trafalgar Square Publishing, 1997.

20. Virginia Woolf, *Roger Fry*. Diane F. Gillespie, ed. The Shakespeare Head Press Edition of Virginia Woolf. Oxford: Blackwell, 1995. 94, 360.

21. The book was reprinted in 1973 by Tristram Powell who changed some of the photographs and added others together with a preface correcting Virginia Woolf's facts and sources.

22. Virginia Woolf's two versions of *Freshwater* edited by Lucio P. Ruotolo were first published in 1976 (New York: Harcourt Brace Jovanovich).

23. Clive Bell, Introduction, Helmut Gernsheim, *Julia Margaret Cameron: Her Life and Photographic Work*. New York: Aperture, 1987. 7–8; Quentin Bell, *Victorian Artists*. Cambridge, MA: Harvard UP, 1967. 58–9.

6 Old Bloomsbury

1. Strachey Papers, British Library.

2. Quentin Bell, *Virginia Woolf: A Biography*, I. 2 vols. London: Hogarth Press, 1972. 125. The memoir is misdated, for example, in my *The Bloomsbury Group: A Collection of Memoirs, Commentary, and Criticism*. Toronto: U Toronto P, 1975. The 37–page typescript entitled 'Old Bloomsbury' is in the Monks House Collection, University of Sussex, which dates it 'after 1927, perhaps 1929'; a fragment of the last paragraph is in the Berg Collection. When the holograph cancellations and insertions were made in the typescript – at the time of the Memoir Club reading or for the later readings – cannot be determined. The memoir following Quentin Bell's dating was first published in Virginia Woolf's *Moments of Being*, 2nd edn. New York: Harcourt, Brace, Jovanovich, 1976, edited and transcribed by Jeanne Schulkind – who deciphered some nearly illegible passages – in 1976, enlarged in 1985, and revised, but with the dating unchanged, by Hermione Lee in 2002 (the edition used here).

3. See Hermione Lee, *Virginia Woolf*. New York: Knopf, 1997. 517–18.

4. Quoted in Todd Avery, *Close and Affectionate Friends: Desmond and Molly MacCarthy and the Bloomsbury Group*. Bloomington: Lilly Library of Indiana U, 1999. 30.

Works Cited

Avery, Todd. *Close and Affectionate Friends: Desmond and Molly MacCarthy and the Bloomsbury Group.* Bloomington: Lilly Library of Indiana U, 1999.

Bell, Clive. *Art.* J. B. Bullen, ed. Oxford: OUP, 1987.

——. *Civilization: An Essay.* London: Chatto & Windus, 1928.

Bell, Quentin. *Bad Art.* London: Chatto & Windus, 1989.

——. *Bloomsbury.* London: Weidenfeld and Nicolson, 1968.

——. *Elders and Betters.* London: John Murray, 1995.

——. *Victorian Artists.* Cambridge, MA: Harvard UP, 1967.

——. *Virginia Woolf: A Biography.* 2 vols. London: Hogarth Press, 1972.

Bell, Vanessa. *Selected Letters of Vanessa Bell.* Regina Marler, ed. New York: Pantheon (Knopf Doubleday), 1993.

Bishop, Edward. *A Virginia Woolf Chronology.* Boston: G. K. Hall, 1989.

Black, Naomi. *Social Feminism.* Ithaca: Cornell UP, 1989.

——. *Virginia Woolf as Feminist.* Ithaca: Cornell UP, 2004.

Boyd, Elizabeth French. *Bloomsbury Heritage: Their Mothers and Their Aunts.* New York: Taplinger, 1976.

Bywater, William G. *Clive Bell's Eye,* unabridged edn. Detroit: Wayne State UP, 1975.

Cecil, Hugh and Mirabel. *Clever Hearts: Desmond and Molly MacCarthy: A Biography.* London: Victor Gollancz, 1990.

Forster, E. M. *Abinger Harvest: And England's Pleasant Land.* Elizabeth Heine, ed. London: Trafalgar Square Publishing, 1997.

——. *Alexandria: A History and a Guide.* Gloucester, MA: Peter Smith Inc., 1974.

——. *Aspects of the Novel.* New York: Houghton Mifflin, 1947.

——. *The Creator as Critic and Other Writings.* Jeffrey M. Heath, ed. Toronto: Dundurn, 2008.

——. *E. M. Forster: Interviews and Recollections.* J. H. Stape, ed. Iowa City: U of Iowa Press, 1993.

——. *E. M. Forster: The Critical Heritage.* Philip Gardner, ed. London: Routledge & Kegan Paul, 1973.

——. *The Hill of Devi and Other Indian Writings*. Elizabeth Heine, ed. London: Edward Arnold, 1983.

——. *Journals and Diaries and Letters of E. M. Forster*. Philip Gardner, ed. London: Pickering & Chatto, 2011.

——. *The Story of the Siren*. Richmond: The Hogarth Press, 1920.

——. and Ronald Edmond Balfour. *Goldsworthy Lowes Dickinson*. New York: Harcourt, Brace, 1934.

——. *Two Cheers for Democracy*. New York: Harcourt Brace, 1951.

Fry, Agnes. *A memoir of the Right Honourable Sir Edward Fry, G.C.B: Lord Justice of the Court of Appeal, ambassador extraordinary and first British plenipotentiary to the second Hague Conference, 1827–1918*. Ann Arbor: University of Michigan Library, 1921.

Furbank, P. N. *E. M. Forster: A Life*. 2 vols. New York: Harcourt, 1978.

Garnett, Angelica. *Sketches In Pen And Ink: A Bloomsbury Notebook*. Lia Giachero, ed. London: Chatto & Windus, 1997.

Garnett, David. *The Familiar Faces*. New York: Harcourt, Brace & World, 1963.

Gernsheim, Helmut. *Julia Margaret Cameron: Her Life and Photographic Work*. New York: Aperture, 1987.

Glendenning, Gloria. *Leonard Woolf: A Biography*. New York: Free Press, 2006.

Harrod, Sir Roy Forbes. *The Life of John Maynard Keynes*. New York: W. W. Norton Inc., 1982.

Hart, Francis R. 'Notes for an Anatomy of Modern Autobiography'. *New Literary History*, I (1969–70). 485–511.

Haule, James M. 'Reading Dante, Misreading Woolf: New Evidence of Virginia Woolf's Revision of *The Years*.' *Selected Papers from the Eighteenth Annual Conference on Virginia Woolf*. Denver: University of Denver, 2009. 232–44.

——. ' "Le Temps passe" and the Original Typescript: An Earlier Version of the "Time Passes" section of *To The Lighthouse*.' *Twentieth Century Literature*, 29, No. 3 (Fall 1983), 267–311.

——. *Virginia Woolf: Editing and Interpreting the Modernist Text*. With J. H. Stape. Basingstoke: Palgrave Macmillan, 2002.

——. 'Virginia Woolf's Revision of *The Voyage Out*: Some New Evidence.' *Twentieth Century Literature*, 42, No. 3 (Fall 1996), 309–21.

Holroyd, Michael. *Lytton Strachey: The New Biography*. New York: Random House, 2005.

——. ed. *Essays on John Maynard Keynes*. Cambridge: CUP, 1980.

Keynes, John Maynard. *The Economic Consequences of the Peace.* New York: Harcourt, Brace, and Howe, Inc., 1920.

——. *The Collected Writings.* Donald Moggeridge and Elizabeth Johnson, eds. 30 vols. London: Macmillan, 1971–89.

——. and Lydia Lopokova. *Lydia and Maynard: The Letters of Lydia Lopokova and John Maynard Keynes.* Polly Hill and Richard Keynes. New York: Scribner, 1990.

Keynes, Milo. *Lydia Lopokova.* Basingstoke: Palgrave Macmillan, 1983.

Lee, Hermione. *Virginia Woolf.* New York: Knopf, 1997.

Linett, Maren Tova. *Virginia Woolf: An MFS Reader.* Baltimore: Johns Hopkins UP, 2009.

MacCarthy, Desmond. *Portraits.* London: MacGibbon & Kee, 1949.

MacCarthy, Molly. *A Nineteenth-Century Childhood.* New York: New Adelphi Library, 1931.

Moggridge, Donald. *Maynard Keynes: An Economist's Biography.* London: Routledge, 1992.

Moore, G. E. *Principia Ethica.* Cambridge: CUP, 1903.

Partridge, Frances. *Everything to Lose: Diaries 1945–1960.* London: Gollancz, 1985.

——. *Hanging On: Diaries, 1960–63.* San Diego: Phoenix Publishing, 1999.

——. *A Pacifist's War: Diaries 1939–1945.* London: Orion Publishing Group, 1999.

Pearsall Smith, Logan, and G. A. Gere, eds. *Bensoniana and Cornishiana,* by Arthur Christopher Benson and Blanche Warre-Cornish. York, UK: Stone Trough, 1999.

Raper Grant, Elizabeth. *The Receipt Book of Elizabeth Raper and a Portion of Her Cipher Journal.* London: The Nonesuch Press, 1924.

Reid, Panthea. *Art and Affection: A Life of Virginia Woolf.* Oxford: OUP, 1996.

Rosenbaum, S. P. *Aspects of Bloomsbury: Studies in the Literary and Intellectual History of the Bloomsbury Group,* Basingstoke: Macmillan, New York: St. Martin's Press – now Palgrave Macmillan, 1998.

——. *The Bloomsbury Group: A Collection of Memoirs, Commentary, and Criticism.* Revd. edn. Toronto: U Toronto P, 1995.

——. *A Bloomsbury Group Reader,* selected and edited. Oxford, UK; Cambridge, MA: Blackwell, 1993.

——. *Edwardian Bloomsbury: The Early Literary History of the Blooms-bury Group*, Vol. Two. Basingstoke: Macmillan, New York: St. Martin's Press – now Palgrave Macmilllan, 1994.

——. *English Literature and British Philosophy: A Collection of Critical Essays*, edited with an Introduction and Bibliography. Chicago: U of Chicago P, 1971.

——. *Georgian Bloomsbury: The Early Literary History of the Blooms-bury Group*, Vol. Three. London and New York: Palgrave Macmillan, 2003.

——. *Victorian Bloomsbury: The Early Literary History of the Blooms-bury Group*, Vol. One. London: Macmillan, 1987.

——. *Virginia Woolf's Women & Fiction: The Manuscript Versions of* A Room of One's Own, transcribed and edited with an Introduction and Notes by S. P. Rosenbaum. Oxford: Basil Blackwell, 1992.

——. *Virginia Woolf, The Platform of Time: Memoirs of Family and Friends*, edited and introduced. Expanded edn. London: Hesperus Press, 2008.

Skidelsky, Robert. *John Maynard Keynes: 1883–1946: Economist, Philosopher, Statesman*. New York: Penguin, 2005.

Spalding, Francis. *Vanessa Bell*. Boston: Ticknor & Fields, 1983.

Stape, J. H. *An E.M. Forster Chronology*. London: Macmillan, 1993.

——. *Virginia Woolf: Interviews and Recollections*. Iowa City: U of Iowa P, 1995.

Stephen, James. *Essays in Ecclesiastical Biography*. Oxford: Longmans, Green, Reader, and Dyer, 1867.

Stephen, Leslie. *Hours in a Library*. London: Smith Elder, 1894.

——. *The Mausoleum Book*. Oxford: Clarendon Press, 1977.

Strachey, Giles Lytton. *Characters and Commentaries*. Westport, CT: Praeger, 1979.

——. *Eminent Victorians*. John Sutherland, ed. Oxford: Oxford UP, 2009.

——. *The Letters of Lytton Strachey*. Paul Levy, ed. New York: Farrar, Straus and Giroux, 2005.

——. *Lytton Strachey by Himself*. Michael Holroyd, ed. New York: Abacus/Little, Brown, 2005.

——. *Queen Victoria*. New York: Harcourt, Brace, 1921.

——. *The Shorter Strachey*. Michael Holroyd and Paul Levy, eds. Oxford: Oxford UP, 1980.

Strachey, Julia: *A Portrait of Julia Strachey*. Frances Partridge, ed. London: Victor Gollancz, 1983.

Sutton, Denys, ed. *Letters of Roger Fry*, 2 vols. New York [1st USA edition]: Chatto & Windus, 1972.

Thackeray, Anne (Lady) Ritchie. *Blackstick Papers*. New York, London: G. P. Putnam's Sons, 1908.

Todd, Andrew, ed. *Memoirs of a Highland Lady*, by Elizabeth Grant of Rothiemurchus. Newton Abbott, 1988.

Tolley, Christopher. *Domestic Biography: The Legacy of Evangelicalism in Four Nineteenth-Century Families*. Oxford: OUP, 1997.

Woolf, Leonard. *The Autobiography of Leonard Woolf*. 5 vols. *Sowing: An Autobiography of the Years 1880 to 1904; Growing: An Autobiography of the Years 1904 to 1911; Beginning Again: An Autobiography of the Years 1911 to 1918; Downhill All the Way: An Autobiography of the Years 1919 to 1939; The Journey Not the Arrival Matters: An Autobiography of the Years 1939 to 1969*. New York: Harcourt, 1975.

——. *The Letters of Leonard Woolf*. Frederic Spotts, ed. New York: Harcourt Brace Jovanovich, 1989.

——. and Trekkie Parsons. *Love Letters of Leonard Woolf & Trekkie Parsons, 1941–1968*. Judith Adamson, ed. London: Chatto, 2001.

——. and James Strachey (editors). *Virginia Woolf and Lytton Strachey: Letters*. London: Hogarth Press, 1956.

Woolf, Virginia. *Between the Acts*. Susan Dick and Mary Millar, eds. The Shakespeare Head Press Edition of Virginia Woolf. Oxford: Blackwell, 2002.

——. *The Complete Shorter Fiction of Virginia Woolf*. Susan Dick, ed. London: Hogarth Press, 1989.

——. *Congenial Spirits: The Selected Letters of Virginia Woolf*. Joanne Trautmann Banks, ed. London: Random House, 2003.

——. *The Diary of Virginia Woolf*. Anne Olivier Bell, ed. 5 vols. London: Hogarth Press, 1977–84.

——. *The Essays of Virginia Woolf*. Andrew McNeillie, ed., vols. 1–4; Stuart N. Clarke, ed., vol. 5. London: Hogarth Press, 1986–.

——. *Flush*. Elizabeth Steele, ed. The Shakespeare Head Press Edition of Virginia Woolf. Oxford: Blackwell, 1999.

——. *Freshwater*. Ed. Lucio R. Ruotolo. New York: Harcourt Brace Jovanovich, 1976.

——. *Jacob's Room*. Edward Bishop, ed. The Shakespeare Head Press Edition of Virginia Woolf. Oxford: Blackwell, 2004.

——. *The Letters of Virginia Woolf*. Nigel Nicholson & Joanna Trautmann Banks, eds. 6 vols. London: Hogarth Press, 1975–80.

——. *Moments of Being.* Jeanne Schulkind, ed. 2nd edn. New York: Harcourt Brace Jovanovich, 1976.

——. *Mrs Dalloway.* Morris Beja, ed. The Shakespeare Head Press Edition of Virginia Woolf. Oxford: Blackwell, 1996.

——. *Night and Day.* J. H. Stape, ed. The Shakespeare Head Press Edition of Virginia Woolf. Oxford: Blackwell, 1994.

——. *Orlando.* J. H. Stape, ed. The Shakespeare Head Press Edition of Virginia Woolf. Oxford: Blackwell, 1998.

——. *Roger Fry.* Diane F. Gillespie, ed. The Shakespeare Head Press Edition of Virginia Woolf. Oxford: Blackwell, 1995.

——. *Three Guineas.* Naomi Black, ed. The Shakespeare Head Press Edition of Virginia Woolf. Oxford: Blackwell, 2001.

——. *To The Lighthouse.* Susan Dick, ed. The Shakespeare Head Press Edition of Virginia Woolf. Oxford: Blackwell, 1992.

——. *The Voyage Out.* C. Ruth Miller and Lawrence Miller, eds. The Shakespeare Head Press Edition of Virginia Woolf. Oxford: Blackwell, 1995.

——. *The Waves.* James M. Haule and P. H. Smith, Jr., eds. The Shakespeare Head Press Edition of Virginia Woolf. Oxford: Blackwell Publishers, 1994.

Woolmer, J. Howard. *A Checklist of The Hogarth Press, 1917–1946,* 2nd edn. New Castle, DE: Oak Knoll Press, 1986.

Index